STORM
FORCE

A DI Tanner Mystery
- Book Seven -

DAVID BLAKE

www.david-blake.com

Proofread by Jay G Arscott

Special thanks to Kath Middleton, Ann Studd, John Harrison, Anna Burke, Emma Porter, Emma Stubbs and Jan Edge

Published by Black Oak Publishing Ltd in Great Britain, 2021

Cover Photograph 73064094 © Philip Bird | Dreamstime.com

ISBN: 9798450409740

DEDICATION

For Akiko, Akira and Kai.

DAVID BLAKE

THE DI TANNER SERIES

*"For where jealousy and selfish ambition exist,
there will be disorder and every vile practice."*
James 3:16

- PROLOGUE -

Saturday, 21ˢᵗ August

THE OPULENT MOTOR yacht's grandiose cockpit pitched and rolled over the ocean's waves, sweeping gently underneath its bulbous white hull. Spread out over a dark folding teak table lay the body of a beautiful young woman, her translucent blue eyes staring up at a blanket of stars, her unblemished skin glowing in the light from a steadily rising moon.

Around her stood three middle aged men, their mouths hanging open, their own bodies as naked as the girl lying before them.

'What are we going t-to d-do now?' stuttered the fattest of the three, his small piggy eyes blinking fast as they remained fixed on the girl's.

'You mean, what are *you* going to do?' replied the older man standing to his side, his body thin, loose folds of skin hanging down from its sides.

'Don't try and make out that this was my fault,' the fat one replied, turning to stare up at his skinny balding friend. 'You're the one who was choking her!'

'But it wasn't me who slipped the LSD, ecstasy and cocaine into her vodka bloody tonic, all at the same time, now was it!'

'Iain. Tubbs. Do me a favour and shut the hell up.'

The two men turned to stare over at the third man, busily stuffing a vibrant pink shirt down into a pair of faded blue designer jeans.

A sudden feeling of exposed vulnerability had the two still naked men start scrabbling frantically about for their clothes, pulling them over their sun-bronzed bodies before standing once again to stare down at the girl.

A silence as cold as the surrounding sea crept its way over the luxury yacht, leaving the only sound to be the tops of the waves, lapping gently against its gleaming white hull.

'Is she definitely d-dead?' came the uncertain voice of the man who was being called Tubbs, peeling his eyes off the girl to stare over at the person standing on the opposite side of the table.

'What do you think?'

'I don't know, Mike. Unlike you, I'm not a doctor.'

'Well, after the convulsions, vomit, and blood that came pouring out of her nose, she stopped breathing. She hasn't moved since, not even enough to blink. Bearing all that in mind, I don't think you need five years in medical school to know that she's definitely fucking dead!'

'Shit.'

As they'd been talking, Iain had been furtively glancing about. 'I think the solution is obvious enough,' he soon began, casting his eyes over at the sea, glistening in the moonlight like a carpet of slithering slugs. 'We simply tie something around her feet and throw her over the side. Then we motor our way home and pretend none of this ever happened.'

'Agreed,' Mike replied. 'One-hundred percent!'

A sudden giant beam of light swept over the boat.

Panicking, they all ducked their heads.

'What the hell was that?' demanded Tubbs, his bottom lip trembling.

Mike slowly lifted his head to peer out over the side towards where Norfolk's coastline lay. When the exact same light swept over them again, he stood up to stare down at his two cowering friends. 'It's the bloody lighthouse, for fuck's sake. Now, get up and help me find something to tie around her ankles.'

As the light arced around again, the remaining two lifted themselves cautiously to their feet, gazing over to where Happisburgh Lighthouse stood, its distinctive bands of red and white stark against Norfolk's starlit sky.

Without waiting for them, Mike threw open the nearest lazarette bench seat, delving down into its contents. 'We just need an anchor, or something, and a length of rope to attach it to.'

Tubbs looked back at the body. 'Are you sure we should be doing this?'

'I suppose you'd prefer to take her body straight to the police, making sure to tell them exactly what we'd been doing to her, just before she happened to overdose on the various illegal drugs that one of us decided to slip into her drink?'

'But...we didn't kill her. At least, not on purpose, we didn't.'

'It may not be murder, but I can't see it being classed as anything other than manslaughter. Then there's the question of where we got the cocaine, LSD and ecstasy from. So unless you want to spend the next twenty-odd years being gang-raped by your overly affectionate homosexual prison mates, I suggest you help me find some bloody rope!'

A few frantic minutes passed as they all searched the depths of the cockpit's lockers, until eventually

Tubbs pulled out a tangled clump of blue frayed nylon, attached to which was a long length of rusty old chain.

'Will this do?' he asked, holding it up for the others to see.

'Looks like it'll have to,' Mike replied, snatching the rope out of his hands to begin tying it around the girl's thin delicate ankles.

After checking the knot, he skirted around the table to take hold of her arms. 'I'm not doing this on my own,' he stated, shooting a glance at his fellow co-conspirators, neither of whom were doing anything more productive than staring vacantly at the girl's angelic stone-like face.

'Are we absolutely sure about this?' Iain questioned, a flicker of doubt catching at the corners of his eyes. 'The moment we throw her over, there'll be no turning back.'

'It was your bloody idea,' Mike scoffed. 'Anyway, the moment we do, she'll be fish food, so I don't see how it matters. Even if her body was to wash up on a beach somewhere, I doubt there would be anything left of her to identify. Certainly nothing to indicate that any of us had been within a hundred miles of her. Now, if one of you can throw the chain over, the rest should follow.'

His two more reluctant friends glanced nervously around at each other.

'I'll do the chain,' Iain eventually mumbled. 'You can grab her ankles.'

Tubbs shuddered, the fat on his face wobbling like chilled jellied eel. 'I'm not touching her.'

'That's hilarious, Tubbs, really it is, especially given the fact that you couldn't stop yourself about half an hour ago.'

'That was b-before – b-before she was...' Tubbs'

began, his trembling voice trailing away as his eyes drifted over the length of her body.

'For fuck's sake,' lamented Iain. '*I'll* take her feet. I assume you'll be able to manage the chain?'

'Of course I can manage the chain,' Tubbs grumbled, stooping down to gather the heavy cast iron links into his brown chubby arms.

Through short shallow breaths, he hauled it slowly over to the boat's side. There he stopped to look over at Mike, still holding onto the girl's arms. 'What do I do now?'

'What d'you think you do? Throw it over!'

Seeing him swing his arms back, Mike suddenly shouted, 'Not all at once!'

'What!' Tubbs exclaimed, hurling the entire length of chain over the side for it to instantly vanish into the cold uninviting sea beneath.

The three men watched in stunned silence as the rope attached to its end caught at the girl's ankles, whipping her body around to drag it across the table, straight over the side; the back of her head cracking against the hard fibreglass edge before it too disappeared.

'I said, not all at once, you brainless moron!'

'You said throw it over the side, so I threw it over the side.'

Mike shook his head with a bemused sigh. 'Anyway, it's done now,' he eventually continued, nudging himself around the table to a set of steps that led up to the flybridge above. 'I suggest we start heading back.'

'Are you sure she's gone?' questioned Iain, barging past Tubbs to peer down over the side.

'As long as the rope holds,' came Mike's apathetic response, disappearing up through a hole in the cockpit's roof.

'And if it doesn't?'

Hearing the motor yacht's engine rumble into life, they glanced up to see his head appear over a gleaming stainless steel railing.

'Then, as I said, she'll either be carried out to sea, or washed up on a beach somewhere, but not before being feasted upon by about a billion fish.'

The two remaining men turned to stare silently out over the vast undulating ocean.

Feeling the yacht begin motoring away, Iain was about to join Mike up on the flybridge, when something caught at the edge of his eye. Stopping where he was, he spun his head around to stare out once again.

'Did you see that?' he asked, turning briefly to look at Tubbs.

'See what?'

'I thought I saw...' He stopped mid-sentence, casting his eyes back out over the ocean's gently rolling waves.

'Are you going to tell me or not?'

Iain shook his head. 'It doesn't matter. For a minute there I thought – I thought I saw the girl, swimming away. Just my imagination, I suppose.'

- CHAPTER ONE -

Friday, 27th August

JOHN TANNER WAS feeling unusually nervous as he turned his polished and recently fixed jet-black Jaguar XJS into Christine Halliday's modest circular drive, and not only because he'd come to pick her up for what was to be their first official date. He'd only just had his car back from the garage having been forced to spend a small fortune getting it through its MOT. If it happened to break down now, or if anything important fell off, like the exhaust for example, he'd be left with little choice but to sell it. The garage's hefty and somewhat extortionate bill left him living off not one, but two credit cards, neither of which had all that much actual credit left. And as he wasn't due to be paid until the end of the month, the first time he had in almost two years, he simply couldn't afford for anything else to go wrong.

Climbing out, he closed the driver's side door as gently as he could to take an admiring step back. He'd always appreciated the lines of the XJS, ever since he'd seen one of his wealthier school friends being picked up in one, some thirty-odd years before. It was one of the aspirational vehicles of its day. It was also the first car he'd seen that he found himself desperate to own. The association with his childhood was one of the reasons why he'd bought it. It reminded him of simpler times, when everything was possible, and all he had to worry about was finishing his homework on time; that and if any of the girls in his class fancied him, of course.

'Nice car!' exclaimed a voice, echoing out from the modest house ahead.

Glancing up, he saw Christine beaming a warm smile over at him.

'Really?' he asked, an anxious frown sending waves rippling over his forehead. He'd always known his car was an unusual choice. It was for that reason he was never quite sure what people's reaction would be.

'Of course!' she replied, with apparent sincerity. 'I mean, what's not to like?'

Tanner shrugged. 'Some people think it's...well, a little eighties.'

'And what's wrong with that? Some of my best memories are from the eighties.'

'They're not exactly known for their reliability, either.'

'It's a classic car. They wouldn't be as much fun if they didn't keep breaking down all the time.'

'I suppose,' Tanner shrugged, his mind taking him back to the numerous occasions when it had, and how much he'd had to fork out each and every time. 'Anyway,' he continued, turning to take her in. 'You look stunning!'

'Oh, please,' she replied, glancing down at her worn jeans and scuffed boots.

'OK, that might have been a slight exaggeration, but in my defence, this *is* the first time I've seen you wearing anything other than your life jacket, that and your rather threadbare blue uniform.'

'It's not quite the first time you have, but I'll take

it anyway. Thank you!'

Skirting around to the other side of the car, he eased the door open for her.

'So, the rumours are true,' she mused, casting her eyes up into his thin, sun-bronzed face. 'You *are* a gentleman.'

'Not really. The handle's been sticking recently, leaving me worried that if someone pulls on it too hard, the entire door will fall off.'

A most unladylike snort blasted out through Christine's nose.

'Are you alright?' Tanner enquired, raising an inquisitive eyebrow.

'Sorry. You caught me off guard with that one. That was all.'

'OK, but you should know, I'm not only holding the door open for you, I'm holding it up as well. And it's not the lightest of car doors either. To be honest, probably the opposite.'

'I suppose I'd better get in then, hadn't I.'

'I suppose you had,' Tanner smiled, taking a moment to watch as she lowered herself down into the car's sumptuous cream leather seats.

Carefully closing the door, he scooted back around to the other side.

Watching him climb in, Christine flipped the sun visor down to check what little makeup she had on in the mirror she found lurking behind it. 'So, how was your day?'

'Busy, unfortunately.'

'Any news on that missing girl?'

'Not a word.'

'Well, it's only been a few days. She'll probably turn up at a boyfriend's house somewhere.'

Tanner clipped in his seatbelt before starting the engine. 'Unfortunately, it will be a week tomorrow since she disappeared. We ran out of family and friends to ask four days ago.'

'Didn't anything come from the press conference?'

'Just the usual round of pointless crank calls,' he replied, shaking his head. 'I still don't think we should have told them that she had a butterfly tattooed on her arm. Giving the press such details only seems to give every man and his dog jumping on the phone something to talk about. It doesn't exactly help that we've still got Professional bloody Standards sniffing about, either.'

'How *is* DI Cooper, anyway?'

'Well, he's still with us, more's the pity.'

'But not for long, though, surely?'

Tanner cast his eyes over his shoulder to begin reversing the car. 'According to Forrester, they've yet to find a single shred of evidence to suggest that he was being coerced by the Clayton family.'

'Then why was he behaving so erratically?'

'Frankly, I've no idea. All I can think of is that he was so pissed-off with me for showing up when I did, he was trying to do everything he could to make me look like an incompetent idiot.'

Christine shook her head. 'I'm not buying that. Not from what you've told me.'

'I don't know. Maybe I was reading more into it than was actually there. Maybe we all were.'

'How's he been taking it?'

'He still seems to hate me, if that's what you mean. More so since Forrester made me the SIO for the missing girl investigation. I wouldn't be surprised if he was scurrying about looking for a transfer.'

'Not before being cleared by Professional Standards, though?'

'Probably not,' Tanner agreed, just as his phone began to ring from inside his salt-encrusted sailing jacket. 'Shit,' he cursed, tugging on the handbrake. 'Please don't tell me that's the office.'

Christine waited patiently as he scrabbled around for his phone.

'Tanner speaking.'

A moment of silence followed.

'OK. Understood. I'll be there in ten minutes.'

'Er...' began Christine, watching as he tucked his phone away, 'we're supposed to be at the restaurant in ten minutes.'

Tanner offered her an apologetic grimace. 'I'm really sorry. Looks like we're going to have to re-schedule. A body's been found over at Thorndike Manor. Forrester wants me to head straight over.'

- CHAPTER TWO -

L IKE MOST PEOPLE living in and around the Norfolk Broads, Tanner had heard of Thorndike Manor. He'd even seen pictures of it. But as he was waved through its towering black wrought iron gates, nothing could have prepared him for just how imposing the estate was, especially the main building planted squarely in the middle.

With his car parked between DCI Forrester's gleaming black BMW 7 Series and Cooper's equally luxurious bullet-grey Audi A5, Tanner levered himself out to peer up at the 16th Century mansion.

As his eyes climbed steadily up its crumbling red brick walls, all the way to a series of triangular crow-stepped gables, they paused to rest on four elongated rectangular chimney stacks, leaving him wondering how the whole thing had remained standing for such a long time. The chimneys alone looked as if they'd topple like dominos if someone was to so much as breathe on them.

Finding the entrance, he nodded briefly at a uniformed constable, standing to attention underneath the building's wide arched alcove before ducking inside. There he found himself gazing around a resplendent wood-panelled foyer; portraits of long-dead members of the British aristocracy staring down their aquiline noses at him, as if he was of no more significance than a stray speck of dust.

With the sound of voices drifting down from the floor above, he made his way up an ornately carved staircase to a half-open door.

Stepping through, he found himself inside a sumptuous stately bedroom in the centre of which stood an impressive Regency-styled four poster bed, one that was surrounded by his colleagues from CID, as well as numerous overall-clad police forensics officers.

Craning his neck to see what, or more likely *who* it was lying on the bed who they all seemed to be staring at, an all-too familiar voice boomed out from behind him.

'Ah, there you are!'

Tanner turned to see DCI Forrester's shining bald head peering at him from around the door he was still standing beside.

'You made good time.'

'I was already in the car,' he replied, with a sanguine smile, stepping forward to find someone else lurking behind the door; a tall, stick-thin man with a stern bony face, dressed head to foot in the pristine uniform of a high-ranking police officer.

'Superintendent Whitaker, this is Detective Inspector John Tanner.'

'Evening, sir,' Tanner responded, bringing himself to attention.

'As I think I mentioned,' Forrester continued, his attention remaining with the superintendent, 'Tanner will be acting as the Senior Investigating Officer.'

'I will?' Tanner enquired, that being the first he'd heard of it.

Forrester whipped his head around to fix his eyes on him. 'Well, you don't expect *me* to do it, do you?' he enquired, before turning to offer the superintendent an amused grimace.

Either unwilling or perhaps unable to appreciate Forrester's rather poor attempt at humour, the superintendent took a moment to look Tanner up and down. 'Forrester has always spoken very highly of you, Detective Inspector.'

Unsure quite how to respond to that, Tanner held the man's gaze to shift his weight from one foot to the other.

'As has Commander Bardsley.'

'Right,' Tanner eventually replied, but only because he felt it necessary to say something.

'For both your sakes,' Whitaker continued, his eyes taking them in, 'I sincerely hope he's right!'

'I can assure you,' interjected Forrester, 'John is our very best man.'

Whitaker sent an imperious snort shooting out through his expansive flaring nostrils. 'That's as maybe, but it's not exactly saying much now, is it. You've only got two other DIs, one of whom is currently being investigated by Professional Standards.'

'For which no evidence has been found.'

'In my experience, where there's smoke there's fire.'

The flippant remark left Forrester clearing his throat. 'You mean, of course, that everyone is innocent until proven guilty, something which naturally extends to our own members of staff. And from what I was told before leaving the office, they're intending to clear Detective Inspector Cooper of all charges.'

'Yes, well,' came Whitaker's dismissive response, his steely blue eyes returning to Tanner's. 'I suppose I'd be a little happier if he was the *only* member of your CID department who'd been under the microscope of Professional Standards.'

'Which is probably why they've gained a reputation for being somewhat overenthusiastic,' Forrester continued, rallying to Tanner's defence.

The superintendent slowly peeled his eyes off Tanner to gaze over towards the bed. 'Anyway, that aside, whoever did this needs to be found, and sooner rather than later. The media attention is going to be huge.'

It was Tanner's turn to clear his throat. 'Forgive me, but does that mean we know the body's identity?'

'It's none other than Lord Blackwell's son, Sir Michael Blackwell,' Whitaker stated, lifting his chin to glare down his nose at first Tanner, then Forrester. 'Which, simply put, means that under absolutely no circumstances are either one of you going to fuck this thing up. Is that understood?'

'Fully, sir,' Forrester replied, pulling his shoulders back to shift the attention over to his most senior officer. 'Isn't that right, Tanner?'

'Er...absolutely, sir,' Tanner replied, albeit with considerably less conviction.

- CHAPTER THREE -

LEFT REELING FROM the news that he'd been made the SIO for what was looking likely to be the single most high-profile investigation of his career to date, without Forrester having even bothered to ask if he wanted to be, Tanner excused himself to slink away from the unwelcome scrutiny of Norfolk's most senior police officer.

Skulking over to where he could see their medical examiner, Dr Johnstone, deep in conversation with DI Vicky Gilbert, together with the still relatively new to CID, DC Mark Townsend, in a tired despondent tone he made the effort to catch the doctor's eye. 'OK, so...what've we got?'

As his colleagues turned their strangely ashen coloured faces towards him, a narrow gap opened up, just enough for Tanner to see for himself.

'Jesus Christ!' he gagged, the acidic taste of uninvited bile catching at the back of his throat.

Lying on the bed was the naked body of a middle aged man, his eyes staring up at the bed's silk-lined canopy, sun-bronzed limbs handcuffed to its ornately carved dark wooden posts. But none of that was what had made Tanner retch so badly. The body's chest cavity had been prised apart, the curved tips of its ribs jutting out like the jaws of a feasting lion. And bulging half-out of his mouth was what Tanner suspected to be the man's blood-filled heart.

'Pretty much as you can see,' Johnstone replied, taking a moment to follow Tanner's gaze. 'But there are some interesting aspects, which I suspect are worth making a note of.'

'Some *interesting* aspects?' Tanner repeated, his eyes unable to tear themselves away from what had been shoved down into the man's wide, open mouth.

'Well, interesting to me, that is,' the medical examiner continued, offering Tanner a nonchalant smile.

Tanner shook his head clear as he struggled to fathom how it was possible for anyone to describe the horrific scene set before them in such a casual manner.

'Anyway,' Johnstone continued, returning his attention back to the body. 'He'd had sexual intercourse shortly before this happened. How long before is difficult to tell, but I'd say he died about twenty-four hours ago, so probably sometime yesterday evening.'

'With a man or a woman?' Tanner enquired; his mind left to consider the likelihood that the person he'd been intimate with was the same person responsible for leaving him in such a state.

'Oh, a woman, at least I'm fairly sure it was. There's a film of what I believe to be vaginal transudate on his, er...*manhood*,' Johnstone muttered, giving Vicky a brief but obviously embarrassed glance, 'but I will of course need to confirm that.'

'Do you think it's possible for a woman to have done *that* to him?'

'If you're asking if a woman would have been able to open up his chest cavity, surgically remove his heart to place inside the mouth of the person she'd only just been having intimate relations with, then yes, of course. From a purely physical perspective, just about anyone could have done this, male or female.'

'Not with their bare hands, though?'

'Well, no, but they wouldn't have needed anything fancy. A simple hacksaw would have done the trick. You can see where the breastbone's been cut, here,' he gestured, leaning over the body, 'so allowing his ribs to be pulled apart. There's nothing to suggest that a surgical spreader was used, either; at least nothing obvious.'

'May we at least assume that he was dead before all this happened?'

'I'm afraid that's probably the worst part,' Johnstone began, slowly pushing his glasses up the bridge of his nose, 'at least for our victim here. He was still alive when whoever was responsible got to work. How long he lasted is difficult to tell, but there are no immediate signs that his heart stopped before eventually being removed.'

- CHAPTER FOUR -

LEAVING JOHNSTONE TO continue with his work, Tanner pulled Vicky to the side of the dimly-lit wood-panelled room. 'Do we know who found the body?' he asked, keeping his voice respectfully low.

'A housekeeper by the name of Margorie Wilson.'

Tanner glanced furtively about. 'Any idea if she's still here?'

'I assumed you'd want a word, so I asked her to wait downstairs.'

'OK, good. Thank you.'

Vicky glanced surreptitiously over Tanner's shoulder to watch Forrester usher a high ranking uniformed police officer out through the door. 'Who's the brass?'

'That, my dear, is Superintendent Whitaker.'

'I thought he looked familiar. Dare I ask what he was doing here?'

'I think he just wanted to make his presence felt, given the size of the house we're standing in, and the identity of the man lying spread-eagled on one of its larger than average four poster beds.'

'I assume that means we're proceeding on the basis that the victim is who everyone's saying he is.'

'Well, the superintendent seems to think so. He probably plays golf with his father. Do we know anything else?'

'Only what Johnstone told you.'

'What about the housekeeper?'

'She was too upset for me to get much out of.'

They both took a moment to gaze over at the body.

'At least we won't be short of DNA evidence,' Vicky continued, her eyes steering themselves over towards the victim's limp sexual organ.

'Perhaps, but only if it *was* the woman he was with who cut out his heart. Even then, she's going to have to have prior form for us to find her.'

Vicky's eyes remained transfixed by the body. 'If it was her, she must have been seriously pissed-off to have done *that* to him. I appreciate the saying that hell has no fury like a woman scorned, but I think this would take that particular idiom to a whole new level.'

'I must admit, it does seem to be just a tad over-dramatic to be the result of a lover's tiff, although choosing to remove the man's heart would perhaps suggest otherwise.'

'I suppose there's always the possibility that she's some sort of deranged psychotic nut-job.'

'Christ!' Tanner exclaimed, 'Not another one, surely!'

Vicky's gaze brought Tanner's attention to Dr Johnstone, skulking his way over towards them; a tablet in one hand, a clear plastic evidence bag in the other.

'Sorry to interrupt,' the medical examiner began, holding the bag up for both Tanner and Vicky to see, 'but I was just handed this by forensics. It was found in the bin beside the bed.'

Vicky peered up at the half-burnt piece of paper that seemed to be hovering inside. 'A scorned lover's note?'

'Looks more like a blackmail letter,' Tanner responded, squinting his eyes in an attempt to read what was left of the words in bold type.

'Judging by the amount of money requested,' Johnstone continued, 'unless the woman he was with was the man's wife, and she was using the opportunity to demand a rather hefty divorce settlement, I'd say Tanner's answer was more likely to be correct.'

Vicky caught the attention of the two men standing before her. 'We're not honestly considering the possibility that some hitherto unknown woman, possibly the man's wife, decided to blackmail him, but when she found her letter left discarded in the bin, she became so enraged that she hand-cuffed him to the bed, forced him to have sex with her before sawing open his rib cage with the hacksaw she just happened to have in her handbag, removing his still beating heart to eventually leave it hanging half-out of the man's rather surprised looking mouth?'

'I suppose that depends on what the argument was about,' Tanner mused. 'And, of course, whether or not her handbag was big enough to fit a hacksaw inside.'

Vicky folded her arms. 'Joking aside, it's hardly the most plausible explanation.'

'In as much as it's probably unlikely that the woman was the one doing the blackmailing. However, I think it would be unwise for us to rule out the possibility that she was the one who murdered him.'

'But she'd have still needed one hell of a motive to have done *that* to him.'

Tanner glanced thoughtfully up towards the high elaborately plastered ceiling. 'I suppose it's possible that it was the blackmailer who simply got tired of waiting for him to pay up. But again, that doesn't seem very likely either.'

'That leaves only one other option – that we have

three separate events taking place at the same time; the girl tying the man up to have sex with him, someone else who opened up his chest with a hacksaw immediately afterwards, and a third party who was trying to blackmail him?'

'I guess that's what you get for being a Knight of the Realm,' Tanner replied. 'Was there anything else written on the note, other than the demand for money?' he continued, glancing around at Johnstone before returning his attention to the bag with the letter inside.

'Just the amount. Fifty thousand in cash.'

'Not a huge amount to go on,' said Vicky, lifting her eyes to Tanner's.

'How long until we can expect the results from the post-mortem?'

'As half the work's already been done for me, I'll probably be able to get something over to you for...shall we say, lunchtime tomorrow?'

'Could we have anything sooner, being who it is?'

Johnstone sighed as he gazed back at the body. 'I suppose I'll be able to get an early summation over to you for first thing in the morning, but that's the best I'll be able to do.'

- CHAPTER FIVE -

W ITH JOHNSTONE RETURNING his attention to the scene of the crime, Tanner led Vicky out of the bedroom in search of the housekeeper who'd discovered the body.

Asking around, they soon found her sitting at an island table, inside a large Victorian kitchen; a female police constable keeping a watchful eye on her from beside an old ceramic Butler sink.

'Mrs Wilson?' Tanner enquired, his line of sight partially blocked by an eclectic mix of pots and pans hanging down from a wrought iron ceiling rack.

The woman glanced up, her rosy crumpled face blinking confirmation at him through round tear-strained eyes.

'Detective Inspector Tanner and my colleague, Detective Inspector Gilbert, Norfolk Police. Is it OK if we ask you a couple of questions?'

After seeking the female constable's approval of their two uninvited guests, the housekeeper turned back to open her mouth. 'I – I don't think I can tell you very much.'

'May we start by asking when you found him?'

The woman stared vacantly down at the china teacup she had cradled in her surprisingly large, masculine hands. 'It was when I came up to change the sheets. Sir Michael likes me to do it every evening, before he goes to bed.'

'What time was that?'

'It would have been just before eight o'clock.'

'Would you have done the same thing yesterday evening?'

'Of course.'

'At the same time?'

'Near enough.'

'Was anyone inside the bedroom when you did?'

'Nobody then.'

'But there was – at some point?'

The woman hesitated, her eyes shifting over to Vicky before narrowing themselves back to Tanner's. 'Like most single men, Sir Michael had a tendency to enjoy the company of women.'

'He wasn't married?'

'His wife died in a horse riding accident, some ten years ago.'

'Children?'

The housekeeper shook her head.

Tanner took a moment to glance about. 'You're saying he lived here all on his own?'

'It's the Blackwells' principal residence. It has been since the 16th Century.'

'So...where's everyone else?'

'His father, Lord Blackwell, had a stroke shortly after his wife died, forcing him somewhat reluctantly into a nursing home. Sir Michael is their only child.'

'And staff?'

'These days, it's only me. The gardens are looked after by a contractor.'

'Am I safe to assume that it wasn't always like that?'

'Good Lord, no! When I first started here there were over a dozen staff, but that was back in the seventies.'

'You've been here for fifty years?' Tanner

questioned, with genuine surprise.

'Fifty-two,' the woman confirmed, her pale blue eyes sparkling with pride.

'Then you must know the family inside and out.'

'Better than most.'

'Sir Michael as well?'

'I was in attendance at his birth.'

'So you can tell us what he was like?'

The elderly woman hesitated for the briefest of moments. 'As you'd expect from someone of his social standing.'

Tanner raised a curious eyebrow. It was an odd thing for her to have said, but fairly obvious what she'd meant; that her employer was like most people he'd met born with a silver spoon in their mouth; pompous, egocentric, and generally speaking rather arrogant.

'Did he have a profession?'

'He studied Medicine, like his father.'

'Did he ever practice?'

'He never needed to.'

'But – he must have had an income from somewhere?'

'I wouldn't know anything about that,' she replied, shaking her head to glance away.

With the lack of staff and the house's crumbling external structure, Tanner made a mental note to look into the family's finances before moving the subject along.

'Going back to yesterday evening, did you see, or maybe hear anyone come into the house, either before or after you changed Sir Michael's bedding?'

The housekeeper continued staring over the kitchen floor, her mouth remaining stubbornly closed.

'It's important, Mrs Wilson.'

'As I said before,' she eventually continued, turning to fix Tanner's eyes, 'like most single men, Sir Michael enjoyed the company of women.'

'Then you know that he was here with someone?'

The housekeeper reached up to wrap her fingers around a small gold cross, hanging lightly down from her neck.

'Do you know who she was?'

'I'm sorry, inspector, but I'm unable to say.'

'You can't, or you won't?'

With still no answer forthcoming, Tanner glanced briefly over at Vicky. 'Mrs Wilson, you do know that it's a common law offence to knowingly withhold information from a criminal investigation.'

'I can't tell you because I don't know.'

'Did you see her?'

Her already rosy cheeks flushed with colour, as her eyes sank slowly to the floor.

'I'll take that as a yes,' Tanner muttered, quietly to himself. 'Are you able to describe her?'

'To be perfectly honest, inspector, they all looked the same.'

'They?'

'Sir Michael hasn't been in a relationship since his wife passed away.'

'I'm sorry, I don't understand.'

'He used working girls for that sort of thing.'

'You mean prostitutes?'

'I've no idea if he paid them or not, but they certainly looked like they were.'

Tanner exchanged a brief glance with Vicky, just to make sure she'd made a note of that before returning his attention back to the housekeeper. 'Do you know if he had any enemies? Anyone who may have held a grudge against him?'

'I'm sure a man in his position had literally dozens

of people who openly resented him.'

'Anyone specific? Someone who'd perhaps come round to the house to threaten him?'

'Good Lord, no! I'd have called the police if they had.'

'OK, what about friends?'

'What about them?'

'Did he have any in particular?'

'One or two.'

'Any chance you could be more specific?'

'There were two he'd spend most of his time with.'

'I don't suppose you know their names, by any chance?'

'A Mr Sanders and a Mr Wallace, neither of which I liked the look of.'

'Any idea as to their first names?'

'I'm not sure I was ever told.'

'And what did they like to do together? Play golf?'

'From what I could gather, they spent most of their time messing about on board their boat.'

- CHAPTER SIX -

ADVISING THE HOUSEKEEPER that she'd need to provide their forensics team with her fingerprints and a DNA sample, with nobody else left to speak to, Tanner led Vicky out of the house onto its expansive unkept gravel driveway.

'Any thoughts about Mrs Wilson?' he asked, stepping over towards their respective cars.

'Only that she seemed to be doing her best to protect the Blackwell family's reputation.'

Tanner zipped up his sailing jacket against the cool summer night's air. 'Do you think she was being protective, or more that she was doing her best to hide her disgust?'

'How d'you mean?'

'Did you see the cross around her neck?'

'I can't say that I did,' Vicky conceded.

'If she turns out to be some sort of Christian fanatic, I can't imagine she'd have been too pleased to find herself having to show an endless stream of prostitutes in through the front door of the house she'd spent the vast proportion of her life working at. Who knows, maybe she snapped when she accidently walked in to find him handcuffed to the bed whilst being ridden like a donkey.'

'If that was the case, wouldn't she have killed the girl as well?'

Tanner shrugged. 'Maybe she tried but found

herself hindered by the fact that she wasn't chained to the bed in quite the same way as her lord and master.'

'And would she really have been able to saw open his chest like that?' continued Vicky, her tone drenched in doubt.

'Johnstone did say that just about anyone would have been capable of doing so, at least from a physical point of view, and it's not as if she had the appearance of being a weak and feeble old lady. Far from it! Maybe her idea was to make it look like the girl had done it, thinking that being banged-up for first degree murder was a suitable punishment for her sacrilegious profession.'

'I've just thought of something else,' Vicky began, stopping beside Tanner's car. 'What if she'd been included in his will, and came to the conclusion that she couldn't wait another thirty-odd years to cash in?'

Tanner gave her a sideways glance. 'Do you think that's likely?'

'Not really, but I suppose it's possible.'

'If she has been included in his will, we're soon going to find out. I suggest we make that the first thing to take a look at. The second will be the state of Sir Michael's finances. She may not have been willing to comment, but even if he couldn't be described as broke, it's fairly clear that he wasn't exactly rolling in cash, not if he couldn't afford to keep his estate in anywhere near the condition it must have been when the place was crawling with servants.'

'Anything else?' asked Vicky, pulling out her notebook.

'The girl he was with. We have to find her. Even if she wasn't directly responsible, there's every chance she was part of the plan. It's simply too much of a coincidence that she just happened to handcuff him to the bed shortly before someone else dropped by with a hacksaw. Maybe she was told to go there with the instructions to ensure he was tied down before letting someone else in through the back door. For all we know, she was there at the time he was cut open. Her testimony is going to be vital.'

'OK, I'll tell Dr Johnstone that we need her DNA sample as a priority. Hopefully, we'll then be able to find her on the database.'

'Next on the list will be to identify the two men the housekeeper said he used to hang out with. What were their names again?'

Vicky turned back a page in her notes. 'Mr Sanders and Mr Wallace.'

'It's a shame she didn't know their first names. I'd hate to think how many Sanders' and Wallace's there are in Norfolk.'

'She did say they used to spend most of the time on board their boat.'

'Yes, she did, didn't she,' said Tanner, tapping a pensive finger against his square-shaped chin. 'I wonder if that meant that they owned a boat together?'

'If Sir Michael was as skint as is being suggested, then it would make sense if they did.'

'It would certainly make them easier to find,' Tanner continued, suppressing an exhausted yawn whilst glancing down at his watch. 'I suggest we give the Broads Authority a call, to ask if they have any boats registered to either Sanders, Wallace, Sir Michael Blackwell; or maybe all three. But for now I think we should call it a day, at least what's left of it. What with who the victim is, the manner by which he's been killed, and the complications surrounding it, I think we're going to need some sleep before all the news media vans start piling up outside the station again.'

- CHAPTER SEVEN -

AYING GOODBYE TO Vicky, Tanner climbed into his car to start digging his fingers into the corners of his eyes. He was both mentally and physically exhausted. There'd normally be months, sometimes years between murder investigations. By that time he'd be praying for something more substantial to work on, other than the normal run-of-the-mill burglary and domestic violence cases that seemed to permanently litter his desk. This time around, not only had it been only two weeks since he'd had to watch Thomas Longshore murder his brother, moments before having his throat torn open by his estranged father's sole remaining Rottweiler, but to suddenly find himself the SIO for the murder of none other than Lord Blackwell's son already had him feeling the pressure.

With the sudden image of Christine entering his mind, and the perturbed look on her face when he'd told her that he was going to have to abandon their plans for the evening, he dug out his phone to give her a call before catching the clock on his Jag's varnished wooden dashboard. It had already gone ten. *Was it too late to call?* he asked himself. If it wasn't, and he did, what would he say? Apologise again for having to bail on what was to have been their first official date together?

He also knew what she'd end up asking. When

would he be free to have another go? It would have been a natural question, one which she'd no doubt expect some sort of definitive answer to, like Sunday afternoon, or Tuesday evening. It didn't matter. He knew he wouldn't be able to say, at least not with any certainty. His availability for the foreseeable future would rest solely upon the roads this new investigation would take him. Would she understand that, and what would she start thinking when he'd be forced to say that he didn't know? It was hardly going to be a response to leave her thinking that he was desperate to see her again.

'Shit,' he cursed quietly to himself, his finger hovering indecisively over the call button.

Finally deciding that it had to be better to call than to not, he was about to press down on the screen when the phone rang in his hand.

Jumping with a start, his surprised frown melted instantly away when he saw who the caller was.

'Hi Christine,' he replied, a natural smile gently lifting the corners of his mouth. 'I was just about to give you a call myself.'

'I didn't know if I should.'

'Oh, there's no harm. If I couldn't answer, it would have just gone through to voicemail. Anyway, I'm pleased you did. I wanted to say sorry again for earlier.'

'There's nothing to apologise for. It's your job. Besides, if you didn't have it, I can't see how you'd have been able to pay for the meal.'

'I *knew* there was a reason why you agreed to go out with me.'

'Er…of course. Why else would I?'

'Anyway, at this rate, it looks like you won't be able to, whether you wanted to or not. At least, not for a while.'

An almost imperceptible pause followed before Christine's voice came back over the line. 'How come?'

'It's another murder, I'm afraid, and a high-profile one at that.'

'Anyone I know?'

Tanner hesitated. 'It's probably best if I don't say who, for the time being at least. Suffice to say, I'd be surprised if you hadn't heard of him. Anyway, Forrester decided to make me the SIO, without even bothering to ask.'

'You wouldn't have wanted to work under Cooper again, would you?'

'Well, no, but it would have been nice to have been given the choice.'

'Couldn't you have refused?'

'Not really. He told me in front of Superintendent Whitaker.'

'Superintendent who?'

'He's Norfolk's most senior police officer. The fact that he was anywhere near the crime scene should give you an idea as to just how high-profile this investigation's going to be.'

'OK, well, no problem. Just give me a call when you know you're going to be free, and we'll re-schedule for another time. But don't leave it too long. I might have to log myself back into my Tinder account.'

Tanner grinned with relief. She was being neither unnecessarily pushy, nor belligerently distant.

He was about to thank her again when her voice came back over the line.

'I did actually call for a reason, other than to remind you that you owe me a night out.'

'That's good to know.'

'I just had a call from my own boss. He told me there's a storm heading our way from Eastern

Europe. It's currently only classed as a category two; but it's forecast to increase up to level three by the time it hits.'

Tanner's thoughts immediately turned to his boat. 'When is it expected?'

'The wind will start building from tomorrow night, but the centre isn't expected to reach us for another couple of days. Anyway, I thought I'd better warn you, ahead of time.'

'OK, thank you. I don't suppose you have any recommendations for my boat?'

'The Broads Water Authority will be advising all liveaboards to seek alternative accommodation for the storm's duration. If it was mine, I'd probably have it craned out. The last time we had a storm like this, there were at least half a dozen swept off their moorings.'

'I'll have to look into it,' Tanner replied, his mind already worried about the cost of having it lifted out.

'If you'd prefer to keep it in the water,' Christine continued, as if reading his mind, 'then I'd suggest finding a floating pontoon to moor it up against. At least then you won't have to worry about the water level. Preferably somewhere that can offer you some shelter from the wind as well.'

'I don't suppose you have any suggestions?'

'I'd have to clear it with my boss,' Christine continued, 'but I think your safest bet would be to moor it up alongside our patrol boats at Potter Heigham. I'm sure he wouldn't mind. The pontoons there are designed to cope with the highest tides.'

'Would you mind asking him for me?'

'Of course. No problem. Assuming he agrees, I still wouldn't risk staying on board.'

'That's not a problem. I'll just have to check myself into a hotel.'

'OK, but just so you know, you can always crash at my place if you like. After all, you did put me up when my house was being overrun by men in white overalls.'

'Thanks for the offer,' he eventually replied, his mind racing to find a suitably diplomatic response, 'but I wouldn't want to impose.'

'Listen, John, I know what you're thinking. I'm keen to take this just as slowly as I'm sure you are. I have a spare bedroom, which is rarely used. You'd be most welcome – no strings attached.'

Tanner smiled. 'Thanks again, Christine. Let me have a think. Meanwhile, I'd better get back to my boat. With an approaching storm and another murder investigation that I'm apparently in charge of, it sounds like I'm going to need my beauty sleep.'

- CHAPTER EIGHT -

Saturday, 28th August

EARLY THE FOLLOWING morning, Wroxham Police Station bustled with activity as its staff gathered inside the main office.

'If I can have everyone's attention, please?' came DCI Forrester's commanding voice, reverberating around the room.

After patiently waiting for numerous conversations to come spluttering to an eventual conclusion, he sucked in a breath before continuing. 'Firstly, I'd like to thank you all for giving up your weekend. Your families as well. I know it's never easy when you have to cancel plans at such short notice, but unfortunately, with what – or should I say *who* was discovered last night – frankly, I didn't feel I had any choice but to drag you all in. I'd also like to apologise for being unable to say why it was necessary, but Headquarters is keen for us to keep what has happened as quiet as possible; for as long as possible as well.'

He paused for breath, leaving the office staff waiting in a state of silent anticipation.

'At around eight o'clock last night, the body of Lord Blackwell's son, Sir Michael Blackwell, was found in an upstairs bedroom at Thorndike Manor.'

As expected, a flurry of whispered remarks hurtled

their way around the room, leaving Forrester raising his hands in an effort to refocus everyone's attention.

'We're still awaiting confirmation from our medical examiner,' he was eventually able to continue, 'but for reasons that will be made clear shortly, there doesn't appear any need for us to question the manner of his death. Subsequently, unless we hear otherwise, we're treating this as first degree murder.

'It only remains for me to hand you over to DI Tanner,' Forrester continued, glancing over to his senior detective inspector, beside whom stood the handsome DC Townsend, a slim file clutched awkwardly in his youthful hands. 'Despite having only been back with us for a few weeks; and having barely had a chance to catch his breath after bringing our last major investigation to a successful conclusion, Tanner has been kind enough to put his name forward to head this one up as well.'

The idea that he'd somehow volunteered had him offering the cheap wiry carpet tiles he was standing on a petulant smirk.

'Whilst on the subject of who heads up what,' Forrester continued, casting his eyes around the room, 'I'd like to add that the decision for Tanner to take the lead once again bears no reflection on DI Cooper's abilities in any way, shape or form.'

Tanner followed Forrester's gaze to find him staring at his younger male counterpart, who in turn was forcing a smile directly back at their DCI.

'Cooper did an outstanding job during Tanner's somewhat lengthy absence,' Forrester continued, 'especially in light of his overall lack of experience.'

Tanner watched with pitying amusement as Cooper's face darkened with humiliated rage, his eyes ricocheting off Forrester's to bury themselves into the farthest wall.

'But as our most senior DI, both myself and Superintendent Whitaker believe that with such a high profile murder investigation, it's only right that the role of SIO went to our most experienced officer.

'Right then!' Forrester stated, briefly lifting himself up onto the balls of his feet. 'I'm sure I don't need to mention anything about the extreme sensitivity that this investigation presents. I subsequently expect you to treat what you're about to hear with the strictest confidence. In other words, I don't want any of you discussing this with your family, or down the pub with your friends. And if I hear of a single instance of someone breaking ranks to talk to the press, you'll be facing disciplinary charges. Assuming that's understood, here's DI Tanner to fill you in on what we know so far.'

'Thank you, sir,' Tanner began, glancing over his shoulder to see Townsend begin attaching a series of photographs onto the whiteboard behind him. 'As DCI Forrester has already mentioned, Sir Michael Blackwell's body was found yesterday evening. He was discovered lying face-up on a four poster bed by the estate's one and only full-time employee, a housekeeper by the name of Mrs Wilson. As you can see from the photographs, he'd had both his wrists and ankles handcuffed to each of the bedposts after which someone cut open his rib cage to remove his heart, leaving it placed somewhat indiscreetly inside his open mouth.'

Tanner let his eyes meander about the room where he found a number of those in the audience glancing away, as the increasingly graphic images continued to be posted up.

'What you won't be able to see is that he's thought to have had sexual intercourse with a woman, shortly before meeting his untimely end. We've also been told that the victim's chest was cut open whilst he was still alive. How long he would have lasted isn't clear,' he continued, 'but it's worth noting that, according to the ME's preliminary report, a heavy dose of adrenaline was administered before the process began. We can only assume that this was to help keep the victim conscious for as long as possible without dulling his ability to feel the surgical procedure being carried out.'

'*Jesus Christ!*' came a horrified muttering from someone out in the audience.

'Yes, quite!' Tanner agreed, taking a moment to glance around at the whiteboard behind him. 'Bearing all that in mind, I think it goes without saying that we're dealing with a particularly dangerous individual, one who either had an extremely strong motive for wanting Sir Michael killed, and in the most horrific way imaginable, or worse still, a deranged psychopath medically incapable of feeling a single shred of empathy towards the manner of their victim's death.

'The perpetrator's motive aside – for now at least – I believe our first priority is to identify the woman he was with. It seems far too much of a coincidence for her not to have been involved somehow, either directly, or as a means to ensure the victim had been secured to the bed with minimal fuss. The housekeeper seemed to be of the opinion that the woman he'd been with was a working girl. If that is the case, and she's spent time with us before, then it should be a straightforward enough process to work out who she is. We just need to await the relevant DNA sampling. There is, however, one more complication which has yet to be mentioned.'

Tanner nodded again at Townsend, leaving him to

post up what was to be the final photograph.

'What was left of the following typed letter was found in the bin beside the bed. The demand for fifty thousand pounds leads us to assume that it was some sort of blackmail attempt. For reasons which should hopefully be obvious, we're assuming that it's unlikely the blackmailer is the same person who took Sir Michael's life, unless of course that person came to the conclusion that he was never going to pay, which leads neatly on to the subject of his financial situation. Judging by the lack of staff, the dilapidated state of Thorndike Manor and the fact that Sir Michael didn't seem to have any obvious means of income, we need to take a look into his current financial situation. We also need to find out if he owed large amounts of money to anyone other than a reputable bank, and if there was someone in his life who had a particular reason to hold a grudge against him. With that in mind, I suggest we start by talking to his friends. Fortunately, the housekeeper was able to provide us with the surnames of two people she thought he'd been spending the bulk of his time with recently. Thanks to an early start by DI Gilbert, we've managed to identify them as being a Mr Iain Sanders and a Mr Toby Wallace, also Norfolk residents. According to the Broads Authority, a fifty-foot Fairline Squadron is registered in their names; Sir Michael's included.

'The only other item we need to consider is Sir Michael's will. As an only child without children of his own – at least none that we know of – and with his wife having died about ten years ago, we need to know who he's left the estate to, and the whereabouts of that person at the time of his death.

'So, whilst waiting for forensics and our medical examiner to come back to us with their final reports,

DI Gilbert and myself are going to see if we can have a chat with his two named friends. Meanwhile, DC Townsend is going to find out all he can about Sir Michael's life, in particular his movements over the last few days. DC Beech, I'd like you to first start by requesting a copy of his will from his solicitors; then start looking into his finances. Where did he get his money from, and did he owe it to anyone in sufficient quantities to justify him being killed over it?

'Right, that's it,' Tanner concluded, clasping his hands together. 'Please tell me the moment you find out anything, whether you think it's important or not, and a reminder once again – no talking to anyone; friends and family included.'

As the room broke into a cacophony of noise, Tanner saw Cooper skulk out through the dispersing crowd towards him, a disgruntled look of wounded resentment etched out over his face.

'What about me?' he asked as he approached, unable to look Tanner directly in the eye.

Realising he'd managed to forget that he was even there, Tanner took a hesitant moment to clear his throat. At the end of the day, despite having been cleared by Professional Standards, he still didn't trust him. However, he also knew that he didn't wish to spend the entire investigation having to fight him at every turn. 'With Forrester's permission,' Tanner began, taking a diplomatic stance, 'I'd like you to head-up an investigation into the blackmail attempt.'

'Oh, right!' Cooper replied, a hesitant look of indecisive gratitude creasing the corners of his eyes.

'Until we're told otherwise, I can't help but think that the two must be separate, so it only makes sense for us to treat them as such. I'll ask DC Townsend to assist you. I'm sure I'll be able to find someone else to cover his work.'

- CHAPTER NINE -

A FTER A BRIEF conversation with Forrester, outlining the thought process behind giving Cooper the lead on the blackmail side of the investigation, Tanner and Vicky made their way out in search of the first of the two men Sir Michael's housekeeper had mentioned, Mr Iain Sanders.

With nobody answering the door at his registered address, they turned to the only other place they thought he might be, the boat the Broads Authority had listed under his name. According to their records, it was supposedly moored up somewhere along Acle Dyke, just off one of the River Bure's many sweeping bends.

'What was it called again?' Tanner queried, climbing out of his car to stare down a long line of boats, each moored aft-end to the purpose built grass-lined hardstanding.

'Medusa,' Vicky replied, slamming the XJS's car door to leave Tanner casting his eyes over it in a state of cautious anxiety.

'Sorry, Vicky. May I ask if you could close the door a little more gently in the future?'

'Why's that?' she asked, sending a mischievous smirk at him over the Jag's sloping low roof. 'Do you think something will fall off?'

'To be honest, I'd rather not take that chance.'

Vicky nodded to offer him a reassuring smile. 'I'll

be more careful next time.'

'It would be appreciated,' Tanner replied, peeling his eyes off the car to begin leading the way down the dyke.

Seeking out each boat's name, it didn't take them long to find the one they were looking for, for no other reason than it was by far the largest boat there.

With nobody in view, either within its wide rectangular cockpit or through its open glass sliding door, Tanner stood back to call out, 'Hello! Is anyone home?'

A scuffling sound from the flybridge at the top of the boat had them both glancing up to find the shaved suntanned head of a thin middle-aged man, staring down at them over a highly polished chrome railing.

'Can I help you?'

'Are you Mr Iain Sanders of 14, Lulworth Avenue?'

'That probably depends on who's asking.'

Tanner held aloft his ID. 'Detective Inspector Tanner, and my colleague, Detective Inspector Gilbert. Norfolk Police.'

The man stood up straight, his eyes shifting between the two of them. 'What's this about?'

'It's concerning someone we believe to be a close friend of yours, Sir Michael Blackwell.'

'Yes, and... what about him?'

'Does that mean you *are* Iain Sanders?'

'OK, yes, but you still haven't told me why you're here.'

Tanner sucked in a fortifying breath. 'I'm afraid I may have some rather distressing news for you. Sir Michael's body was found inside his home yesterday evening.'

'His *body?*'

'Due to the nature of his death,' Tanner continued, 'we're going to have to ask you where you were on

Thursday night from around eight o'clock to twelve?'

'You mean someone...killed him?' Sanders questioned, his eyes widening in shock.

'We're not in a position to say how he died, only that his death wasn't from natural causes.'

Tanner and Vicky watched as the man's narrow bony face visibly paled, disappearing a moment later to be replaced by a pair of long gangly legs tumbling down a series of moulded plastic steps.

'Do you have any idea who killed him?' they heard him demand, his head re-appearing through the opening in the cockpit's ceiling.

'Not yet.'

'But you must have some idea?'

'Naturally,' Tanner said, offering Sanders a thin detached smile, 'which is why we're keen to find out where you were the night before last.'

'You can't possibly think that I had anything to do with it?'

'We don't have any particular reason to think that you did, but it would certainly be useful if we could eliminate you from our enquiries, hence the question.'

The man stopped to stare vacantly down at the cockpit's dark wooden table. 'I was here, with another friend. It was our poker night. We were waiting for Mike, but he never showed.'

'Your other friend wasn't Mr Toby Wallace, by any chance?'

Sanders nodded to sink slowly down into a black folding chair.

'Will he be able to confirm that?'

'Of course.'

'Would anyone else?'

The man glanced up, as if being woken from a dream. 'Huh?'

'Would anyone else be able to confirm that you were here on Thursday night other than your friend, Mr Toby Wallace?'

'Well, no, I mean...I - I don't know,' he stuttered, turning his head to glance around at the boats moored up on either side. 'You can ask our neighbours, I suppose. They probably heard us. We do seem to make more noise than perhaps we should.'

'Am I to assume that this was a regular occurrence?'

'Pretty much. Every Thursday.'

'May I ask how long you'd known each other?'

'Me and Michael? Oh...years! We went to Cambridge together.'

'And Mr Wallace?'

'Not quite so long. Michael introduced me to him a while back. The three of us turned out to be looking to buy at boat at the same time, so after a few drinks we came up with the idea of picking one up together.'

'I don't suppose you know how Mr Wallace knew Sir Michael?'

Sanders nodded. 'They're in business together.'

Tanner raised an intrigued eyebrow over at Vicky. 'Are they still?'

'Not if Michael's dead, they aren't!'

Tanner offered the man a contemptuous smile. '*Before* Sir Michael died.'

Sanders eyes drifted away. 'As far as I know.'

'Do you have any idea as to what sort of business they were in?'

'They owned the Phantom Exchange.'

'Sorry – the what?' Tanner questioned, shooting a glance back at Vicky.

'It's the largest nightclub in Norwich,' she replied. 'Actually, I think it's the only nightclub in Norwich.'

Having never heard of it before, probably because

he'd not stepped inside one since dating his ex-wife at university, as he turned his attention back to Sanders, Tanner suddenly felt rather old. 'And Sir Michael was into that sort of thing, was he?'

'He did seem to be.'

'As I assume is your other friend, Mr Wallace?'

'It was he who approached Michael, looking for finance.'

'How about you?'

'He asked me as well, but it's not my thing. Too loud for my liking.'

Tanner took a moment to run his eyes over the smooth elegant lines of the luxury yacht they were standing beside. 'May I ask what you do for money?'

'If you mean my profession, I used to work in banking. Risk Management, to be precise.'

'Not anymore?'

'I retired a few years ago. The riskiest thing I do these days is to take this out sea fishing,' he laughed, the grin evaporating a moment later.

Tanner studied his face. 'When was the last time you saw Sir Michael?'

'It was, er...' the man started, his head turning to the cockpit's floor. 'It must have been last Saturday.'

'And what did you do?'

'What we always did. Took the boat out to see what we could catch, or as was more normally the case, what we couldn't.'

'The three of you?'

The man looked up to hold Tanner's gaze. 'That's right.'

'How did he seem?'

'Sorry, I'm not with you?'

Tanner shrugged. 'Did he appear worried about anything?'

'Who, Michael?' the man snorted. 'He wasn't

exactly the type to spend his life worrying about things. I'm not sure it's something the British Aristocracy are even capable of.'

'He didn't have money troubles, or anything?'

'He never seemed to be short of cash; if that's what you mean.'

'But he couldn't afford to buy his own boat.'

'Oh, right. To be honest, I'd never thought about it like that before. I suppose it's possible that he wasn't as wealthy as he liked to make out. He did talk about selling Thorndike Manor when his father died, but only because he said it was too big for him to live in on his own.'

'Do you know if he was in a relationship with anyone?'

'Not that I know of. His wife died a while back. Horse riding accident.'

'Yes, we heard.'

'He made out that it didn't bother him all that much, but I suspect in reality it hit him pretty hard. Anyway, after that, he swore an oath to remain single.'

'You're saying that he wasn't interested in woman?'

'Quite the opposite,' Sanders smirked. 'He just wasn't interested in being with any one in particular.'

'Any idea why?'

Sanders shrugged. 'Personally, I think he had trust issues. When you're born into the British aristocracy, I can imagine it being difficult to know if a woman is interested in either you or your title.'

'Fair enough,' Tanner mused. 'How about you?'

'Was I born into the British aristocracy, or do I have trust issues?'

Tanner folded his arms over his chest in an attempt to display his lack of amusement. 'Are you in a relationship, Mr Sanders?'

'I am, thank you very much. Happily married with three teenage children, none of whom I probably deserve.'

'Going back to these girls you say Sir Michael would hang out with. Any idea who they all were?'

'Nope!'

'You never met them?'

'He didn't exactly bring them round for dinner.'

'You didn't see one in particular he'd be hanging around with?'

'I thought I just told you!' Sanders exclaimed, glaring out at Tanner. 'He was never with one woman more than once.'

'You did, yes, but how would you know,' Tanner continued, a sagacious frown weaving its way over his forehead, 'if, as you said, you never met any of them?'

Sanders rubbed hard at his eyes before staring back. 'Look, why all the interest in his bloody girlfriends, anyway?'

Tanner offered the man a seemingly indifferent shrug. 'No particular reason. At the moment, we're simply endeavouring to find out as much about Sir Michael's life as possible.'

'Do you think one of them could have killed him?'

'It's possible, but then again, it's also possible that his murderer was one of his friends, someone he used to go sea fishing with, for example.'

'I've already told you where I was.'

'So you did. Anyway, going back to the subject of his various girlfriends. I don't suppose you have any idea where he'd meet them all?'

'Not a clue, sorry,' Sanders replied, his gaze falling to the cockpit's floor.

- CHAPTER TEN -

ARRANGING TO HAVE Sanders' fingerprints and DNA collected, they began making their way back to the car when Tanner noticed somebody moving about inside one of the other much smaller boats.

Stealing a glance back down the dyke to see Sanders' head duck down inside his yacht's luxurious main cabin, Tanner stepped lightly onto the boat they'd stopped besides to rap his knuckles gently against one of its thick glass windows.

'Excuse me,' he called, fishing out his ID as a mop of ginger hair appeared through the doors at the back. 'DI Tanner, Norfolk Police. You wouldn't happen to live on board, by any chance?'

'Only during the summer,' the woman replied, offering him an affable enough smile.

'I don't suppose you would have been here on Thursday evening?' Tanner continued, watching a well-fed tortoiseshell cat weave its way between the woman's legs.

'I'm not sure where else I'd have been,' she replied, scooping the cat up into her arms.

Tanner tilted his head to glance surreptitiously back down the line of boats. 'You wouldn't be able to verify if there was anyone on board the large motor yacht at the end of the dyke?'

'If you mean the over-sized Fairline, then

unfortunately, yes.'

'Why unfortunately?'

'Because of the constant bloody noise they make. I've made countless complaints to the guy who owns the moorings, but he's never bothered to do anything about it.'

'And that was the case on Thursday?'

'Well…maybe not *quite* as much as normal, but I suspect that was because there were only two of them that time.'

'I don't suppose you know which two they were?'

'The tall skinny one and the short fat one. It was the posh good-looking one with the fetish for wearing horrendous pink shirts who wasn't.'

Tanner glanced around at Vicky, busily taking notes behind him.

'But what they get up to during the week is nothing compared to the weekends,' the woman continued.

'And what happens then, may I ask?'

'What *doesn't* happen then!' the woman exclaimed, shaking her head in apparent disgust. 'Music to all hours, drugs as well, and enough alcohol to sink the Titanic all over again.'

'What about women?'

'If you can call them that.'

Tanner raised an eyebrow. 'What would you call them?'

'Prostitutes!' the woman spat, lifting her head to stare directly at the boat under discussion. 'At least, they dress as if they are.'

- CHAPTER ELEVEN

'AT LEAST WE know Sanders can't be trusted,' commented Vicky, as they continued their journey back to the car.

'With regards to what?'

'He said he never met any of Sir Michael's women, when it sounds like they all did, and on what would appear to be quite an intimate basis.'

'Yes, well; I'm not sure we can blame him for lying about that. He's probably just trying to prevent his wife and children from finding out.'

'But we can blame him for spending his weekends with women who need to be paid to perform. We could arrest him, as well.'

'Only if they'd been coerced into doing so,' Tanner continued. 'Anyway, at this stage, we don't even know if they even were prostitutes.'

'But it fits with what Sir Michael's housekeeper said – about the women who'd come round to see him.'

'Who could have just as easily been girls he met at his nightclub. As one of the owners, I can imagine he'd have had his pick. All we've really learnt so far is that our Mr Sanders isn't the most faithful of husbands; that and his alibi would appear to be sound. And as there isn't any obvious motive for him wishing Sir Michael harm, at least not to the extent of feeling it necessary to open up his rib cage with a hacksaw, then I suspect he's not our man. However, saying that, I couldn't help think that there was something else he was lying about.'

'What was that?'

'When I asked him about the last time he'd seen Sir Michael,' Tanner explained, coming to a halt beside his car. 'When he said they went fishing together, he looked me straight in the eye and said it was just the three of them.'

'Don't psychologists say that people are only lying if they look away?'

'I think that depends on the person. From my own experience, more calculating individuals know they're supposed to look away, so in an attempt to convince you that they're telling the truth, they do the opposite.'

Vicky shrugged. 'Then they probably had some girls on board the boat with them, and he didn't want us to know.'

'Probably,' Tanner mused, pulling open the driver's side door, 'although, saying that, it was the only time he did. Anyway, it was just an observation.'

The sound of his phone ringing had him digging it out to stare down at the screen. 'It's Forrester. No doubt checking up on us.'

Taking the call, he stood up straight to pull his shoulders back. 'Tanner speaking!'

'Just calling to see how you've been getting on?'

Tanner rolled his eyes at Vicky before turning away. 'We've just finished talking to the first of Sir Michael's friends, Mr Iain Sanders.'

'Did you hear the news?' Forrester continued.

'What news?'

'Sir Michael's murder. The media's found out about it. The story's running across all major broadcasters.'

'But – how? Surely it wasn't one of us?'

'Looks like it was the housekeeper, probably doing her best to cash in; at least, she's the only person who's been interviewed. If that isn't bad enough, what's she's been saying is potentially worse.'

'What's that?'

'That the last person to see Sir Michael was the woman he was with.'

'Then I suppose it's a good job she doesn't know who it was.'

'Unfortunately, it looks like she does.'

'That's not what she told us!'

'Well...she's gone and given them all a name, so it looks like she did after all. The problem is, it's not the same one we have.'

'OK, now I'm confused. I didn't even know we had one.'

'We've just this minute had a match with a DNA sample Dr Johnstone sent over. Apparently, the woman Sir Michael was with that night was a Miss Claire Metcalf. She's on our database for soliciting prostitution. I've asked Sally to email you her address.'

'And what's the name our housekeeper's being telling everyone?'

'Amber Vale.'

'Does that mean there were two girls with Sir Michael that night?'

'I've no idea, but one thing I do know; at this precise moment in time just about every journalist in the UK is trying to find her, so I suggest you speak to Claire Metcalf. Hopefully she'll be able to point us in the right direction.'

- CHAPTER TWELVE -

ENDING THE CALL to find an address waiting for him in his inbox, it wasn't long before they were parking up in front of a large sandstone coloured block of flats on the outskirts of Norwich.

After leading the way up a set of cold grey concrete steps to the third floor, Tanner was soon leaning his finger against a cheap plastic bell as Vicky dug out her ID beside him.

'Miss Claire Metcalf?' Tanner enquired, holding up his own to the face of the attractive young woman who'd answered the door, her natural beauty hidden by layers of garishly coloured makeup.

'Christ!' the woman replied, glaring first at Tanner, then over at Vicky. 'What've I done now, for fuck's sake?'

'DI Tanner and DI Gilbert, Norfolk Police,' Tanner stated. 'We just have a couple of questions. May we come in?'

'Er, no, you may not. Now, get on with it. I was about to go out.'

'Anywhere nice?'

'Not that it's got anything to do with you, but some of us have got to work for a living.'

'And what sort of work is that?'

The woman looked Tanner up and down. 'Nothing you could afford, darlin', at least, not if that suit is anything to go by.'

'Is that an open confession to soliciting sexual favours in return for someone's hard earned cash?'

'I'm an exotic dancer, thank you very much.'

'Oh, I see. And where abouts is it that you "exotically dance"?'

Metcalf folded her arms over her ample-sized chest. 'The Riverside Gentleman's Club; if you must know.'

Tanner turned to raise a questioning eyebrow at Vicky.

'Don't look at me,' his colleague replied, tilting her head to give him an accusatory glare.

'It's a private club, about two bus stops that way,' Metcalf interjected, pointing off towards where they could see Norwich Cathedral's spire rising majestically up from its burgeoning city's centre.

'I see,' Tanner continued. 'And that's what you were doing on top of Sir Michael Blackwell on Thursday evening at around nine o'clock; exotically dancing?'

The woman's eyes darted erratically between the two detectives before coming to an eventual rest on Tanner's. 'I was his escort for the evening.'

'Right, yes, of course. And where did you escort him to?'

'Oh, you know, around,' she replied, offering him an irreverent smirk.

'Around where? His bedroom?'

Metcalf shrugged back in response.

'After which you just happened to find yourself on top of him, having accidently handcuffed his wrists and ankles to the bed posts?'

'I don't know what he's been telling you, but whatever it is, it isn't true.'

'Unfortunately, for him at least, he hasn't told us anything.'

'Then what makes you think I was there?'

'You're honestly trying to tell us you don't know?'

Her eyes stared blankly into Tanner's, the mascara lined lids remaining fixed and unblinking.

Tanner drew in an impatient breath. 'Sir Michael's body was found by his housekeeper yesterday. Someone had cut open his rib cage with a hacksaw to remove his still beating heart before stuffing it down into his throat. Apparently, it's been all over the news this morning.'

'But – I...' she began, her voice trailing away as the skin beneath her foundation rapidly drained of all colour.

'But you...what? Didn't mean it? I see. So I suppose you're going to tell me that you lost the keys for the handcuffs, and the hacksaw slipped when you were trying to cut them off?'

'No – I – I d-didn't...' she spluttered, her former proud countenance crumbling before their very eyes.

'OK, listen, Claire,' Tanner began, adopting a more gentle tone of voice, 'to be completely honest, we believe you; at least the part about you not having been the one who cut him open with a hacksaw. And whether or not you were there to provide Sir Michael with sexual favours is frankly of little interest. What is, however, is how you ended up being there?'

'How'd you mean?'

'Did he call you?'

She nodded her head.

'You don't use some sort of an intermediary?'

'I don't have a pimp; if that's what you mean,' she stated, her eyelids batting away at an escaping tear.

Tanner took a moment to study her face. 'OK, so...how often would you see him, roughly?'

'I don't know. Once a month?'

'Did he see any other girls?'

'I've no idea.'

'What happened afterwards?'

Metcalf shrugged. 'I just un-cuffed him, got dressed, and left.'

'There wasn't anyone else there with you?'

She shook her head. 'I was on my own.'

'Are you sure about that?'

'Yes.'

'So...how come you say you left him alive and well having uncuffed him from the bed, only for the housekeeper to find him back in the exact same position, that time with a hole in his chest where his heart used to be?'

'I d-don't know. Someone must have come in after I left. All I know is that he was alive and well when I left him.'

'You're sure you weren't sent there at someone's behest?

'I swear!'

'And that there was nobody else with you?'

'On my mother's life!'

'You do know that we can take you down to the station to ask you all this again, this time under caution, don't you?'

'Be my guest, but it won't change my answer.'

'What if I said that we've heard from a reliable source that someone *was* with you at the time?'

Tanner watched her full red lips tighten as her eyes continued to stare.

'A woman by the name of Amber Vale, for example?' Tanner continued.

Metcalf's countenance remained unchanged for a split second longer before she suddenly snorted with laughter, leaving her face cracked in half by a wide broad grin.

Tanner glanced curiously around at Vicky. 'Did I

say something funny?'

'Not at all,' Metcalf continued, straightening her face. 'You're hardly the first person to make that mistake.'

It was Tanner's turn to look confused. 'And what mistake was that?'

'Amber Vale is my stage name. I'd never be stupid enough to use my real name for work.'

- CHAPTER THIRTEEN -

'A T LEAST WE know that there was only one
girl with him that night,' Vicky commented,
stepping around a hunched-over old lady at
the base of the communal stairs.

'I'm not so sure we even know that,' replied
Tanner.

'We don't?'

'Well, if she wasn't the one who left him
handcuffed to the bed, then someone did.'

'Oh, please! Don't tell me you believe her?'

'I suppose that depends on which part. At this
stage, all I know is that she didn't kill him.'

'You seem very sure.'

Tanner shrugged. 'I just can't see her as being the
type capable of doing such a thing.'

Reaching the car, Vicky stopped to stare at him.
'Then maybe we shouldn't judge a book by its cover.
Don't forget what Johnstone said, that he thought it
would have been possible for anyone to have done it.
All they'd have needed was a hacksaw.'

'And the adrenaline, of course.'

'Yes, well; with the sort of people she must meet
through her line of work, I can't imagine it would
have been too difficult for her to get hold of.'

'Look, don't get me wrong,' Tanner began, 'it's not
that I don't think she could have killed him, it's the
method that bothers me. Had he been stabbed, or

maybe had his throat cut, then I'd be more easily convinced, but not with his chest being opened up like that. She'd have needed one hell of a motive. No! Whoever killed him wanted him to suffer, and when I say suffer, I mean *really* suffer.'

'What if she *was* a furious woman who'd recently been scorned?'

'I wasn't aware she had been.'

'I can think of a least two scenarios which could have led her to be, certainly if she turns out to have psychological problems we don't yet know about. For example, if he'd proposed, only to end up laughing at her face when she found out that he had no intention of marrying her. Or maybe if he'd convinced her that she was the only woman for him, only to find out she was just one of a very long line.'

'Fair enough,' Tanner continued, skirting around to the driver's side door, 'but she's going to need to have some pretty serious mental issues. I don't mind taking a look at her medical history, but if nothing shows up, I think we need to focus our attention on the people she knows from work.'

'OK, well, you're the boss, I suppose.'

'You don't agree?'

'Not really, but hey, what do I know? So anyway, what's next?'

Tanner turned to look over his Jag's sweeping low roof to find her staring vacantly down at her open notebook. Wondering if he'd either said or done something to upset her, he glanced away to tug open the car's door. 'I suggest we make our way over to see the second of Sir Michael's friends the housekeeper mentioned. What was his name again?'

'Toby Wallace,' Vicky replied. 'I've got his address. It's not far from where we are now.'

- CHAPTER FOURTEEN -

'IT SHOULD BE up here on the left,' said Vicky, staring out of the passenger-side window where a long line of elegant stately homes could be seen drifting effortlessly past.

'Quite a contrast from where we've come from,' Tanner observed, keeping one eye on the road ahead, the other peeled for the house number they were looking for.

'Chalk and cheese,' Vicky muttered in agreement, before sitting up in her seat. 'Hold on. This looks like it.'

Just up ahead was a curved wall leading into an impressively wide driveway, the number 42 standing proud against its neatly laid corn-yellow bricks.

Checking his rear view mirror, Tanner indicated to turn in, only to slam on his brakes as an enormous black Mercedes SUV came surging out the other way, skidding to a halt just inches away from Tanner's polished chrome bumper.

As he glared up at the driver, and the guy sitting opposite, both seemingly mouthing abuse at him, Tanner opened his door only to be greeted by the disgruntled sound of the SUV's horn.

'This should be fun,' he muttered to Vicky, levering himself out as the horn blasted out again.

Leaving his door open, Tanner pulled out his ID to step up to the obstructing vehicle, just as the driver's side window wound slowly down to reveal a large anvil-shaped head.

'You gonna get out of my fucking way, or is me and my mate gonna 'ave to get out and beat the living shit out of you?'

A curious frown rippled its way over Tanner's sun-bronzed forehead. 'Do you normally speak to your fellow road users in such an aggressive manner?'

'What the fuck's it got to do with you?'

Tanner held aloft his ID. 'DI Tanner, Norfolk Police.'

The man glared out at it with a look of abject contempt. 'I should've guessed,' he growled, looking Tanner up and down. 'Cheap suit, stupid car.'

Tanner glanced over the driver's shoulder, first at the gorilla-like man stuffed into the seat beside him, then at a shadowy figure sitting immediately behind.

'I don't suppose any of you would happen to be the property's owner; a Mr Toby Wallace, by any chance?'

'Never 'eard of 'im,' the driver replied.

'Even though it would appear that you're driving out of his registered address?'

The man gave Tanner an indifferent shrug. 'We took a wrong turn.'

'Right, yes, I see. May I ask your name?'

'I wasn't aware I'd done anything wrong.'

'Driving with undue care and attention, for a start.'

'Don't make me laugh. You're the one who nearly drove straight into us. If I was you, I'd get them brakes of yours checked.'

Tanner watched as the driver tilted his head back to listen to something being whispered to him from the person behind.

'Anyways,' he eventually continued, bringing his attention back to Tanner. 'we've got some place to be. Now, are you gonna move that gay-looking car of yours, or am I gonna 'ave to drive over the top of it?'

'I'm afraid I'm going to need to see your driver's licence first.'

'Good luck with that,' the man huffed, glancing back over his shoulder to reverse a few feet before revving the engine to wheelspin away, leaving Tanner and Vicky standing in a swirling cloud of burnt rubber and noxious diesel fumes.

After taking a peaceful moment to watch the vehicle career off down the otherwise quiet tree-lined avenue, Tanner glanced around to find Vicky standing beside him. 'What delightful characters. Please tell me you got that guy's numberplate?'

'That, together with the make and model,' she confirmed, offering Tanner a satisfied grin.

- CHAPTER FIFTEEN -

WITH VICKY CALLING the SUV's numberplate through to the office, they climbed back into Tanner's car to continue the short journey through the property's curved bricked entrance. Once inside, they found themselves driving through a spacious Mediterranean-styled courtyard; a large over-hanging pergola leaving dappled sunlight over smooth terracotta flagstones.

'This is all rather nice,' commented Vicky, casting an admiring eye over a line of matching miniature fir trees, each one rising gracefully out of a giant metallic oval-shaped flowerpot.

'A tad gaudy for my tastes,' Tanner replied, with perhaps a touch of jealousy to his tone.

'Nice car as well,' she added, nodding over at a curvaceous Bentley Continental, languishing next to a modern rectangular front door, it's dark gunmetal colour perfectly matching the car's glistening paintwork.

'Perhaps, but you'd have to be a certain type to feel comfortable driving around in one.'

'What, you mean...rich?'

'I actually meant someone with all the characteristics of being pompous, overbearing and arrogant, but lying in the depths of their core is a shallow pool of insecure vulnerability.'

Vicky raised an intrigued eyebrow at him. 'You're

not doing an online course in psychiatry, by any chance?'

'Er, not exactly. That's Christine's professional assessment of why I choose to drive around in a fuel-guzzling twelve-litre Jaguar XJS.'

Vicky smiled before glancing away. 'How're you two getting along, anyway?'

'Oh, um...not sure, really,' he replied, his mind taking him back to the time when Vicky had asked him out, a few weeks before, or at least when he thought she had. Deciding that it was probably best to play their relationship down, which wasn't exactly difficult, he caught the corner of her eye. 'We haven't been on an actual date yet. To be honest, at this rate, we probably never will.'

Pulling up beside the Bentley, he turned the engine off to begin clambering out. 'Shall we see if anyone's home?'

With Vicky following behind, Tanner briefly cast his eyes up at the house before stepping up to the front door, his gaze taking in the elegant brushed-steel handle that ran all the way from the top down to the bottom.

Ringing the bell, they stood listening to its hollow chime dissipate through the house beyond to be replaced by nothing but the sound of a cold sterile silence.

Vicky leaned forward to peer through a narrow strip of frosted glass running parallel with the elongated doorhandle. 'It doesn't look like anyone's home.'

Tanner turned his head to cast a questioning eye over at the Bentley. 'Either that, or they'd prefer not to be disturbed. Let's try again, shall we?'

Pressing the doorbell once more, this time he was rewarded by the sound of a curt metallic voice, barking at them from a speaker hidden somewhere to the side of the door.

'Can I help you?'

'It's, er, Detective Inspectors Tanner and Gilbert, Norfolk Police,' Tanner replied, his eyes roaming about, trying to work out where the voice was coming from. 'We're looking to speak to a Mr Toby Wallace?'

'What's it about?'

'Would it be possible for you to come to the door, to talk to us in person?'

A brief pause followed.

'OK, but you'll need to show some identification first. There's a camera above you, to the left.'

Glancing up to see a blacked-out glass ball, tucked into the corner of the door frame, they each dug out their IDs to hold them awkwardly aloft.

'That's fine. Hold on.'

Approaching footsteps could soon be heard, followed by the door being nudged open to reveal a round red face of a short fat middle-aged man.

'Mr Toby Wallace?'

The man nodded. 'I assume this is about what happened to Mike?'

'Sir Michael Blackwell,' Tanner confirmed, noting the man was wearing what appeared to be a pair of silk black pyjamas.

'May I also assume that that you want to know where I was at the time of his death, whilst requesting samples of my fingerprints and DNA?'

'That is correct, Mr Wallace! You know, it sounds like you've done this before.'

'Not at all. A friend of mine phoned earlier, telling me to expect a visit.'

'I take it you mean Mr Iain Sanders?'

'That's the one.'

'I see. It sounds like he was keen to make sure your

alibis were going to be the same.'

'There was no need,' Wallace smiled. 'It was as he said. We were both on board our boat at the time. If our riverside neighbours aren't able to verify that, then you'll be able to ask Jim.'

'Jim?'

'He's the guy who owns the moorings. I don't know his surname. He said hello to me when I arrived, and he was still there when I reached the boat.'

Tanner glanced over at Vicky. 'Could you make a note for us to have a chat with a man called Jim?'

'Already have.'

'Excellent!' Tanner exclaimed, returning his attention back to Wallace. 'Would I be correct in assuming that Mr Sanders was also kind enough to tell you how Sir Michael died?'

'He didn't need to. I'd already seen it on the news. What I fail to understand is why you're standing here talking to me? Wasn't it a woman who killed him? A psychotic floosy by the name of Amber Vale, flying off the handle in some sort of demonic jealous rage?'

'Er...' Tanner began, 'I'm not sure where you heard that one from.'

'The Norfolk Herald. It's on the front page of their website.'

'Ah, right! Of course it is! Well, if I were you, I wouldn't believe everything you read in the newspapers, that one in particular.'

'It was on TV as well. At least the part about you looking to speak to an attractive young woman, supposedly the last person to have seen him alive.'

'It sounds like they know more about the investigation than we do. Perhaps we should give them a call when we're done here?' Tanner added, glancing around at Vicky. 'Maybe they've got the whole thing on video?'

With her smiling back, Tanner returned his attention to the man standing in the doorway. 'But as we're here, maybe you could tell us a little about what your good friend, Mr Sanders mentioned to us. Something about you and Sir Michael owning a nightclub together?'

Wallace shrugged. 'What about it?'

'I was just thinking that now he's no longer with us, you must have become the sole owner.'

'And that's why I killed him,' Wallace stated. 'Now why didn't I think of that?'

'Perhaps you had, Mr Wallace, which was why you went to the trouble of making sure you were seen on board your boat at the time of his death.'

'That's it, yes, of course! Oh, but hang on. If I was on board my boat, which at least one person will be able to verify, how could I have been inside Mike's bedroom, bashing him over the head with a candlestick?'

'There's more than one way to skin a cat.'

'I see, yes. Actually, sorry. No, I don't.'

Tanner turned his head to gaze over the elegant courtyard, over to the curved wall where they drove in. 'May I ask who your visitors were?'

'Which visitors were those?'

'The ones who nearly drove straight into us on their way out.'

'I've no idea.'

'Are you really trying to tell me that you don't know?

'Nobody's been round here for days. They must have turned in by mistake.'

Tanner offered Wallace an accommodating smile. 'OK, well, fair enough. I do hope you're not planning on going anywhere over the next few days. A backpacking trip around Europe, for example?'

'There's nothing like that in my diary.'

'And am I to assume that you won't mind if we send a forensics team around to collect your fingerprints and DNA?'

'Anytime. My door is always open; apart from the times when it's closed, of course.'

- CHAPTER SIXTEEN -

'FUNNY MAN,' MUTTERED Tanner, the moment Wallace's head disappeared back inside his grandiose mansion.

'Hilarious,' Vicky agreed, in a similar sarcastic tone. 'What did you mean about there being two ways to skin a cat?'

Tanner turned to begin leading the way back to his car. 'I thought of another reason why our friends in the SUV may have been here, other than to turn their car around, of course.'

'What was that?'

'To collect payment for services rendered. Probably in cash.'

'You think he might have hired them to kill Sir Michael?'

'Well, they weren't here on behalf of the RSPCA, I know that much. And both parties seemed equally keen to deny having ever met. As it currently stands, our Mr Wallace is the only person with even the vaguest sort of a motive for wanting him dead.'

'Apart from Claire Metcalf, of course.'

'Yes, well,' Tanner snorted. 'I'm still not convinced about her, but we'll have to see.'

'I assume you're thinking that Wallace and Sir Michael had some sort of falling out?'

'Either that, or Wallace simply wanted the business all to himself. Maybe Sir Michael was refusing to sell it to him?'

'OK, but doesn't it seem just a little extreme, to have someone killed over a business deal?'

'To you and I, maybe.'

'What about the manner of his death? Removing someone's heart to leave it hanging out of their mouth sounds far more like the result of psychotic jealous rage than the work of a hired assassin.'

'That probably depends on who the hired assassin was,' Tanner replied, as the muffled sound of Vicky's phone could be heard ringing from somewhere inside her coat. 'Any chance that's news on the numberplate?' he asked, catching her eye as she fished it out.

'It's the office,' she confirmed, lifting it to her ear, 'so it could be.'

Leaving her to take the call, Tanner took a quick tour around the Bentley, occasionally stopping to peer inside, all the while doing his best to overhear his colleague's conversation.

'OK, thanks Sally,' he eventually heard her say, ending the call to exchange the phone for her notebook.

'Anything?'

'McMillan International Investments and Entertainment Ltd,' she replied, busily making notes.

'I'm sorry?'

'The business that owns the Mercedes.'

'And who owns the business?'

'A man by the name of Terrance McMillan. He's a London-based property developer and businessman. He also just happens to own the Riverside Gentleman's Club, of which there would appear to be quite a few dotted up and down the country.'

'Wasn't that where Claire Metcalf said she worked?'

'The very same.'

'Do we know where it is?'

'Back towards Norwich; near the university.'

'Then I suggest we head straight over there, to see if we can find its owner.'

'No probs, but before we do, Forrester wants us back in the office.'

'What, seriously?'

'That's what Sally said.'

'Did he tell her why?'

'She said she didn't know. Do you want me to phone him up to ask him?'

'Maybe not,' he replied, glancing down at his watch, 'but it better be important. Norwich is back the other way.'

- CHAPTER SEVENTEEN -

D ISCOVERING THE REASON for the long tailback down Stalham Road to be a number of badly parked news media vans cluttering up the pavement outside Wroxham Police Station, Tanner was finally able to edge his way into its entrance to leave his car parked discreetly in the farthest corner.

With Vicky's ear glued to her phone, endeavouring to track down the owner of the Riverside Gentlemen's Club, they entered the main office where Tanner hovered beside his desk, unable to decide if he should take a moment to check through his emails before heading over to see what Forrester had dragged him back for, or if he had time to make himself a coffee first. Reaching the conclusion that coffee was a definite priority, he turned on his heel to make a beeline for the kitchen, only to find DC Sally Beech trotting out the other way.

'Oh, hi John!' she exclaimed, a massive mug of steaming hot coffee cocooned by her smooth delicate hands. 'Did you hear that my uncle wanted to see you?'

'Vicky did mention something about it,' he replied, glancing over her shoulder to see if she'd been kind enough to leave any coffee for him.

'OK, I'll leave you to it,' she continued, batting her eyelids whilst nudging her way past.

Relieved to see the carafe was still half-full, he forged his way inside, reaching up to grab a mug from the cupboard above the kettle, when young DC Townsend's head appeared around the door.

'Afternoon, sir. Did anyone tell you that DCI Forrester wanted to see you?'

'One or two people,' Tanner muttered, shaking his head.

'OK, just so you know.'

With the coffee poured and the milk added, he turned to make his way out, only to nearly walk straight into DI Cooper.

Apologising, he took a half-step back.

'My fault,' Cooper replied, somewhat awkwardly. 'Did you hear Forrester wanted to see you?'

'Oh, for fuck's sake!' Tanner muttered under his breath.

Glancing up to see a look of wounded discontentment drawn out over Cooper's face, he hastily put forward what he felt was a necessary apology. 'Sorry, Cooper, it's just that you're the third person to tell me that since I walked in, and that was only about thirty seconds ago.'

'Then I suppose it must be important,' Cooper huffed, standing to one side to allow Tanner to pass.

Stopping next to Forrester's door, Tanner knocked briefly at it before nudging it open. 'You wanted to see me, sir?'

'Ah, there you are. I was about to send out a search party.'

Tanner frowned with irritation. 'I was out interviewing suspects. I thought you knew.'

'I was under the impression you'd be bringing that woman in for questioning.'

'Sorry, sir; which woman was that?'

'The one I was talking to you about on the phone,' Forrester continued, glancing around at his monitor. 'Claire Metcalf.'

'Er...I'm fairly sure you didn't.'

'Maybe not in so many words, but to be honest, I thought it should have been fairly obvious. I mean, she was the last person known to have seen him alive, we've already proved that she'd just had sex with him, she has a criminal record as long as my arm...'

'...for prostitution,' Tanner interjected, '*not* first degree murder.'

'And...' Forrester continued, '...we've just found out that she has a documented history of mental illness.'

'What?'

'You heard me.'

'But – nobody told me.'

Forrester gave him an indifferent shrug. 'She should have been brought in, whether you knew that or not.'

'Had I known her state of mind before being sent over to talk to her, I would have, *sir*.'

'You can't blame me for that.'

'I'm not blaming you; I'm simply stating my reasoning.'

'OK, fair enough. You did speak to her, though?'

'We did.'

'And?'

'From her answers to my questions, I felt that she was unlikely to have been responsible for Sir Michael's death.'

'I suppose she told you she was innocent, so you believed her?'

Tanner took up a defensive stance. 'Not exactly.'

'So...what *did* she say?'

'That she was his escort for the evening, and that

she'd handcuffed him to the bed to have sex with him, after which she removed them, got dressed and left.'

Forrester was left staring at him with his mouth hanging open. 'And it was on that basis you made the executive decision that she was innocent?'

Tanner shifted awkwardly from one foot to the other. 'Not *just* that, sir, no.'

'Jesus Christ, Tanner. Sometimes I wonder if you left that brain of yours at the bottom of the North Sea. You are still capable of doing this job, I hope? If not, please tell me, and I'll be happy enough to hand the reins over to Cooper.'

'I suppose that depends if you want to find out who killed Sir Michael, or if you simply want to give Cooper the chance to start lining his pockets again.'

Forrester paused for breath. 'I think you're going to have to shake off this idea of yours that Cooper is some sort of corrupt policeman, Tanner.'

'At some point no doubt I will, but unlike Professional Standards, it's going to take me a little more than a couple of weeks.'

'Any chance we could stay on subject?'

'You're the one who brought up Cooper.'

'And you're the one who believed some psychotic prostitute, just because she had a nice pair of tits!'

The room fell into a stunned silence, with Tanner left reeling by what he'd heard his DCI blurt out, whilst Forrester looked equally appalled.

Breaking the embarrassed silence, Tanner raised a hand to clear his throat. 'To be honest, sir, I can't say I noticed.'

'Yes, well,' the DCI muttered, glancing sheepishly out through the partition window to see if anyone out in the main office had overheard him. 'You get my point.'

'I can assure you that my judgement was in no way

clouded by the fact that she was an attractive young woman. It was based purely on her reactions to the questions being asked, and what I felt at the time was a distinct lack of motive for her having murdered the victim, certainly in the manner by which he met his untimely end. I admit that had I known about her psychological history, I would have brought her in, but I still wouldn't have thought she was the party responsible.'

Forrester took a moment to study his face. 'Did she know anything about the other woman – Amber Vale, wasn't it?'

'Not exactly.'

'What do you mean, not exactly?'

'The two are one and the same.'

'I'm sorry, Tanner, I'm not with you.'

'Amber Vale is her stage name.'

'Oh, right. I see. Well, at least that clears that one up.'

'But it was the person we nearly drove into whilst on our way to see the second of Sir Michael's friends, a Mr Toby Wallace, that I believe to be of far greater interest.'

'And who was that?'

'The owner of a local strip club. We saw a car registered in his name coming out of Wallace's drive as we arrived.'

'The connection being?'

'The strip club he owns is where Claire Metcalf, AKA Amber Vale, works.'

Forrester leaned back in his chair.

'On top of that, neither Toby Wallace, nor the guy driving the car, seemed willing to admit that they knew each other, which was odd, being that one was driving out of the other's property.'

'May I assume you were able to speak to this Toby

Wallace character?'

'We were.'

'Anything of interest?'

'Only that Iain Sanders had already phoned him up to warn him that we were on our way, so ensuring their alibis were identical; that and the fact that he must know the guy we saw leaving his property.'

'Do we know the strip club owner's name?'

'Terrance McMillan. He's a London-based businessman and property developer.'

'And the strip club?'

'The Riverside. Apparently, it's part of a national chain.'

'OK, then I suppose you'd better have a word with him.'

'Funny that, but that's exactly what Vicky and I were going to do before we were ordered back.'

Forrester suddenly sat up in his chair, staring at his watch. 'Christ, I almost forgot. I've organised a press conference. It's supposed to start in ten minutes.'

Tanner stared over at him with a confused curious expression. 'You're holding a press conference?'

'Er, no; you are.'

'Me?'

'You are the SIO for this investigation, are you not?'

'I'm not sure I can be. If I was, I'm fairly sure someone would have asked my opinion before making the decision to hold a press conference. Failing that, I'd have at least been given a little more notice than ten bloody minutes before it was about to start.'

'The decision was made by Superintendent Whitaker.'

'Oh, I see. So *he's* the SIO now, is he?'

'No, Tanner, but he is in charge of the Norfolk Constabulary, the organisation for which you work.'

'That doesn't give him the right to tell me how to do my job, though, does it.'

'Er, I think it does, Tanner.'

'Then you'd better show me that written in a manual somewhere, because as far as I know, *I'm* the one who has overall responsibility for this investigation, not Superintendent bloody Whitaker. And in my personal opinion, holding a press conference at this moment in time is the last thing we should be doing.'

'Then you'd better tell him that yourself, hadn't you.'

Tanner pulled his shoulders back to look Forrester straight in the eye. 'Alright – hand me the phone and I will.'

'Look, Tanner; just do the bloody press conference, will you?'

'And say what? Sir Michael Blackwell is dead, and all we know so far is that it wasn't the butler – for a change – but only because he didn't have one.'

'For a start, it will give us the chance to lay out the facts of the investigation whilst correcting what the housekeeper told them all; that the girl he was with didn't kill him.'

'We don't know that she didn't.'

'That's not what you told me five minutes ago.'

'I said that I thought she was unlikely to have been responsible. That's not the same thing at all.'

'Are you going to do the press conference, or not?'

Tanner gave Forrester one last defiant glare before letting out a heavy sigh of forced capitulation. 'Fine! But I'm not going out there on my own.'

'Don't worry, I've told Cooper to join you.'

'Oh, great. That's just what I needed.'

'And I'll be there as well.'
'Even better.'

- CHAPTER EIGHTEEN -

'HOW'D IT GO?' asked Vicky, watching Tanner approach from reception, a look of tired despondency hanging from his face.

'Assuming you mean the press conference,' he replied, reaching her desk, 'about as well as can be expected. Still, at least it's done. Any luck locating that strip club owner?'

'He's normally there between three in the afternoon and about one in the morning. Otherwise he should be at the hotel he's staying at.'

Tanner took a moment to glance down at his watch. 'Then I suppose we'd better get ourselves over there before Forrester sends me out to pick up Superintendent Whitaker's uniform from the dry cleaner's.'

'Huh?'

'Never mind,' Tanner replied, spinning back to fetch his coat, only to see Forrester bounding his way towards him, an unusually cheerful expression stretched out over his face.

'I thought that went rather well,' the DCI called out, capturing Tanner's attention with a cheerful smile.

'Which bit?' Tanner queried in response; his tone drenched in condescending sarcasm.

'Yes, well. I suppose they're never exactly easy. Anyway, at least they've got the facts now.'

Tanner gave his shoulders an ambivalent shrug. 'Perhaps, but it won't stop them from writing whatever comes into their tiny little minds between now and when they get back to their desks.'

'I didn't think they brought their desks with them!' Forrester exclaimed, grinning demonically at first Tanner, then Vicky, as if expecting them to burst into uncontrollable fits of hysterics.

With Tanner's face remaining a mask of stoic indifference, and Vicky barely managing a smile, Forrester cleared his throat. 'Anyway, so...what are your plans now?'

'Well, I *was* going to head back to my boat to put my feet up, being that it's already gone five o'clock, but unfortunately, we still need to drive all the way over to Norwich to interview the owner of the Riverside Gentleman's Club.'

'Can't it wait till tomorrow?'

Tanner raised a surprised eyebrow. 'Well, it could...' he replied, realising Forrester must have been feeling a rare sense of guilt for having prevented them from making the trip earlier.

'It's up to you, of course,' Forrester continued, spinning around to head back to his office.

'*It is?*' Tanner muttered, under his breath.

Just before reaching his door, Forrester stopped to turn his head back. 'Whilst I remember, I had someone from the Broad's Authority on the phone earlier. They said there's a storm on its way. Quite a big one, apparently. It should hit the coast tonight.'

Tanner kicked himself for having managed to completely forget all about it.

'Not sure what we're supposed to do about it,' Forrester continued. 'More something for the Broads Rangers to worry about, but I suppose it's good to be forewarned. No doubt we'll be roped in to help clean up the mess afterwards. Anyway, I thought I'd better let you know, being what you live onboard, and everything.'

'Actually, sir,' chirped Tanner, 'would you mind if I did head home?'

'I'm sorry?' Forrester replied, stepping forward with a bemused look.

'It's the storm, you see. I was told about it yesterday. I was going to move my boat to a safer mooring, but then I got the call about Sir Michael.'

'Oh, right. I see. Then perhaps Vicky could go?'

'Er...sorry, sir,' Vicky spluttered, having opened and closed her mouth a few times, 'but I really can't say I'd be comfortable going to what is effectively a strip club; not on my own, at least.'

'Then maybe Cooper could go with you?'

Vicky turned to give Tanner a look of pleading desperation.

'If it's alright by you, sir,' Tanner began, realising the predicament he'd placed Vicky in, 'I'd be happier if Cooper could remain focussed on the blackmail side of the investigation.'

'Then how about taking young Townsend?'

Tanner glanced over at Vicky. 'Is he even old enough to go inside?'

Forrester let out a heavy sigh of reluctant capitulation. 'Very well. I suppose it will just have to wait till tomorrow.'

- CHAPTER NINETEEN -

L OOKING FORWARD TO a pleasant evening's sail, Tanner arrived at his old 1930s yacht only to find the wind had dropped to virtually nothing. Assuming it had to be the calm before the forecast storm, he was forced to change his plan, motoring out from his moorings instead, heading for Horning and the River Thurne beyond.

Thanks to Christine, the Broads Rangers had offered him free temporary moorings in amongst their patrol boats at Potter Heigham, and although it meant having to make a long four-hour journey, he was grateful to have found somewhere safe to keep his yacht during what looked likely to be a particularly savage summer storm. He also knew the journey would do him good. There was no better way for him to relax than to chug along at a sedate four miles-an-hour with nothing better to do than take in the gentle beauty of the Norfolk Broads and the majestic rivers that meandered their way through it.

'Ahoy there!' came a familiar voice, as he began steering his yacht in towards a line of near identical patrol boats, each glowing pink in the light of a steadily setting sun.

Lifting his head to see Christine waving at him from one of the bows, he raised a hand with a grateful smile, the other easing back on the yacht's stubby brass throttle.

With the noise from the engine ebbing steadily away, the boat's forward momentum gradually began to slow.

'You didn't have to meet me,' he called, his words echoing out over the river's gently rippling surface.

'It's no problem. I've only just finished work. Besides, it's not every day I get to meet someone famous.'

'Huh?'

'I saw you on TV earlier.'

'Oh, that!' Tanner replied, rolling his eyes with a bashful smirk.

'I don't suppose I could have your autograph?' she teased.

'I suppose that depends on what you want me to sign.'

'How about a cheque for two-million?'

'Er...that might be a problem.'

'Fifty-quid?'

Tanner laughed. 'Tell you what, if you can help me moor up, I'll think about it.'

'OK, but you'd better throw me a line before the tide takes you.'

Realising she was right, and the boat was already being swept past the mooring towards the ancient brick base of Potter Heigham's low medieval bridge, Tanner leapt out of the cockpit. Picking his way down the narrow walkway to the bow at the front, he fetched up a neatly coiled rope from off the deck to send it spiralling over the water towards her. Leaving Christine to pluck it out from the air to begin heaving on its end, Tanner hurried back to the cockpit to place the tip of his foot onto his yacht's tiller, nudging it gently away. As the yacht's nose crept slowly in towards a space between two of the Broads Rangers' patrol boats, he leaned over to retrieve the second mooring line coiled up beside his other foot, waiting until the rear transom lined up with the port-side patrol boat before stepping lightly off.

'That'll be fifty pounds, please!' Christine announced, tying off her line to send him a broad cheeky grin.

'Ah, yes, right,' he began, tying his own off to begin searching his pockets. 'How about I make you something to eat instead?'

'I wasn't aware you could cook?'

'I suppose that depends on your definition.'

'If you were in Bake Off, would you make it through to the final?'

'If it was a ready meal special, I'd probably win!'

Sending him a look of scolding disapproval, she placed her hands firmly down on her hips. 'There's nothing funny about what is without doubt the greatest show on British television.'

'I'd no idea you were such a fan,' Tanner replied, struggling to work out if she was being serious.

'I'm more than just a fan, I'm an applicant!'

'You've actually applied to be on the show?'

'I have.'

'Wow. That *is* impressive.'

'So, no more Bake Off jokes, please. It's all far too serious.'

'Understood. So, anyway, I can cook you up a tasty Sainsbury's lasagne with a serving of freshly heated up baked beans, if you like?'

'To be honest, I think I'd rather have my brain removed with a spatula.'

'I can do peas; if you prefer?'

'I'm not sure that would make much difference. Anyway, joking aside, I should be getting home. I've got a homemade Boeuf Bourguignon waiting for me in the fridge.'

'I must admit, that does sound a little more tempting. I don't suppose I could tag along?'

'Only enough for one, I'm afraid.'

They exchanged a flirtatious smile.

'Look,' Tanner eventually said, 'why don't you stay?'

'For the night?'

'You may as well. You're going to have to come all the way back here tomorrow anyway. If you did, you'd be able to have a lie-in.'

Christine hesitated for the briefest of moments before shaking her head. 'I can't. I'm sorry, John. I've told you before how I feel about staying on board the boat you used to live on with your fiancée.'

'You're right, of course,' came Tanner's reluctant reply, unable to hide the disappointment in his voice.

'Besides, we need to go on a date first.'

'OK, then how about I take you out for dinner tomorrow night?'

Christine paused for the briefest of moments. 'Are you sure you'll be free?'

'Not sure, no, but I can't see what possible reason Forrester would have to object to me taking a few hours off on a Sunday evening.'

- CHAPTER TWENTY -

Sunday, 29th August

EVERY SINGLE DAY for the last sixty-three years, William Appleyard had taken the bus to Fairbrother's in Norwich, the locally renowned department store where he'd worked with loyal diligence for the entirety of what he now considered to be a wasted career. Throughout that time, he'd only ever missed two days; the first being when he'd woken up to find his wife lying dead in the bed beside him, and the second the day after he'd been made redundant. The weeks, months, and years that followed, he'd continued to make the very same journey; not because he had to, at least not for financial reasons. He'd been given a surprisingly generous retirement package, which combined with decades of savings and the normal state pension, was more than enough for him to live on. His reason for continuing his daily commute was purely psychological. Having made the exact same journey every day since he was sixteen-years-old had become such an integral part of his being, the idea of not being able to filled him with the most inexplicable sense of dread. And so he'd continued to drag his now fragile arthritic body out of bed every morning at half-past six, no matter what day of the week it was, to shuffle his way to the road at the end of the bleak narrow alley that ran along the back of his small terraced house. There he'd catch the number thirty-two bus into Norwich City Centre where he'd walk to Fairbrother's main entrance, stare longingly up at the building he'd spent all those years working in before dropping his shoulders to turn slowly around to begin the exact same journey home.

Taking a seat at the very back of the bus, apart from the somewhat blustery conditions, so far this particular day had been no different. But his journey home became a special moment in time when the bus jerked to a halt to let on a gorgeous scantily-clad young woman who immediately began making her way past rows of empty seats towards him, the undulating tops of her half-exposed breasts rippling with every seductive step.

When she reached the line of seats he was slumped at the end of, instead of choosing the opposite side, to be as far away from him as possible, to his absolute astonishment she offered him the most alluring smile he could have possibly imagined before nestling herself down next to him, her skin-tight miniskirt riding so far up her smooth naked thighs that by leaning forward and tilting his head, he could see that she wasn't wearing a stitch of clothing underneath.

With his heart thumping hard with voyeuristic excitement, every time she looked away he stole another glance. After a while, he hardly cared if she saw him doing so or not, surreptitiously slipping his right hand down inside his sagging suit trouser pocket to absorb himself in the pure hedonistic pleasure of gently massaging his already throbbing manhood.

When he realised she was purposely levering open her legs to offer him a better view, he honestly couldn't believe his luck. As the motion of his hand increased, he quickly approached a state of orgasm when she suddenly snapped her legs closed to reach up and press the bell, indicating for the driver to stop.

Watching as she stood to quickly smooth down her skirt, he was about to carry on regardless, when it suddenly dawned on him that it was his stop as well.

Panicking that he might miss it, he wrenched his hand out of his pocket to haul himself up, his eyes remaining glued to the woman's perfectly formed heart-shaped bum. As it swayed back and forth like a hypnotist's pendulum, he followed as fast as his wretched body would allow, up until the moment she stepped lightly down from the bus to immediately disappear from view.

'Wait a minute!' he called out to the driver, lurching his way forward as the doors began hissing to a close.

Relieved to see them jerk to a stop to start juddering open again, he continued forward, stopping to step carefully down to the pavement.

With the doors closing awkwardly behind him as the bus pulled away, he stared about for the woman, longing for another chance to see her sumptuous young body. But she was nowhere to be seen.

A savage gust of wind tugged at his threadbare black suit as he let out a disappointed sigh. Hunching himself over against the stiffening breeze, he shuffled his way into the narrow alleyway that would take him back to his house, his mind feverishly replaying the events on the bus. With a wandering hand re-entering his pocket, he'd only just started flirting with the idea of finding somewhere quiet to finish what he'd started, when something caught his eye, lying on the path ahead. It almost looked like the woman from the bus, the one who'd left him in such a state of deprived sexual arousal. But he knew it couldn't have been, not unless she'd fallen over and hurt herself.

Removing his hand, he continued along the shadowy path, his eyes continuing to question whether it was her or not. It wasn't long before he knew, without a shadow of doubt, that it was. He also knew that she hadn't simply tripped and was now catching her breath, preparing to get up. The woman was lying sprawled out on her back, her unblinking mascara-lined eyes staring up towards the twisted branches that hung over the path like a shop crammed full of broken umbrellas.

He continued to stare at her face for a moment longer, before allowing them to wander down the length of her curvaceous body, first resting gently on the smooth milky curves of her ample young breasts, then down to where the hem of her skirt met her pale naked thighs. Instinctively, he knew she was dead. There was no other explanation for her eyes to be staring up like that if she was anything but.

With his mind picturing what he'd been stealing glances at on the bus, his manhood swelled once again. Ungluing his eyes from the hem of her skirt, he lifted his head to stare down the lane, first at where he'd come from, then the other way, towards where he lived. There was nobody about. There never was!

His eyes drifted back to her skirt, a billion years of animalistic evolution yearning desperately for what he knew lay underneath.

Could I? he asked himself, glancing up again. *There's nobody about.*

His hand snuck back into his pocket as his eyes ran themselves back up the smooth bare skin of her legs. *I could*, he continued to think, glancing over his shoulder at the thin line of trees that lay only a few feet behind, *but not here.*

With his heart thumping hard behind his ears he

glanced up and down the lane again, listening for the slightest sound. Without a soul in sight, he quickly navigated himself around to the woman's head, fetching up her arms to begin heaving her back. As beads of sweat erupted over his head and face, the heels of his polished office shoes soon began digging into the soft earth behind. Less than a minute later, with only the woman's feet remaining on the path, he was about to heave her body back again for what he hoped would be the final time, when a flicker of fluorescent yellow began dancing through the trees towards him.

Panic rising, he placed a frantic foot behind him to heave back again, only for his office shoes to slip on the inky black mud, sending him crashing to the ground, his ears to be met by the jarring screech of a bicycle's rusting brakes.

- CHAPTER TWENTY ONE -

TANNER WOKE THAT morning with that all-too familiar sense that he'd hardly slept a wink. As the night had worn steadily away, a building breeze had left his yacht slamming into the patrol boats lashed to either side of his. More annoying still, he'd neglected to put a spacer between the mast and the rope used to hoist the mainsail, leaving it slapping against the vertical wooden beam every time there was even the slightest gust of wind.

It wasn't until he was dragging himself out of bed that it dawned on him he'd forgotten something else as well; two things in fact. Firstly, that his car was still sitting in the carpark next to his former moorings, all the way over at Wroxham, leaving him with no immediate way of getting into work. The second was that he was supposed to have reset his alarm, to give him the additional time needed to commute in from his new, more distant location.

Kicking himself for having forgotten both, with the wind howling like a banshee above his head, he scrabbled around for his phone to put an urgent call through to a local taxi firm.

With a car booked to come as soon as possible, his next call was to Vicky, asking her to let Forrester know that he was going to be late.

By the time the taxi had dropped him off outside the station, it was already gone half-past nine.

Hurrying inside, he'd only just started wrestling himself out of his coat when he saw Vicky, forging her way through the middle of the office towards him.

'I wouldn't bother if I were you,' she said, the moment she was within earshot.

'I'm sorry?'

'Your coat. We've been called out.'

'But...' Tanner began, his eyes gazing longingly towards the kitchen, 'I haven't even had a coffee yet!'

'We'll have to get one on the way,' Vicky continued, plunging her arms into a coat of her own. 'Claire Metcalf's body's just been found along a lane near where she lives. The man who's thought to have killed her is being held for us on site.'

- CHAPTER TWENTY TWO -

A RRIVING AT A cordoned-off bus stop at the edge of Salhouse village, Tanner stepped out of Vicky's car to the sound of Police Do Not Cross tape flapping vigorously in a steadily stiffening breeze. Zipping his old sailing jacket up to the top of its broad high collar, he sent a glance spiralling up towards the brooding grey clouds above before leading Vicky over towards where a fluorescent-clad police constable could be seen standing to attention, just to the side of a narrow alleyway entrance.

After offering the man the briefest of nods they made their way into the alley, down towards where a small group of forensic officers could be seen, their pristine white overalls flickering between gaps in the trees to their left. When he saw Dr Johnstone's head emerge out onto the path ahead, he raised his voice above the sound of the wind. 'What've we got?'

'Thankfully, nothing like last time,' the doctor replied, directing their eyes down towards a pair of pointed feet resting on the path's uneven concrete edge. 'At the moment, my best guess is that she was killed by a single blow to the back of the head. However, there is a possibility that she simply passed out, hitting her head on the concrete. You can see a patch of blood just there,' he continued, directing their attention down towards the middle of the path.

'So, it might have been purely by chance?'

questioned Tanner, removing his eyes from the blood to run them along the length of the woman's stretched out body, her pale slender arms snagged above her head by a series of jagged low-hanging branches.

'Well, it's a possibility, but to be honest, I don't think it's very likely,' Johnstone continued, following Tanner's gaze. 'Apart from the obvious fact that her body was moved shortly afterwards, most people who faint generally fall forwards, leaving them with facial injuries, and the force is rarely enough to kill them.'

Tanner glanced down at the body's heavily mascara-lined eyes staring unblinkingly up towards the tangle of branches above. 'Are we sure of her identity: Claire Metcalf?' he asked, tilting his head as he tried to determine if it was the same woman they'd spoken to the day before.

'At the moment we are. What we're presuming to be her handbag was found on the far side of the path. The credit cards inside all bear the same name.'

'Had anything been stolen?'

Johnstone shook his head. 'There was a fair amount of cash in there as well.'

'So, she wasn't mugged then. How about rape?'

'At this stage I'd say probably not. She'd had sexual intercourse recently, though, but there are no obvious signs of trauma. So unless I find some when I get her back to the lab, I'd have to say it was consensual.'

Johnstone's attention shifted from the body to look up at Tanner. 'I assume you heard that someone was caught, dragging her into the trees?'

'As we left the office,' Tanner replied, turning to look back down the alleyway from where they'd come. 'I don't suppose you know if he's still here?'

'I'm sorry, I don't.'

'OK, no problem.'

A sudden gust of wind tore through the trees above, bringing a shower of leaves and twigs tumbling down through the branches.

'I'd better get on,' Johnstone commented, watching with concern as a small branch landed on top of the corpse. 'Hardly ideal conditions to be conducting the forensic examination of a murder scene.'

'I suppose you can't put a tent up?'

'Not with all these trees. Anyway,' he continued, with an optimistic look, 'it could be worse. It could be raining.'

The moment he said it, a heavy drop of water smacked into the path beside them, missing the woman's feet by inches.

'That'll teach me to open my mouth,' he lamented, a sanguine smile tugging at the corners of his mouth. 'Sorry folks, but it looks like I'm going to have to get back to work.'

- CHAPTER TWENTY THREE -

WITH A RAPIDLY increasing number of raindrops smacking into the concrete path surrounding them, they turned to hurry back the way they'd come, Tanner reaching behind his head to lever out the fluorescent yellow hood kept hidden inside his sailing jacket's collar, whilst Vicky rummaged around inside her bag for a collapsible umbrella.

Reaching the end, Tanner stopped to face the constable they'd passed on the way in.

'Is the person who was found with the body still here?'

The constable nodded. 'We assumed you'd want to speak to him.'

'Good man,' Tanner replied, his eyes darting about, briefly studying the faces of the various people he could see standing nearby. But with the only civilian being a frail old man taking shelter under a bus stop, his hands held behind a smart but ill-fitting suit, he turned back to the constable. 'Sorry, I can't see him.'

'It's the old man, under the bus stop,' the constable continued, re-directing Tanner's attention, 'where Constable Dickens is standing.'

Tanner gave the officer an incredulous look. 'What, him?'

'Er...that's correct, sir.'

'Are you sure?'

'That's what the guy said who caught him - in the act, so to speak. He said he was cycling down the lane when he saw him dragging the victim into the bushes.'

'And where's this so-called cyclist?'

'We took his statement and said he could go. I hope that's OK?'

'I'd have preferred to have been able to talk to him as well,' muttered Tanner in a disapproving tone, 'but at least the suspect's still here, I suppose. Has he said anything?'

'Only that he didn't kill her.'

'Yes, well; I suppose he would. How about a name?'

The officer tugged out a notebook. 'A Mr William Appleyard; retired.'

'If he's retired, what's he doing in a suit?'

The officer gave him a guilty shrug. 'I'm sorry, sir; we didn't think to ask.'

Rolling his eyes, Tanner nodded over to Vicky to begin hurrying their way over to the bus stop where the old man was now sitting, perched on the edge of one of its narrow plastic seats.

'Mr Appleyard?' Tanner queried, stepping under the bus shelter to pull out his ID.

The man glanced up with a nod, paper-thin skin clinging to the sides of a long haggard face.

'Detective Inspector Tanner, and my colleague, Detective Inspector Gilbert, Norfolk Police.'

'I didn't kill her!' he suddenly declared, his eyes darting briefly between them.

'But you were caught trying to hide the body.'

'That doesn't mean I killed her though, does it!'

'Not on its own, perhaps, but you'd have to admit that it was an unusual thing to have done, presuming that person was innocent, of course. I'd have thought most people finding themselves stumbling over a corpse would have the good sense to leave it well alone.'

Appleyard returned his attention to what he'd been staring at before, the space between the pavement and the road, and a faltering trickle of water running gently between the two.

'So...what were you doing?' Tanner continued. 'And please don't tell me you were worried someone might trip over her.'

His face remained unchanged.

'OK, but you'd better know that if you're not prepared to tell me, I'll be left with no choice but to charge you with first degree murder.'

Appleyard paused momentarily before opening his mouth. 'We were on the same bus together. She sat next to me.'

'Go on.'

'I thought she was nice.'

'Nice in what way?'

'She smiled at me,' the man continued, his voice vacant and flat. 'Not many people smile at me anymore. I can't even remember the last time a girl did.'

'I assume you found her attractive?'

Appleyard offered Tanner a solitary nod.

'I can't blame you for that, I suppose,' Tanner continued. 'So, you decided to follow her off the bus and down the lane where you attempted to have your disgusting way with her. But finding she wasn't quite as consenting as you may have hoped, you hit her over the head before dragging her off to find somewhere a little more...private.'

'I didn't kill her!' Appleyard repeated, tugging painfully at the handcuffs securing his hands behind his back.

'OK...so you were attempting to rape her, only for her to end up slipping on the concrete to end up dead? Either way, you're still looking at spending the rest of your life, at least what's left of it, locked up inside a maximum security prison.'

'I admit, I did follow her off the bus, but only because it was my stop as well. And I didn't follow her down the lane. My house is at the end. I found her when I was about halfway down. At first I thought she'd simply fallen over, so I went to help. But when I got there, it was obvious she was dead.'

'And...what happened then?'

The suspect remained quiet and still, the only sign of life being the tears falling silently from his eyes.'

'Mr Appleyard?'

'I'm sorry,' he eventually began, his voice nothing more than a faltering whisper. 'I didn't mean anything by it. And it's not as if she'd have minded.'

'Minded what?'

'It's just – it's just been such a long time – over twenty years since my wife passed away.'

The suspect's head rolled slowly forward as he openly began to cry.

'And she was just so beautiful. I know I shouldn't have. I was wrong to even think it. I tried not to, honestly I did. But I – I just couldn't – I just couldn't help myself.'

Tanner saw Vicky gag involuntary beside him.

Hearing her response, the suspect glared up at her, his sagging grey eyes now red with tears. 'Don't look at me like that!' he spat. 'You've no idea what it's like to get old. I mean *really* old. You see yourself in the mirror, but the person staring back – it's not you. It's someone else. You spend year after year forced to watch your body decompose before your very eyes, but inside you remain the same. You still want the same things. You still have the same basic human needs. But they can never be satisfied because women think you're disgusting. You can't even look at them without being called a pervert.'

He turned back to face the ground, rain drumming off the top of his polished office shoes.

'Anyway, I didn't, as I'm sure your forensics officers will clarify. That do-gooder on his decrepit old bike saw to that. Besides, it may be frowned on by society, but it's hardly illegal.'

'Assuming you're talking about necrophilia, Mr Appleyard,' Tanner began, 'then I'm afraid it is. I'd have to look it up, but from what I remember, the carnal penetration of a corpse was criminalised under the Sexual Offences Act back in 2003.'

'Then I suppose it's a good job I didn't then, isn't it!' the man responded, glaring up at the two detectives before his attention returned to the ground.

'Going back to the bus, Mr Appleyard. Apart from the victim and yourself, did anyone else get off?'

The man shook his head.

'Are you sure?'

'It was just her and me. Nobody else.'

'How about when you were walking down the lane?'

'I didn't see anyone. Only the girl – and that stuck-up twat on his crappy old bike.'

- CHAPTER TWENTY FOUR -

'**I**T'S NOT HIM,' stated Tanner, leaving the bus shelter as they hurried back to Vicky's car.

'I don't suppose there's a law against *attempted* necrophilia?'

'Remind me to look it up when we get back to the office, but even if there was, it would be challenging to prove. Not without a living witness. It would also be difficult to find an aggrieved party who was either willing, or indeed able to press charges, being that the victim would need to be dead for the offence to be relevant.'

'Can't we arrest him for something else?'

'Any ideas?'

'Well, he did move the body, and not exactly by accident.'

'But not in an attempt to cover up a crime.'

'Endeavouring to instigate one instead,' Vicky muttered, barely loud enough for Tanner to hear.

'To be honest, I think we have bigger fish to fry. Assuming he was telling the truth, that nobody else got off the bus, then we know she wasn't being followed. That means someone must have known she'd be walking down the lane, and at what time she'd have done so.'

'Unless it was just a random attack. Maybe someone tried to mug her? Or maybe it was an attempted rape that went wrong? She was certainly dressed provocatively enough.'

'Being hit on the back of the head suggests she was attacked from behind,' Tanner continued. 'If she'd been mugged, or if someone had tried to rape her, I'd have thought the attack would have come from the front. Saying that, we don't even know if she *was* attacked. As Johnstone said, it's possible she may have simply fainted.'

Stopping besides Vicky's car, they turned to look back through the rain towards the alleyway's entrance, just in time to see Johnstone emerging, the hood of his coat pulled up over his head.

'Another problem we're going to have is this bloody weather,' Tanner continued, watching the doctor glance briefly up at him before hurrying over. 'With the amount of rain we've had just in the last ten minutes, if there *was* someone waiting for her before launching their attack, it's going to be virtually impossible to find any evidence, either at the scene or on the body.'

They took a moment to watch in silence as Johnstone splashed his way through the rain.

'I thought I'd missed you,' he called out, looking over at them through rapidly steaming-up glasses. 'We've found a couple of things we thought might be of interest.'

Seeing him pull out his phone, Vicky did her best to angle her umbrella against the wind to help protect its screen from the now driving rain.

'The first was a photograph we found hidden in the depths of her handbag,' Johnstone continued, holding the phone out for them to see.

Tanner and Vicky stared down at a picture of a young couple, one of whom Tanner knew to be the victim, cosying up to a good-looking young man with dark olive skin.

'Any ideas?' Tanner asked, catching Vicky's eye.

'I think it's the guy who owns that strip club. Terrance McMillan.'

'Then there was this,' Johnstone added, swiping a finger over the rain-splattered screen. 'It was found on the back of her hand.'

Tanner screwed up his eyes to stare down at it. 'Is it some sort of tattoo?'

'It's a stamp,' stated Vicky. 'The sort you get when you go to a nightclub. If that's an R, then I'd say it was for the Riverside Gentleman's Club.'

- CHAPTER TWENTY FIVE -

CLIMBING INTO VICKY'S car for her to immediately pull away, Tanner put a quick call through to Forrester, updating him with what they'd found at the scene and where they were subsequently heading.

Half an hour later they were turning off the road into Norwich to see a large flashing neon sign shimmering at them through the rain, the glowing silhouette of a curvaceous naked woman propped seductively up against the words Riverside Gentlemen's Club.

After parking up next to a familiar looking Mercedes SUV, they threw open the doors to pelt their way over the water-logged gravel to huddle under a shallow torn awning that helped make up the building's dark uninviting entrance.

'Looks like it's closed,' Vicky observed, shaking out her umbrella.

Tanner glanced down at his watch before cupping his hands against the door's smoke-glass window. 'Well, it is eleven o'clock on a Sunday morning. Their clientele must all be at church.'

Trying the door, he raised an eyebrow at his colleague when he found it swinging open. 'Shall we go in?'

'After you,' she smiled, gesturing for him to lead the way.

Entering a dark narrow passageway they soon found themselves in a large oppressive space, an unlit stage on one side, a similarly shadowy bar on the other.

'Nice place for it,' commented Tanner, his nose sniffing cautiously at what smelt like an unsubtle mixture of stale alcohol and undiluted vomit.

'I suppose that depends on what "it" is?' queried Vicky, her attention drawn down to their shoes, and the sticking noise they were making as they crept their way over the floor.

Stopping where they were, Tanner took a moment to glance cautiously about. 'There doesn't seem to be anyone around.'

'I can hear voices, though.'

'You can?'

Vicky pointed over towards the bar beside which was a small door with the words STAFF ONLY painted in bold white lettering. 'Sounds to me like someone's having an argument.'

Tanner waggled a finger inside one of his ears. 'You know, I'm going to have to get my ears tested. I can't hear a thing.'

'Don't worry. It's very faint, but it's definitely the sound of people shouting.'

Making their way over the curiously sticky floor to where the door was, with the voices growing steadily louder, Tanner nudged it open with his foot.

'I assume you can hear it now?' questioned Vicky.

Tanner levelled his eyes at her. 'I'm possibly a little hard of hearing – not as deaf as a post.'

'Just checking,' she smirked.

Opening the door to its fullest extent, Tanner was about to forge his way through when they heard a more distant one being slammed, closely followed by the sound of footsteps heading in their direction.

Preparing himself for what felt likely to be an aggressive confrontation, Tanner pulled out his ID, just in time to see a well-built young man dressed in an immaculate charcoal suit come charging around the corner, fury etched over his handsome suntanned face.

'Who the fuck are you?' they heard him bark, unnaturally white teeth flashing as he stormed his way down the corridor towards them.

'Detective Inspector Tanner, and Detective Inspector Gilbert, Norfolk Police.'

Pulling up just inches away, the man cast an unnerving eye at the IDs being held up in front of him. 'You're a bit keen aren't you? We don't open till five.'

'We're looking for the owner; a Mr Terrance McMillan?'

The man's eyes narrowed. 'What am I supposed to have done now?'

'I take it that means that you are him?'

Pausing for a moment, the man took a half-step back. 'It's a fair cop, I suppose,' he eventually smirked, holding out his hands as if awaiting to be handcuffed.

Tanner sucked in an impatient breath. 'Do you happen to know someone by the name of Michael Blackwell?'

'Never heard of him.'

'His full name is *Sir* Michael Blackwell; if that helps.'

'I'm sorry, why would it?'

'Apparently, he's been all over the news recently.'

McMillan shrugged. 'I don't have time for lounging about watching TV, I'm afraid. Speaking of which,' he added, making a point of glancing down at his over-sized jewel-encrusted watch, 'is this going to take long? I have a business to run. Several in fact.'

'How about a Mr Toby Wallace?' Tanner continued, digging out his notebook to begin flicking through its pages.

'Again, no, sorry.'

Tanner glanced up with surprise. 'That is your car outside? The black Mercedes with the tinted windows?'

'What about it?'

'It's just that we saw you yesterday, driving out of Mr Wallace's property.'

'Must've been someone else.'

'You nearly drove straight into us. My colleague here made a note of your numberplate before you left us standing in a cloud of dust.'

'I was here all day yesterday.'

'Well, that *is* odd!'

'It must've been my security guys. I did tell them to pop out to fetch some milk. They must have got lost on the way.'

'Oh, right. That must be it. At least, it would have been had Mr Wallace not lived over ten miles away. That's quite a journey to make, just for some milk.'

'You can tell that to them. They may be good at security, but they've got a crap sense of direction. Anyway, are we done?'

'Nearly,' Tanner replied, with a thin detached smile. 'We just have a couple more questions regarding a woman who we believe was working here last night.'

'Yes, well; we have been known to employ the odd woman every now and again, but that shouldn't come as too much of a surprise, given what we do, and everything.'

'We found a photograph of you both together, tucked away inside her handbag.'

'Again,' he smirked, 'she could be one of a hundred.'

'No doubt, except this particular one was found dead this morning.'

'Oh dear, how awful.'

'Don't you want to know who it is?"

'Not really.'

'Her name's Claire Metcalf. I assume you must know her?'

'Nope, sorry. Maybe she's another customer? We do get women in here as well as men,' he added, turning to offer Vicky a sleezy wink.

'Perhaps you know her by her professional name. Amber Vale?'

McMillan whipped his head back to fix his eyes on Tanner. 'What?'

'So, you do know her then?'

'Of course I know Amber. She's one of our very best performers.'

'I therefore take it that you don't know how she ended up sprawled out down a quiet alleyway, just down from where she lived?'

'Why the hell should I?'

'May I ask where you were this morning, between the hours of eight and nine?

'I was at the hotel I'm currently staying at.'

'Which is…?'

'The Southern Lodge. It's the closest one I could find.'

'Will anyone be able to vouch for you?'

'The receptionist. She saw me leave at around that time.'

Turning briefly to make sure Vicky was taking notes, Tanner continued. 'What about on Thursday night between eight and twelve?'

'Why? What happened then?'

'That's when Sir Michael Blackwell, the man you say you've never heard of before, despite his name being plastered all over the national news, was murdered in his bedroom, or at least one of them. He'd had his wrists and ankles handcuffed to the corners of a rather large four-poster bed before someone opened up his chest to remove his still beating heart.'

'News to me.'

'It should be, especially as the woman you've already admitted to having known, Claire Metcalf, otherwise known as Amber Vale, was seen entering Sir Michael's home shortly before he met his untimely end.'

'Then I suppose it's a shame she's dead, else you'd have been able to ask her why she killed him.'

'Actually, we were able to speak to her, before she was murdered, of course.'

McMillan held Tanner's eyes. 'Don't tell me she denied it?'

'Surprisingly, she did. What's perhaps even more of a surprise was that we actually believed her.'

'Well; more fool you.'

'At the end of the day, she just didn't seem the type to saw open a man's chest with a hacksaw, at least not whilst he was still alive.'

'Then I suppose she must have neglected to mention her on-going psychological problems?'

'You know what, she did, but don't worry; we found out about them shortly afterwards.'

A contented smile spread out over McMillan's face. 'Well then, there you have it. Case closed!'

'Despite that, we still thought she was telling the truth.'

'Oh, right. And why was that? Actually, I think I already know. You allowed her beguiling beauty to persuade you; that and her quite extraordinary pair of breasts.'

'Actually, there were two other reasons, neither of which were related.'

Tanner fell momentarily silent as the two men continued glaring at each other.

McMillian eventually opened his mouth. 'Sorry, was I supposed to guess?'

'Well, I think they're fairly obvious, at least the second one is. First up, she seemed to lack motive.'

'Oh, right. But I didn't think deranged psychopaths needed one?'

'And secondly,' Tanner continued, happy to ignore the remark, 'because she's just turned up dead.'

'So you don't think she killed herself during a bout of psychotic remorse for having murdered some rich guy with a hacksaw, just because he wouldn't tell her that he loved her?'

'That would have been difficult, being that she was killed by a single blow to the back of her head, leading me to perhaps, unsurprisingly believe that someone else must have done it, possibly because she knew who'd actually murdered him, someone who wasn't too keen for her to start going around telling everyone.'

'Unless she was mugged, of course.'

Tanner offered him a thin smile. 'Not very likely.'

'What, you mean people don't get mugged in Norfolk? Blimey! I'd no idea. It happens all the time down in London.'

'Don't worry, people get mugged around here as well, it's just that the assailants normally remember to take the person's money, especially when this one in particular had a purse crammed full of the stuff.'

'Maybe they just forgot. From what I've seen during my brief stay so far, everyone around here is as thick as shit. Must be all the inbreeding,' he sneered, staring first at Vicky, then Tanner.'

'I'm from London,' Tanner remarked.

McMillan shrugged. 'Fair enough. Although, to be honest, there are plenty of stupid people down there as well.'

'Which does lead me to ask what you're doing all the way up here, Mr McMillan? I understand your main residence is in London.'

'I'm here on business.'

'What sort of business is that?'

McMillan glanced over at Vicky again. 'Are you sure he's not from Norfolk?'

'I think my colleague is curious to know if you're involved in anything other than the ownership of a chain of seedy strip clubs that stink of vomit and are so disgusting your shoes stick to the floor,' Vicky replied, ungluing one of her feet to the sound of Sellotape being peeled from off its reel.

'Yes, well,' he replied, following her gaze. 'I must admit to having been somewhat lackadaisical in my hands-on management approach recently.'

'So, you're here to get things back on track, are you?' Tanner questioned.

'Something like that.'

'Is that all the shouting was about?'

McMillan offered him a look of confused innocence. 'Sorry, what shouting?'

'When we came in. I assume that was you?'

'Oh that! Right, yes, well. If you don't raise your voice occasionally, nobody seems to pay any attention.'

'May I ask what it was about, specifically?'

McMillan glanced behind him. 'Oh, you know, the normal. Anyway, if there's nothing else? As I said before, I've got a lot to be getting on with.'

- CHAPTER TWENTY SIX -

WITH THE DOOR being both closed and locked behind them, Tanner and Vicky found themselves staring out over the carpark, once again taking shelter under the club's ripped narrow awning.

'What did you make of him?' asked Vicky, giving her umbrella another shake before endeavouring to open it.

'Just your average wannabe gangster, Tanner replied, pulling his fluorescent hood over his head. 'Subsequently, I didn't believe a word he said; apart from one thing, that is.'

'That he didn't know anything about what happen to Claire Metcalf?'

Tanner nodded. 'He seemed genuinely shocked, which now that I think about it, does make me wonder if he was telling the truth about Sir Michael as well.'

'How d'you mean?'

'The only reason I can think of for Metcalf being killed was because she knew who'd murdered Sir Michael; and couldn't be trusted to keep her mouth shut. On that basis, whoever murdered her must have killed him as well. If that wasn't our new friend Terrance McMillan, then it looks like we're back to where we started.'

'Makes sense,' agreed Vicky, her attention

appearing to be more focussed on the clasp at the base of her umbrella than the ins and outs of their current investigation.

'Saying that,' Tanner continued, 'I can't help but think that he's involved somehow. He clearly knows Toby Wallace; else we wouldn't have nearly driven straight into him on his way out of his drive. We've already established he knew Claire Metcalf, even if he didn't know her real name. Then there's the business connection.'

'What connection is that?'

'Wallace and McMillan are in a very similar line of work in that they both own a late night entertainment venue. In fact, the only difference I can think of between the two is that the employees of one expose slightly more flesh than the clientele of another. Maybe they're trying to do some sort of deal together?'

'Maybe the deal went wrong,' Vicky mused, 'a bit like my umbrella.'

'What's wrong with it?' queried Tanner, glancing down.

'I can't seem to get the bloody thing open.'

'Here. Let's take a look.'

Shaking her head in frustration, she handed it to him before gazing out at the rain rattling down onto the roof of her car like the wayward bullets of a Gatling gun. 'If there *was* a business deal, one that had perhaps gone sour, I suppose it could have given McMillan motive for feeling it necessary to open Sir Michael up with a hacksaw, being that he was a joint owner of the Phantom Exchange. Maybe that's why McMillan was at Wallace's house,' she continued, 'to show him pictures of the state they'd left him in?'

'That's *if* he went to Wallace's house,' said Tanner, sagaciously studying the umbrella's opening mechanism.

'Well, if he didn't, then I'm not sure who we nearly drove into yesterday.'

'If you remember, we never actually saw who was in the back. Only the driver, and the guy sitting next to him.'

'Maybe McMillan has a business partner we don't know about,' suggested Vicky, 'and it was him in the back of the Mercedes? Maybe *he* killed Sir Michael, going on to silence Metcalf, all without McMillan knowing, and that's who he was arguing with when we came in?'

'That's a lot of maybes,' muttered Tanner, who'd given up attempting to fix the umbrella and was now doing his best to open it using brute force instead.

'Well, he was definitely shouting at someone about something, and it didn't sound like it was simply because whoever it was had forgotten to mop the floor.'

Hearing his phone ring, Tanner stood up to hand the umbrella back. 'I think its broken,' he commented, delving a hand inside his sailing jacket.

'Yes, thank you,' Vicky replied, taking it from him to find the handle bent, as was the clasp.

'Let me just answer this, and I'll take another look at it.'

'Er...you're OK, thanks,' she replied, glancing around for a bin.

'Tanner speaking!'

'Tanner, it's Forrester. Are you done speaking to that strip club owner?'

'Just finished, sir.'

'OK, good, then you can head back to Toby Wallace's place.'

'Right,' Tanner replied, pausing for a moment to catch Vicky's eye. 'Er...for any particular reason?'

'The guy's neighbour has just called to say that he can see him lying face-up in the middle of his garden, directly next to his swimming pool.'

'Is he dead?'

'Presuming it's raining there as well, I'm fairly sure he's not out there sunbathing.'

'No, right, of course,' Tanner replied, kicking himself for having asked such a stupid question. 'We'll head over there straight away.'

- CHAPTER TWENTY SEVEN -

TANNER AND VICKY stood staring out through a pair of rain-splattered patio doors as they watched Dr Johnstone jogging through the rain towards them. Sliding them open to the sound of the wind howling outside, they stood back as the medical examiner burst in through the opening to stand dripping on a section of white plastic sheeting that had been laid out over the floor.

'Nice day for it,' Tanner commented, sliding the door back.

'You know, Tanner,' the doctor responded, removing his already steamed-up glasses, 'we really must stop meeting like this.'

'It's hardly my fault people keep getting themselves killed around here.'

'It isn't?' he questioned, throwing a glance up at him as he rotated a tissue around each of the lenses. 'No, well, I suppose not, but in this particular case, I don't think they have been.'

Tanner returned his attention to the expansive lawn outside, and the body of a man he could see dressed in a scarlet dressing gown thrown over what appeared to be a pair of black silk pyjamas, his short fat body lying face up on the grass beside a large rectangular swimming pool. 'So, he's just taking a nap?'

'Er...not exactly. From what I can make out, it

looks like he had a heart attack.'

'What, out there?'

'I'm not sure it matters where you happen to be at the time,' Johnstone replied, replacing his glasses to follow Tanner's gaze.

'I meant, what would he have been doing hanging out by his swimming pool dressed in what looks to be his pyjamas on a day like this?'

'My job is to establish a cause of death, Tanner, not to figure out what they were doing at the time.'

'Fair enough,' Tanner replied, turning to glance around at the shiny bright orange units of the expansive modern kitchen they were standing in. 'How about a time of death?'

'I'd say no more than two hours ago.'

'Are there any signs that anything's been taken?'

'Again, not my job, but I haven't heard of anything.'

'What about a forced entry?'

'The front door was locked when we arrived, as were all the windows. A neighbour told us how to get into the garden from a gate around the side.'

'Is this the same neighbour who reported seeing the body?'

'I've no idea, but I believe he's in one of the rooms at the front; if you'd like to have a word.'

- CHAPTER TWENTY EIGHT -

H AVING A POLICE constable show them into a generously proportioned living room at the front of the house, Tanner pulled out his ID to address the middle-aged man they found pacing up and down, his hands clasped behind a stuffy-looking tweed jacket.

'Detective Inspectors Tanner and Gilbert, Norfolk Police,' Tanner announced, closing the door behind them.

The man came to an abrupt halt in front of a stainless steel fireplace. 'And about bloody time,' he muttered, in a distinctly clipped British accent. 'I've been waiting here for an absolute age.'

'Sorry to have kept you. Your name?'

'Marsh. Henry Marsh,' the man replied, pulling his shoulders back.

'You don't mind if we ask you a few questions, do you, Mr Marsh?'

'I don't see what they could be about. All I did was call for an ambulance after seeing our moronic neighbour lying flat-out in the middle of his garden, again. I doubt I'd have even bothered had it not been for the fact that it was raining.'

'Am I to assume that seeing him do so wasn't an unusual occurrence?'

'Well, it wasn't exactly the first time I'd woken up to find he'd spent the night outside, together with numerous of his so-called friends.'

'A bit of a partygoer, was he?'

'A bit of a party-holder, more like. My wife and I don't mind so much during the winter, but his constant summer pool parties drive us up the bloody wall. It's not just us, I may add. The entire neighbourhood have been up in arms. Music to all hours, shouting, screaming, people constantly coming and going.'

'Oh dear. That sounds dreadful. I'm surprised you didn't call the police earlier.'

'We did. Several times.'

'And?' Tanner queried, struggling to feel sorry for the man who both looked and sounded like he could afford to live on a quiet island somewhere in the Caribbean, or at least to go on holiday there.

'And you've been of absolutely no use,' Marsh continued. 'Whenever we called to lodge a formal complaint, it was obvious you didn't give a rat's arse, telling us that there was nothing you could do, and that we needed to call the council, which was hilarious.'

'Sorry, but why was that funny?' asked Tanner; a somewhat contradictory question given the fact that he was personally finding the man's story to be highly amusing.

'Because, detective inspector, nobody works there at two o'clock in the bloody morning!'

Struggling to suppress the smirk he could feel tugging at the corners of his mouth, Tanner dropped his head to begin searching his coat pockets for his notebook. Eventually managing to claw it out, he was finally able to meet the man's gaze with a more appropriately aligned expression. 'When you said there were people constantly coming and going, I don't suppose you saw anyone doing so this morning?'

'Not then, no, but at just about every other time.'

'He didn't have any visitors today?'

'I didn't see anyone, and I didn't hear a car pull up, but then again, I don't spend my life camped out by my bedroom window with a pair of binoculars.'

'Only part of it,' mumbled Tanner.

'I'm sorry?'

Tanner cleared his throat. 'When he did have visitors, I don't suppose you noticed if one of them in particular was a well-dressed young man with olive skin and whiter than normal teeth, often accompanied by two men who'd have been about twice his size?'

'Oh him! I actually saw that particular individual relieve himself up against my garden fence last week. He even had the gall to wave at me whilst doing so.'

Hearing Vicky snort through her nose beside him, Tanner glanced around to find her with a hand covering her mouth, her lightly-freckled face a little redder than usual. 'Are you alright?' he queried; a feigned expression of intense concern drawn out over his face.

'Hay fever,' she replied, fishing a tissue from out of her bag.

Tanner's eyes swivelled over towards the nearest window, and the rain outside being pummelled against it.

'Or maybe dust,' she added, following his gaze with a sheepish expression, after which she drew in a breath to give her nose a loud and most unladylike blow.

'I must apologise for my colleague,' Tanner continued, returning his attention to the man now staring at them as if they were a couple of homeless drunks. 'She's always been prone to allergies. So anyway, where were we?'

Marsh folded his arms over his jacket to give them each an equally disapproving glare.

'Oh yes, that's right,' Tanner continued. 'We were talking about the man who you said shamelessly relieved himself against your fence. May I ask when you saw him last?'

'The day before yesterday.'

'Definitely not this morning?'

'As I said,' Marsh continued, still looking a little peeved, 'I didn't see him then, but that doesn't mean he wasn't there.'

'OK, I think that will do. Thank you for your time, Mr Marsh.'

'I assume that means I can go?'

'You may, but don't worry, we know where you live.'

'What?'

'Sorry. That was just my little joke.'

'Oh, right.'

'But if you could give us a call before making any travel arrangements, at least for the next month or so, that would be appreciated.'

Marsh studied Tanner's face for a moment. 'Was that another joke?'

'Not that time, I'm afraid. And we will need to arrange a convenient time to come over to take a sample of your DNA and fingerprints.'

'I'm sorry?'

'Purely to help us eliminate you from our enquiries.'

'I wasn't aware I was even a part of your enquiries.'

'Well, you did find the body.'

'I saw him from my bedroom window.'

'And you were the one who called the police.'

'I phoned for an ambulance, as anyone would.'

'You've also been inside the victim's house.'

'This is the first time I've stepped foot in this sordid little hole, and I only did that because I was asked to wait here for you.'

'I believe you also showed our forensics team around the back of the house?'

'Well, yes, but –'

'And to be honest, Mr Marsh, it is fairly obvious that you didn't exactly *like* the victim. For all we know, you crept around here this morning to beat him over the head with a hockey stick.'

'I can assure you...'

'Actually, now that I think about it, we'd better take a sample of your prints and DNA before you leave, just in case they prove vital to uncovering the truth about Mr Wallace's seemingly untimely death.'

- CHAPTER TWENTY NINE -

'THAT WAS A bit mean, wasn't it?' whispered Vicky, turning to leave the neighbour stranded in the middle of the living room with his mouth hanging open.

'Sorry, I couldn't help myself,' Tanner replied, stopping to pull the door open for her as they made their way out into the hall. 'Anyway, for all we know, he did do it.'

'I wasn't aware there was anything for him to have done, by him or anyone else. Johnstone seems adamant Wallace died of natural causes, there's no sign of a break in, nothing appears to have been stolen, and the person we think most likely to have killed him wasn't even here.'

'According to the neighbour.'

'Why would he lie about that?'

'I've no idea,' Tanner shrugged. 'Maybe he paid McMillan to kill him.'

'How? By chasing him around his swimming pool in the pouring rain until he had a cardiac arrest?'

'He could have.'

Vicky offered Tanner a deeply sceptical frown.

'We have to keep an open mind, young Vicky.'

'I'm not that young.'

'And my mind isn't that open,' Tanner muttered, just as Johnstone's head appeared around the corner.

'Have you got a minute?' the medical examiner

asked.

'Actually, I've got two,' Tanner smirked, glancing down at his watch. 'Why, what've you found?'

Johnstone emerged into the hall to hold up an evidence bag. 'Looks like another blackmail letter. This one, however, would appear to be complete.'

Stopping beside him, Tanner and Vicky took a moment to peer through the see-through plastic.

'Leave fifty thousand in cash at the base of Happisburgh Lighthouse by midnight tonight,' read Tanner, 'or else I'll be doing unto you as you so kindly thought you'd done unto me.'

'I'd have to compare it to the other one,' Johnstone continued, 'but the typeface looks the same, as is the amount being demanded, obviously.'

'So, someone was trying to blackmail both Sir Michael *and* Mr Wallace.'

'And now they're both dead,' Vicky mused. 'Coincidence?'

Tanner thought for a moment. 'I don't know, but I still don't think it can be the same person. Traditionally, blackmailers don't go around killing the people they're trying to extract money from, being that it would be somewhat counter-productive. Where was it found?'

'In one of the kitchen drawers,' Johnstone replied. 'There's an envelope as well,' he added, turning to head back the way he'd come.

'I don't suppose it had the senders address written on the back?' Tanner called out, as Vicky and himself followed after.

'Unfortunately not. It was very clearly delivered by hand.'

Tanner raised a curious eyebrow at Vicky as they re-entered the kitchen. 'How can you be sure?'

Johnstone stopped to stare down at a stainless

steel table piled high with evidence bags. 'Because it has the words, "by hand" written in capitals over the front,' he continued, fishing another bag out to hold up for Tanner and Vicky to see.

'It is very clearly marked "by hand", isn't it?' Tanner observed, taking the bag from him. 'Underlined no less than three times as well, almost as if the sender wanted to make sure Wallace knew it had been.'

Handing it back, he cast his eyes down at the various other bags piled up on the table. 'Anything else that could be of interest?'

'Um...' Johnstone replied, following Tanner's gaze. 'Oh, yes, we found a pen as well.'

'A pen?'

'It was lying on the floor, under the table. One of the forensics officers nearly trod on it.'

'How very clumsy of him.'

'It was a her, actually,' corrected Johnstone, searching through the various plastic bags.

'Either way; why would a pen be of interest?'

'Before someone trod on it again we checked it for prints. None of the ones we found belonged to the victim.'

'OK, I suppose that does make it slightly more interesting.'

'Here it is,' he eventually announced, holding another bag up for Tanner to take.

'Well, it's a pen alright. A black one at that.'

Stooping down, Vicky peered up at it from underneath. 'Have you seen what's written on its side?'

Lifting his arm so that they could both see, he followed Vicky's gaze. 'The Riverside Gentlemen's Club. Well I never.'

- CHAPTER THIRTY -

STEPPING BACK OUT through the front door, Tanner and Vicky stopped under the overhanging pergola to stare out at the rain ricocheting off the various emergency vehicles parked around the property's spacious gravel drive.

'So,' began Tanner, happy enough to wait there for a moment, 'we have a fat little man who decided to take a stroll around his swimming pool during a category three storm in order to have a heart attack, a stuck-up neighbour who didn't see a single person either enter or leave the property – despite spending half his life staring at the place through his bedroom window, a blackmail note that was definitely delivered by hand, and a pen from the local strip club that our victim hadn't touched, but one of our forensics officers had nearly trodden on.'

'Well, the pen was black,' said Vicky, 'and it was lying on a grey tiled floor, so it was probably quite difficult to see.'

'Leaving to one side the fact that a police forensics officer nearly trod on what could prove to be a vital piece of evidence, during the process of looking for vital pieces of evidence, did I forget anything?'

'That the forensics officer in question was a woman?'

'Anything else?'

'Yes,' Vicky continued, staring out at the rain. 'I

don't have an umbrella.'

'Anything relating to the investigation?'

'Only that the blackmail money was supposed to be left outside Happisburgh Lighthouse.'

Tanner thought quietly for a moment. 'Isn't that the one up above Stalham?'

'It is,' Vicky nodded.

'I don't suppose there's any chance somebody lives there?'

'Aren't most of them unmanned these days?'

'What if that one isn't?'

'Then it would be like asking someone to drop the money off directly outside their house. In fact, it would be exactly like asking someone to drop the money off directly outside their house. Nobody would be quite that stupid, would they?'

Tanner shrugged. 'Well, according to McMillan, there are quite a few stupid people knocking about the place these days. Let's just hope the person who wrote those letters is one of them. Are you ready?' he continued, reaching behind his back to pull his fluorescent hood up over his head.

'Ready for what?'

'To drive over to the lighthouse.'

'Er...isn't that something Cooper needs to follow-up? I mean, you did put him in charge of the blackmail investigation.'

'Shit, yes, of course. I'd almost managed to forget about him.'

'I don't mind going with you, but he'll be seriously pissed off when he finds out.'

'No, that's fine. I'll give him a call to let him know what we've found. Hopefully he won't mind if I tag along. In the meantime, I suggest you get back to the station. See if you can find out who *had* touched that pen.'

'One more thing,' added Vicky.

'What's that?'

'How are you planning on getting to the lighthouse?'

Remembering she'd given him a lift there, Tanner turned to give her a sheepish look. 'Any chance of a ride over to pick up my car?'

'I will on one condition.'

'What's that?'

'That you lend me your coat.'

'Er...' Tanner began, staring out at the horrendous weather, 'how about we share it?'

'As you were the one who broke my umbrella, I think the least you can do is to let me have your coat.'

'Er...I think you're forgetting that it was broken when you gave it to me.'

'I believe it was fixable when I gave it to you, which it most definitely wasn't by the time you handed it back.'

'I'm not sure that argument would stand up in court.'

'I'm not sure the umbrella could stand up in court,' Vicky continued, glaring over at Tanner, 'not after your over-exuberant efforts to fix it.'

'It could have if it was propped up against a wall.'

Vicky offered Tanner the hint of a smile. 'Leaving to one side an umbrella's ability to stand up on its own, be it in a court of law or anywhere else, to be honest, I'm surprised you haven't offered me your coat sooner.'

'Tell you what, I'll share half my coat with you now, and buy you a new umbrella later?'

Vicky considered that for a moment. 'OK, deal; but I don't want some cheap crappy one found at the back of a charity shop.'

'You do know that I've got literally no money, don't

you?'

Vicky folded her arms.

'Alright, deal. But I can't afford to spend more than ten pounds,' Tanner replied, peeling off his sailing jacket.

'I suppose that'll have to do.'

'And you may have to lend me the money to buy it,' Tanner added, lifting the coat up for them to both huddle under before quickly trudging their way over towards Vicky's car.

- CHAPTER THIRTY ONE -

WITH VICKY DROPPING him off next to his Jag parked near the river in Wroxham, Tanner was soon heading northeast, through Stalham, making a beeline for Norfolk's dark stormy coast.

After half an hour of driving through buffeting wind and torrential rain, he eventually rounded a corner to see Happisburgh Lighthouse, rising up from a blanket of deep yellow corn, its broad bands of red and white standing resiliently against a growing mass of clouds beyond.

Following a line of telegraph poles, he turned to make his way up a narrow country lane barely wide enough for his car to pass, at the top of which was a carpark surrounded by a thick shoulder-high hedge. As he brought the car around he peered out through the rain, searching the seemingly deserted space for the familiar slender shape of Cooper's car.

'Where the hell is he?' he questioned, leaving the engine ticking over to help keep the windows from steaming up. Having suggested to meet him there only a few minutes after Vicky had brought up his name, Tanner couldn't help but think he should have been there by now, and was about to call him again, when he saw another car's headlights begin sweeping around the carpark behind him.

'Better late than never,' he muttered, donning his

fluorescent hood once more to climb out.

'You took your time,' he called, the moment Cooper had opened his door.

'I wasn't aware that there was any rush,' the young DI replied, stepping out to turn up the trendy slim collar of a black city raincoat. 'As I said on the phone, there won't be anyone here. Nobody's dumb enough to leave their address as the drop off point to a blackmail demand, present company accepted, of course.'

Tanner could feel himself bristle with repressed animosity. 'Maybe so, but it's still our job to look.'

'Of course, but don't you think it could have waited, at least until it had stopped raining?'

'Time and tide,' Tanner replied, with a thin smile.

Cooper glared at him, his face and hair already soaking wet. 'What the hell's the tide got to do with it?'

'Nothing,' Tanner mumbled, unsurprised to learn that he'd not heard the phrase before. 'Shall we go?'

Cooper gazed wildly about. 'Go where? There's absolutely nothing here!'

'You mean, apart from the lighthouse?'

'People don't live in lighthouses; at least not anymore they don't.'

'Well, there's only one way to find out.'

Turning on his heel, Tanner marched over to the wide base of the giant cylindrical tower where a small door could be seen covered with dark green paint. With no sign of either a bell or a knocker he pounded his fist on its hard wooden surface before taking a step back to stare up, searching for even the vaguest signs of life.

'Told you,' Cooper muttered, when no answer came.

Ignoring him, Tanner stepped forward to hammer

again, but by that time it was clear that there was nobody home.

'Looks like you were right,' Tanner eventually conceded, turning to offer Cooper a congratulatory grimace. 'Well done.'

Cooper responded with a conceited smirk. 'Even a complete moron would have known there wouldn't have been. Right, I'm heading back to the office. Thanks for wasting my time. I can't say how much I appreciate it.'

'Anytime,' Tanner replied, grinning with sarcastic glee to watch Cooper stomp back to his car looking every bit like a drowning rat attempting to board a rapidly sinking ship.

- CHAPTER THIRTY TWO -

A FTER WATCHING COOPER slam his car into reverse before wheel-spinning away, Tanner hunched his shoulders over to begin plodding back to his own at a more casual pace, taking a moment to be grateful for his sailing jacket, the one Jenny had bought him all those years before. Without it, he'd have been just as wet as Cooper. As it was, the only part of him that was admittedly drenched was the lower half of his trousers, which he could feel clinging uncomfortably to his shins.

With Cooper's car disappearing back down the lane, he hooked a hand under his car's chrome plated door handle only to hear the distant sound of something being slammed shut. Instinctively, he glanced back at the lighthouse, but it hadn't come from there. The noise had come from behind him, somewhere beyond the surrounding hedge.

Leaving his car as it was, he trudged his way over to find that there was a narrow over-grown gap beyond which was a path leading to a small country cottage, inviting yellow lights glowing gently behind a series of modest lead-lined windows.

After making his way up to the front door, he ducked underneath a carved wooden porch to lift and release a heavy cast iron knocker.

A moment later he heard the sound of a heavy bolt being slid back from the other side, leaving him greeted by a pair of searching eyes staring out from the angular weathered face of a balding middle aged man.

'Sorry to bother you,' Tanner began, digging out his ID, 'Detective Inspector Tanner, Norfolk Police.'

'On a day like this?' the man questioned, staring first at Tanner, then down at his ID.

'I'm making enquiries about the lighthouse.'

'What about it?'

'Do you know if anyone lives there?'

'Not for years. Why?'

'But someone must come around to service it, occasionally?'

'No doubt they do, but its nobody I know. Some private company, I think.'

'How often do they come?'

The man shrugged. 'Once a month. Something like that.'

'I don't suppose you've seen anyone hanging around there recently?'

'Well, we get the occasional tourist. Not in weather like this, mind.'

'Who is it, Daddy?' came the inquisitive chime of a young girl's voice, calling out from somewhere inside.

'Nobody, darling,' the man responded. But if his words had been meant to dissuade her from coming to take a look, they failed in their primary objective as she came bounding into the hallway behind him, a slim pretty face accentuated by a pair of cobalt blue eyes.

'Hello!' the girl said, offering Tanner a curious smile.

'Er, hi,' Tanner responded, his eyes resting awkwardly on hers for the briefest of moments before glancing away. Simply put, the girl was beautiful. She was also extremely young.

'Forgive my daughter,' the father said. 'We don't often get visitors here.'

'No, of course. That's fine.'

'My name's Alice,' the girl continued, holding out her hand with impetuous excitement.

'Er, Tanner, John Tanner,' Tanner replied, finding himself raising his ID again in a bid to avoid having to shake the young girl's hand. 'Norfolk Police.'

The girl stopped to stare at it, her proffered hand falling away as her neck and cheeks flushed with blood.

Noticing her reaction, the father turned to look around at her. 'It's nothing to worry about, darling, he's just asking about the lighthouse.'

'What about it?' the daughter enquired, lifting her eyes to meet with Tanner's.

'I was just asking if anyone lives there?'

'Nobody, no. Not for years.'

'So your father said.'

'Anyway,' the father continued, 'you'd better get yourself back to that homework of yours.'

'Of course,' she replied, with an obedient nod.

Shifting her eyes back to Tanner, she smiled again. 'Nice to have met you,' she suddenly said, as if remembering that it was the sort of thing she was supposed to say having just met someone new.

'Nice to have, er, met you too,' Tanner replied, stumbling over the words as the girl spun away.

Feeling the father's eyes boring into his, Tanner cleared his throat. 'She seems nice,' he eventually said, unsure as to what else to say.

'She's also fifteen,' the father replied, his voice filled with threatening reproach. 'A bit of a handful as well,' he continued, in a more apologetic tone, as if becoming aware that he was being unnecessarily over-protective. 'Always has been. Worse since her mother became ill and passed away.'

Sensing the man's wife must have died quite recently, Tanner pulled in a shallow breath. 'I'm sorry for your loss.'

'That's kind of you. It's been over a year now, but it still feels like it was only yesterday.'

Tanner's heart went out to him. 'These things take time.'

'Yes, well. Anyway, can I be of further help?'

'Er, no. I think that's it. Thank you for your time, and sorry to have disturbed you.'

Turning his head, he was about to head back into the unrelenting rain when he glanced quickly back. 'Actually, I'd probably better take your name and a contact number, just in case I think of anything.'

'Chapman. George Chapman,' the man replied. 'You'll find my number in the phone book.'

- CHAPTER THIRTY THREE -

PLODDING BACK TO his car, with the door closed and the strangely comforting sound of the rain clattering against the roof, he put a quick call through to the office.

'Vicky, hi, it's me.'

'Hello John. I don't suppose you're calling to say that you've bought me a new umbrella?'

'Er...no; at least, not yet.'

'OK, but you will be soon though, right?'

'The second I pass a suitable shop,' Tanner replied, unable to determine if she was being serious.

'How'd it go with Cooper?'

'About average. He left the second we found out that the lighthouse was deserted.'

'I'm not surprised. And you?'

'I stayed on to have a chat with the guy who lives next door, but he was only able to confirm what we already knew; that nobody lives there. The only people who ever turn up are the company who look after it, them and the occasional tourist.'

'So, it was purely a drop-off point then?'

'Looks like it. Good choice, though. It's virtually in the middle of nowhere.'

'I bet Cooper was pleased to have been dragged all the way out there in the pouring rain, for no particular reason.'

'I think delighted would be a better word. Anyway,

how've you been getting on?'

'As it turns out, there were a number of fingerprints on the pen found at Wallace's place, one of which was a partial belonging to our friend the strip club owner, Mr Terrance McMillan.'

'OK, well, it's a start, I suppose,' came Tanner's somewhat despondent response.

'It's more than a start, isn't it?'

'Not by much. It doesn't prove he was at Wallace's house, only that he'd touched the pen at some point. I don't suppose they've found his prints on anything else there, preferably something that isn't quite so easily moved, like a built-in fridge freezer, or a seventy-two inch TV, preferably one mounted to a nearby wall?'

'We've yet to hear back, but I've checked to see if there were any of his found in Sir Michael's bedroom.'

'Anything?'

'Not a single one, I'm afraid. Apart from the housekeeper's, and Sir Michael's of course, the only ones they've managed to unearth belong to the late Claire Metcalf.'

Tanner took a moment to wipe at the rain still dripping down his face. 'I don't suppose there's been any news about her, by any chance?'

'We've had an interim report back, but it only confirms what Johnstone already suspected. She'd had sex between one and two hours before she was killed, but it would appear to have been consensual, and that the cause of death was from a single blow to the back of her head. Apart from the old man's who we interviewed, they've found no other prints or DNA on either her or at the place she was found, something Johnstone has formally put down to their inability to protect the scene from the ensuing storm.'

'OK, well, at least we found that photograph of her

with McMillan,' continued Tanner, endeavouring to sound a little more upbeat, 'that and the fact that she was at his club that night.'

'How do we know that?'

'Because of the stamp on her hand.'

'Does the stamp prove she was there?' questioned Vicky. 'Those things can last for days, can't they?'

'Speaking from experience, are you?'

'Some of us are still young enough to remember going to the occasional night club.'

'Yes, well, fair enough. I can't say it was ever my thing. Right, I'd better start heading back. Any sign of Cooper?'

'Not yet, no. Why?'

'What with our somewhat frosty meeting earlier, I forgot to ask him how his blackmail investigation was coming along. I was also wondering if it was possible that Sir Michael's other friend, Iain Sanders, may have received a letter as well.'

'Shall I give him a call to ask him?'

'Well, you can, but I doubt he'd tell you. If he has received a letter demanding fifty thousand pounds to be left outside a deserted lighthouse, it would have been to cover up something fairly serious. And as we now have two dead people, both of whom had received the same letter, I'm becoming increasingly convinced that we're going to have to find out what that was.'

- CHAPTER THIRTY FOUR -

TANNER LAUGHED QUIETLY to himself as he drove up Stalham Road heading for Wroxham Police Station, outside which he could see the now familiar gaggle of reporters, all looking decidedly wet and even more decidedly miserable. One attractive blonde-headed woman in particular had him suppressing a smirk as he drove slowly past. She was endeavouring to do a news segment to camera, but her tangled mop of soaking wet hair was catching in her mouth each and every time she opened it, forcing her to keep tugging it out with the hand that was supposed to be holding onto a microphone. The other was clamped around the base of an umbrella, desperately trying to keep its ridged dome facing into the twisting turbulent wind.

The moment of self-amusement passed the second he turned into the station's carpark to see none other than Cooper, stepping out of his Audi to pelt his way inside. Assuming he must have stopped off somewhere for petrol on the way back, either that or he'd got lost, he left his car next to Forrester's BMW to follow inside, only to find Cooper again. This time he was standing in the middle of reception, having what appeared to be a somewhat heated discussion with the only other person there, a taller, older man wearing a pristine white sailing jacket, rainwater dripping from its surface down to the reception's floor. It took him a full moment to realise who that person was.

'Mr Sanders!' Tanner called out. 'I was just talking to one of my colleagues about you.'

'I'm here to find out what happened to Toby,' Sanders demanded, glancing around.

'Oh, right. You heard about that, did you?'

'I'm not sure how I couldn't have. It's been all over the news.'

'He wants to know how he died,' Copper commented, watching as Tanner stepped up to join them.

'Does he, now.'

'Of course!' Sanders proclaimed, his eyes darting between the two DIs. 'He's one of my very best friends.'

Tanner took a moment to study the man's face. There was a questioning curiosity there, there were also clear signs of frustration, no doubt brought on by the fact that nobody at the station would confide in him the details of what Tanner considered to be another murder investigation. But there was something else as well, something he'd not expected to find; an emotion he'd seen etched out on so many people's faces during his career that he could recognise it in an instant. It was fear; cold, hard, undiluted fear.

Tanner caught the man's eyes. 'Why are you really here, Mr Sanders?'

'What d-do you mean?' he stammered, glancing briefly away. 'I just told you. I want to know what happened to Toby.'

'Well...' Tanner began, 'what did the papers say?'

'Just that his death was being investigated by the police.'

'Which is exactly what we're doing.'

'So, someone killed him then?'

Tanner raised an inquisitive eyebrow. 'Did I say that?'

'You just admitted that you're actively investigating his death,' Sanders continued.

'As we do in all instances when someone's died in what could be considered to be unusual circumstances. That doesn't mean he was murdered, though.'

'So, what happened to him?'

'That's what we're trying to find out.'

'Can you at least tell me how he died?'

'I'm sorry, but I'm struggling to see what difference it would make.'

'I just told you. He was one of my very best friends.'

'And...?'

'And I think I have a right to know how he died.'

'I'm sorry, Mr Sanders, but I'm afraid that privilege is only extended to members of his immediate family.'

'I'm probably the closest thing the man had to one.'

'Maybe so, but that doesn't make you a blood relative, does it.'

Sanders hunched his shoulders over as he glowered back at Tanner, the fear he'd seen in his eyes being replaced by resent-fuelled anger. 'As you're apparently investigating his death, don't you at least want to know where I was at the time?'

'Why? Did you kill him?'

'Of course I didn't kill him!'

'Then why would we want to know where you were?'

'I'm sorry, I'm confused. Are you investigating his death or not?'

Tanner let out a world weary sigh as he dug his

notebook out from the depths of his coat. 'Go on then. Mr Sanders, where were you at the time of your friend, Mr Wallace's death?'

'You'll need to tell me when he died, first.'

Tanner narrowed his eyes at him. 'I must admit, at this stage I'm becoming more curious to know why you seem so keen to find out how and when your friend died than whether or not you had anything to do with it.'

'As I said, I have a right to know.'

'But to come all the way here to find out, during the middle of a storm as well? Couldn't you have just picked up a phone?'

'Fine!' Sanders spat, spinning around to stomp his way towards the exit. 'If you're not prepared to tell me, and as you've clearly no interest in knowing where I was at the time, I'll be heading back to my boat.'

Knowing he was going to have to ask him at some stage anyway, Tanner waited for him to reach the door before calling out, 'It was between nine and eleven this morning.'

'I'm sorry?' Sanders enquired, turning back to feign surprise. 'Are you talking to me?'

'Your friend, Toby Wallace. He died between nine and eleven this morning.'

'Does that mean you *would* like to know where I was?'

'If you wouldn't mind.'

'I see. Right, let me think. If he died this morning, between nine and eleven, then I suppose I would have been on board my boat.'

'What a surprise,' Tanner muttered, rolling his eyes over at Cooper.

'What was that?'

'Nothing,' he added, realising he must have said it

louder than he thought.

With Sanders still glaring at him, Tanner remembered something he'd wanted to ask him. 'Actually, there was something my colleague, DI Cooper and I were curious about.'

'What was that?' Sanders questioned, as Cooper tilted his head to give Tanner a curious look.

'I don't suppose you've received any threatening letters recently?'

'Threatening letters?'

'You know, something written on a piece of paper demanding the payment of an unfeasibly large sum of money.'

'You mean a blackmail letter?'

'I believe they have been known to be called that.'

'Why would anyone want to send me a blackmail letter?'

'Other than the fact that we found one at both Sir Michael's and Mr Wallace's house? No reason.'

'Then it must have had something to do with their sordid little night club business.'

'That's a no, then?' Tanner sought to clarify, his eyes never leaving Sanders'.

'I can assure you, detective inspector, that had I been in receipt of such a letter, you'd have been the first person I'd have called.'

'Of course you would,' Tanner muttered to himself again, that time making sure that only Cooper could have overheard.

- CHAPTER THIRTY FIVE -

THE MINUTE SANDERS had thrown his pristine sailing jacket's hood over his head to march back out into the rain, Tanner gave Cooper a look of bemused curiosity. 'That was all a bit odd, don't you think?'

'The part when he was demanding to know if his friend had been murdered, or when he seemed strangely keen for you to ask if he'd done it?'

'I think he was using that as an excuse to find out *when* Wallace had died,' Tanner mused, staring at the door the man had just walked out of as it swung slowly back.

'Did you notice that he never once asked if we knew who may have killed his friend?' Cooper queried, following Tanner's thoughtful gaze. 'His only interest seemed to be if he had been.'

'I must admit, I've never known anything quite like it. For someone to come all the way over here – in this weather – demanding to know the details of a person's death; more particularly, if we thought the person had been murdered, without ever thinking to ask if we had any idea who would have done so. As I said – it was all very peculiar.'

'There was something else I noticed as well,' Cooper continued, catching Tanner's eye. 'When he was asking about his friend I thought he looked scared.'

'I'll go one better than that,' Tanner added, finding himself in the unusual position of being in agreement with Cooper, 'I'd say the man looked terrified. So, when you add together his interest in finding out if his friend had been murdered – without thinking to ask if we knew who may have been responsible, combined with the fact that we both agree he look petrified, plus the fact that I thought it was fairly obvious he was lying about not having received any threatening letters, what are we left with?'

'Someone who not only knows who killed Wallace, but also why.'

'Which naturally leads me to my next question.'

'Which is?'

Tanner turned to offer Cooper an affable smile. 'How's that little blackmail investigation of yours going?'

With the corners of the young DI's mouth tilting up into what could almost be considered a smile, he was about to answer when DCI Forrester came charging his way through the doors from the main office.

'There you are, Tanner. Where the hell have you been?'

'We've – er – just come back from the lighthouse, sir,' Tanner replied, trying to remember the last time they'd spoken.

'Lighthouse? What lighthouse?'

'The one mentioned in the blackmail letter found at Toby Wallace's house.'

'News to me,' Forrester grumbled, offering him a blank stare. 'Sounds like I'm due for some sort of an update, don't you think?'

The sucking sound of the entrance door had all three of them glancing around to see a bedraggled soaking wet young woman come stumbling into the reception, a red-faced toddler fighting at the end of one arm, a broken umbrella hanging limp from the other. As the child began tugging with vehement determination at his mother's twisted hand, screaming at the top of his lungs as he did, Tanner turned back to Forrester. 'Would you mind if I updated you somewhere else, sir?' he began, raising his voice above the cacophony of noise. 'Actually, sir, would you mind if I updated you *anywhere* else?'

'Right, you two; my office, now!'

'Me as well?' bleated Cooper.

Forrester turned to glare over at him. 'You do work here, don't you?'

'Well, yes...'

'And am I to understand that you went with Tanner to this mysterious lighthouse, presumably because you're still in charge of the blackmail side of this investigation?'

'I did, but...'

'Then yes, you as well, Cooper! Why the hell wouldn't it be you as well?'

- CHAPTER THIRTY SIX -

'OK YOU TWO, take a seat,' said Forrester, levering himself down into his own. 'And close the door,' he added, planting his elbows down on his desk to watch Tanner follow Cooper inside.

'Right,' the DCI continued, 'where were we? Something about a lighthouse and another blackmail letter?'

Glancing around to find Forrester aiming the question squarely at him, Tanner took the seat next to where he could see Cooper was endeavouring to make himself comfortable. 'The blackmail letter was found in a kitchen drawer at Toby Wallace's house.'

'Who, I've been told, had a heart attack whilst apparently doing a spot of gardening?'

'Dr Johnstone did seem to be under the impression that he'd had a heart attack,' Tanner confirmed, 'but I doubt it was because he was overexerting himself whilst cutting the grass.'

'You think he was somehow murdered?'

'Not murdered, as such. He was spotted by his neighbour, sprawled out beside his pool in his dressing gown.'

'OK, so he wasn't gardening, but I still don't see why you think there's anything suspicious about it.'

'Had it not been for the weather, sir, I doubt I would have.'

'What's the weather got to do with it?'

'His death coincides with when it started raining, making it an odd sort of time for him to venture outside, especially given what he was wearing.'

'Couldn't he have run out to grab something that wasn't supposed to be getting wet? Some washing, perhaps, or maybe a book he'd left by the pool?'

'It's possible, I suppose,' Tanner replied, 'but I didn't see a washing line. I didn't see a book lying beside the pool either, or anything else I could imagine forcing him out into such inclement weather.'

'So what are you suggesting happened?'

'I think he was trying to escape from someone inside his house.'

'Was there sign of a forced entry?'

'No, but...'

'Had anything been stolen?'

'Again, no.'

'Did you find an unexploded World War II bomb in his downstairs toilet?'

'Er...'

'Was he married?'

Tanner exchanged a brief bemused look with Cooper. 'Not that we're aware of, sir, no.'

'OK, so if a gang of armed criminals hadn't broken into his house, if he hadn't found an unexploded bomb in his downstairs toilet, and if he didn't have a disgruntled wife he'd managed to upset about something, what could he have been so desperate to run away from?'

'That's where the pen comes in.'

'The pen?'

'Yes, sir. It was found under the kitchen table.'

'My God! You mean to tell me that an actual real-life pen was found under a table, in his kitchen? Why didn't you tell me this before? I mean, of course the man was murdered!'

Tanner forced an unamused smile over at his DCI. 'I was more interested in what was written on it, than it being the specific reason behind Wallace's death.'

'Which was?'

'The Riverside Gentlemen's Club.'

'So what?'

'It's the strip club Terrance McMillan owns.'

'I'm fully aware of that, thank you, Tanner; but it doesn't mean the owner was there, nor anyone else for that matter.'

'But we do know that McMillan had been there before. His neighbour had seen him coming and going on a fairly regular basis.'

'Did the neighbour see him there at the time of Wallace's death?'

'Well, no sir, but...'

'But what?'

'But the only prints we've identified on it so far belong to McMillan. It doesn't even look like the victim had touched it.'

'So you're thinking that he went to Wallace's house that morning armed with a pen, the sight of which was so terrifying, the homeowner ran out into his garden in the middle of a category three storm in order to have a heart attack?'

'I was thinking more along the lines that McMillan had brought it with him with the intention of forcing Wallace to put his name to something he didn't necessarily want to. When he refused, they threatened to start removing his fingers with a pair of pliers, or something similar, at which point he legged it out into the rain, only to find himself dying of a heart attack.'

'It's a great story, Tanner, really it is, but I've got

no idea how you're going to prove that in court.'

'We're not there yet, I admit, but we've at least managed to link McMillan to each of our three victims.'

'Remind me how you've done that?'

'Through Claire Metcalf, sir. She was the woman Sir Michael was with that night, the one who openly admitted to handcuffing him to his bed. We know she worked at the Riverside strip club, and that McMillan knew her. And now she's been found dead down an alley with her head bashed in.'

'And that's something else nobody's bothered to tell me about.'

'I'm sorry, sir, it's just that there's been quite a lot going on recently.'

'Yes, well, fair enough. So, you think McMillan killed her because she was a witness to Sir Michael's murder?'

Tanner nodded. 'He told us she was their best performer. I think we all know what that means. So it makes sense for him to send her to Sir Michael's house with the specific instruction to secure him to the bed with minimal fuss. Whether or not she was still there when he had his heart surgically removed is probably largely irrelevant. The fact that she'd been seen going inside by the housekeeper, who then unfortunately went and gave her name to the national press – albeit the wrong one – would have probably meant she was too dangerous to leave walking about.'

'I don't suppose we have any proof that either McMillan, or any of his known associates, did actually kill her?'

'Nothing yet, I'm afraid. To be honest, I'm not sure we're going to. It had just started pouring down with rain when we arrived at the scene, and the location of the body made it impossible for forensics to protect the surrounding evidence.'

'Do we have *anything?*'

'Just that it's unlikely she was mugged, as her purse was found stuffed full of cash. And although Johnstone says she'd had sex with someone shortly before her body was found, she hadn't been raped. Apart from a Riverside club stamp found on the back of her hand, the only other thing we found to be of interest was a picture of her inside her handbag, cosying up to McMillan.'

'Do we have any idea who she'd been having sex with?'

'I must admit, I'd assumed it to have been one of the club's patrons, but I'll make a note to give Johnstone a call to find out.'

'Before you do, you still haven't told me why the two of you have been off visiting a lighthouse. Was it part of some informal team building exercise. Cooper?'

Hearing his name, Cooper sat up in his chair. 'As, er, Tanner mentioned earlier, sir,' he began, clearing his throat, 'another blackmail letter was found at Mr Wallace's house, which is thought to be from the same person as the one Sir Michael received, the difference being that it was intact. Its instructions were to leave fifty thousand pounds at the base of Happisburgh Lighthouse.'

'So you thought you'd go over to see if the person who wrote the letter actually lived there?' Forrester queried, both his tone and expression burgeoning with incredulity.

Tanner watched as Cooper's head turned slowly around to stare over at him. Expecting him to say that the whole lighthouse trip was his idea, he drew in a fortifying breath in preparation for having to defend himself. But instead of doing so, Cooper returned his gaze to Forrester.

'We thought it was a possibility, sir; certainly not something we should automatically rule out.'

'Well...?' Forrester demanded. 'Did you find anyone there? Some troubled soul hunched over a dilapidated typewriter, frantically hammering out a few more letters?'

'Er, no sir. The place was deserted.'

Forrester began to slowly rotate his head around until his eyes rested firmly on Tanner's. 'You don't say.'

Feeling it necessary to offer some sort of response, Tanner shifted uncomfortably in his chair. 'We did speak to the people living next door.'

Cooper jerked his head to stare over at him.

'And...?' Forrester questioned, leaning back in his chair.

'They were able to confirm that the lighthouse was unmanned.'

'Really?'

'And that the only people who ever went there were the contractors who serviced it, them and the occasional tourist.'

'You mean, they didn't see anyone hanging about outside holding up a placard with, "Please leave your fifty-thousand pound blackmail demand here," written all over it?'

Tanner gave Forrester another of his not so amused smiles. 'Not that they saw, sir, no.'

'Oh well, at least neither of you has anything better to do. I mean, we only have the deaths of three people to investigate, half the nation's press parked outside, what they're now saying could become the worst storm in over a hundred years, and Superintendent Whitaker phoning me up every five minutes demanding to know what's going on.'

Tanner feigned a confused expression. 'Excuse me, sir, but...are you being sarcastic?'

'OF COURSE I'M BEING BLOODY SARCASTIC!' Forrester yelled back, the vein running vertically down his forehead pumping ominously.

'Sorry,' Tanner responded, doing his best to suppress the smirk that seemed desperate to make what would have been a most inappropriate appearance. 'I wasn't sure.'

'Please don't tell me that you think this is funny, Tanner.'

'Not at all, sir. But in our defence, Sir Michael's body was only found on Friday, and the other two just this morning. Bearing that in mind, I think it's a little presumptuous of Superintendent Whitaker to expect us to already have the person responsible under lock and key. As for the British press, if they wish to spend their sad little lives camped outside our station in the pouring rain, then good luck to them.'

'That's as maybe, Tanner, but we're still going to need to see some tangible signs that you're making progress, and what should have obviously been a pointless wild goose chase off to see some uninhabited lighthouse doesn't count, I'm afraid.'

With neither Tanner nor Cooper offering any form of response, Forrester drew in an exasperated breath. 'So anyway, do we have anyone in mind as being a suspect?'

'For the murders or the blackmail?'

'I don't suppose there's any chance they're one and the same?'

'At this stage, it's difficult to see how. It would certainly be unusual for a blackmailer to start going around murdering the people they're trying to extract money from. If they were to kill anyone, it would be a family member, and they'd only do that out of desperation.'

'If the person didn't have a family, I suppose they could consider targeting a close friend instead,' mused Cooper, catching Tanner's eye.

'I must admit, I'd been considering the possibility of something similar myself.'

'And what's that?' Forrester questioned.

'I think Cooper is suggesting that Sir Michael may have been killed to convince Wallace that their blackmail threat was serious?'

'It could also explain why they murdered him in such a theatrical manner,' Cooper added, 'and why Wallace was so scared when they showed up at his house that he tried to make a run for it, without making the effort to get dressed first.'

'During the middle of a category three storm, as well,' Tanner muttered, his eyes drifting away in thoughtful contemplation.

Forrester replaced his elbows on top of his desk. 'What did the blackmail letter actually say?'

'It sounded like some sort of a bible quote.' Tanner replied, digging out his notebook to begin flicking through its pages. '"Leave fifty thousand in cash at the base of Happisburgh Lighthouse by midnight tonight, or else I'll be doing unto you as you so kindly thought you'd done unto me."'

Forrester raised an eyebrow. 'That's a bit cryptic, isn't it?'

'I think it was supposed to be. Quite clever when you think about it. Discreet enough not to give too much away, but clear enough for the target to know what was being referred to.'

The office fell into a thoughtful silence as the three men each took a moment to consider what was being proposed.

'I don't suppose we have any suspects?' Forrester

eventually asked, his gaze switching between the two DIs.

'Well, sir,' Tanner began, 'if the blackmailer and the murderer are one and the same, at this stage I'd say the most likely suspect is the strip club owner, Terrance McMillan. He clearly fancies himself as a bit of a gangster, and I'd be very surprised if he doesn't have form.'

Forrester laid his hands flat on the desk. 'OK, that will have to do. I suggest you bring him in for questioning.'

Tanner's mouth fell open in surprise. 'You want us to arrest him?'

'No, Tanner, I want you to ask him out for dinner.'

'But...' Tanner continued, exchanging a brief look of bemused uncertainty with Cooper, '...we don't have any evidence to prove his involvement, for either the murders or the blackmail.'

'You found that pen of his at Wallace's house, didn't you?'

'Well, yes...'

'And that dead stripper. Didn't you say she worked for him?'

'But...'

'OK, I know it's not much, but it will have to do. With Whitaker breathing down my neck, and all the reporters parked outside, we have to be seen to be doing something.'

'Even though we won't have enough to hold him for more than twenty-four hours?'

'The way I'm looking at it, the fact that we don't have any evidence means that we haven't got anything to lose.'

'Sorry, sir, I'm not with you.'

'If he walks free, then we haven't lost the means to use the evidence we've acquired against him, being that we didn't have any to start with.'

'You mean, *when* he walks free,' added Tanner, astonished by Forrester's uncharacteristically flippant attitude.

'It will also give us the excuse to search that strip club of his,' Forrester continued, 'and who knows what we'll find in there.'

Tanner once again looked over at Cooper, before glancing down at his watch.'

'Well?' he heard Forrester bark. 'What are you waiting for?'

'You want us to arrest him now?'

'No, you're right. It's probably better if you wait till next week. Hopefully the weather would have cheered up by then.'

'It's just that it's already gone five o'clock,' Tanner continued, his mind thinking what Christine was going to say when he had to tell her that he was going to cancel their planned dinner together, again.

Forrester glared theatrically down at his watch. 'My God, you're right, it has! I'd no idea. That really is rather late, isn't it.'

'Er...and it's Sunday, sir.'

'How very insensitive of me. I suppose you had plans for the evening?'

Regretting having mentioned either the time or the day of the week, Tanner cleared his throat. 'Well, sir, I was just thinking – wouldn't it be better if we were to wait till tomorrow? That would at least give us time to find some actual evidence against him.'

'Is that very likely?'

'Maybe not, but...'

'Then I want him brought in now; if that's all the same to you. At this stage, I think it's more important that we're seen to be doing something than nothing at all.'

'*Speak for yourself,*' muttered Tanner quietly to himself, his mind imagining just how long it was going to take him to locate the suspect in question, drag him back to the station, have him formally processed, await the arrival of his solicitor – presuming he even had one – all before being able to interview him under caution.

Forrester cast a beady eye over at him. 'I'm sorry, what was that?'

'I was just telling myself that if I'm going to be able to start questioning him before eleven o'clock tonight, I suppose I'd better be getting on with it, sir,' Tanner replied, forcing a smile over at his DCI.

'That's the spirit. You'd better take Cooper with you as well.'

'Huh?' the young DI said, looking up with a start.

'You are still heading up the blackmail side of this investigation, are you not?'

'Yes, but it's...' Cooper began, copying both Tanner and Forrester in staring down at his watch.

'...it's gone five o'clock on Sunday afternoon,' Forrester said, finishing the sentence for him. 'I know. Tanner told me that less than a minute ago. But don't worry, I'll be keeping myself busy as well. The moment I get home, I'll be putting my feet up to watch the evening news, and the two of you being filmed marching that strip club owner in through the station's doors.'

Seeing Forrester take hold of his mouse to turn his attention to his monitor, Tanner and Cooper stared around at each other before climbing slowly to their feet.

'We'll be off then, shall we, sir?' Tanner enquired, with the forlorn hope that the DCI would have a change of heart.

'Actually, hold on,' Forrester began, abandoning

his mouse to pick up his phone instead.

Tanner's spirit lifted momentarily, but only until he heard who he was calling, and why.

'Hi Sally; do me a favour, will you? Can you collect together everything we have on Terrance McMillan. Give forensics a call if you have to. Then, if you don't mind, could you see if you can dig out a couple of umbrellas? Tanner and Cooper are about to head off to arrest him, and I don't want them to get any wetter than they would already appear to be.'

- CHAPTER THIRTY SEVEN -

TANNER WAS WET, tired, and starving hungry as he led Cooper inside one of Wroxham Police Station's interview rooms to find a disgruntled looking Terrance McMillan, quietly conferring with a man he presumed to be his solicitor. Subsequently, it probably wasn't too much of a surprise that he was also in a foul mood. It hadn't helped that he'd been forced to cancel his date with Christine three hours before, for the second time in nearly as many days. And although she said she was fine about it, from the despondent tone of her voice, it was obvious that she wasn't.

Without bothering to say anything to either of the men sitting on the opposite side of the small wooden table, both now glaring at him with impatient expectation, Tanner slumped down onto the chair closest to the wall, placed his freshly made mug of coffee beside a surprisingly hefty-looking file he'd brought in with him, and waited for Cooper to take the seat next to his before pressing a button on the wall-mounted recording device.

'Commencing the interview of Mr Terrance McMillan of 14, Bainsbrook Gardens, London at...' Tanner made a point of pulling back his suit jacket sleeve to stare down at his watch, '...twenty-nine minutes past eight. The day is Sunday the 29th August,' he continued. 'Present in the room are

Detective Inspectors Cooper and Tanner, the afore-mentioned suspect, and his solicitor.' Picking up a pen, he glanced up at the remarkably unattractive man sitting immediately opposite him. 'Sorry, I don't know your name.'

'Crabtree,' the solicitor replied.

Tanner stopped for a moment to take the man in. With his bulging eyes and flaky brown skin, he looked almost exactly like the result of crossing a crab with a tree. 'Of course it is,' he eventually replied, imagining what it would have taken for the two to have had such an oddly-shaped human-sized offspring together.

Shaking his head in an effort to refocus his mind, his eyes shifted over to the suspect. 'Mr McMillan, you have been arrested on suspicion of the murder of Sir Michael Blackwell...'

'This should be good,' McMillan muttered in response, smirking around at his solicitor.

'...Miss Claire Metcalf,' Tanner continued, 'otherwise known as Amber Vale, and Mr Toby Wallace. You do not have to say anything, but it may harm your defence if you do not mention when questioned something which you later rely on in court. Anything you do say may be given in evidence.'

'Speaking of which,' the solicitor enquired, his eyes drilling down into Tanner's, 'may we see this so-called "evidence"?

'We're getting to that, thank you, Mr Tree Crab.'

The solicitor sent Tanner an irritated scowl. 'It's Crabtree, and no, we won't be "getting to that". We'll see the evidence now, thank you very much. Failure to do so will have me escorting my client straight out the door, after which I'll be advising him to sue the Norfolk Constabulary for wrongful arrest; police harassment as well, if you're stupid enough to try and stop us.'

'Mr Crab, er, Tree,' Tanner began, making the mistake of glancing up at the solicitor's bulging eyes, 'we are well within our rights to detain your client for a period of twenty-four hours whilst continuing to conduct our investigation into the deaths of no less than three of our local residents.'

'Not without evidence, you're not.'

'Which we'll be coming to shortly. Now, if we may continue?'

The solicitor held his eyes for a moment longer before waving his hand.

Tanner paused for a moment to take a much needed sip from his coffee.

'Mr Terrance McMillan, do you understand why you've been arrested, and the allegations that have been made against you?'

'Yes, thank you,' McMillan replied, sending Tanner an overly appreciative grin.

'May I start by asking where you were on Thursday evening between eight and twelve, this morning at around nine o'clock, and again a couple of hours later?'

'I'd have thought you should have asked him all that *before* you arrested him,' muttered the solicitor, beginning to take notes on the pad in front of him.

'I was at the Riverside,' McMillan replied.

'On all three occasions?'

'Since making the trip up to Norfolk, I've had no choice but to spend the vast majority of my time there.'

'I assume there will be witnesses who'll be able to vouch for you?'

'Everyone who works there.'

'Well, not quite everyone, being that one of them was found lying down an alleyway near Tunstall with her head smashed in.'

'Sorry, my mistake. Apart from Amber.'

'You mean, Miss Metcalf?'

'Again, my error. I've always known her by her stage name.'

'Yes, of course,' Tanner said, taking a moment to review his notes. 'Would you be able to describe your relationship with Miss Metcalf?'

'How do you mean? She was one of my employees.'

'Let me put it another way,' Tanner continued. 'Did you ever have sex with her?'

McMillan's eyes narrowed. 'What's that got to do with anything?'

'My client does have a point,' interjected Crabtree.

'We're simply trying to establish the relationship between your client and one of the victims. If he would prefer not to answer, that's fine by us, although it would lead us to question why he'd choose not to.'

Crabtree thought for a moment before nodding over at his client.

Seeing McMillan open his mouth, Tanner caught his eye to interrupt him. 'But do please remember, Mr McMillan, that you may not be here under oath, but if you are caught lying about anything during these proceedings, it will negatively reduce your credibility both here and in the eyes of a court, making it extremely difficult for us to believe anything you tell us going forward.'

McMillan closed his mouth before opening it again. 'Not that it's any of your business but yes, we had a relationship.'

'Of a sexual nature?'

'Well, she wasn't my grandmother, if that's what you mean.'

'No, of course,' smiled Tanner. 'May I ask when you last had such a relationship with Miss Metcalf.'

'If you must know, it was at around seven o'clock

this morning.

'You mean, about two hours before her body was found?'

'If you say so.'

Tanner allowed the room to fall silent as he made a quiet note in the file in front of him.

'I'm still awaiting to see some of this elusive evidence,' he heard Crabtree mutter.

Ignoring the remark, Tanner looked up to continue. 'And your business relationship with Miss Metcalf. How would you describe that?'

'I've already told you. She was an employee.'

'In what capacity was she employed?'

'She's a dancer. One of our best. But I've told you this as well, haven't I?'

'When you say dancer, I take it you actually mean a stripper?'

McMillan smiled. 'Our dancers do seem to have a tendency to take their clothes off during their performances. I'm not sure why, but whatever the reason, I'm fairly sure that there isn't a law against it.'

'And what happens then?'

'I'm sorry?'

'After they've taken their clothes off.'

'Er...they go back to their dressing room to put them back on again.'

'You don't offer your clientele any...additional services?'

'Not me personally,' he grinned, 'but to be honest, I doubt I'm their type.'

'I suspect you know what I mean, Mr McMillan.'

'If my dancers wish to make some money on the side by taking our clients off somewhere in order to have sex with them, then that's their business. Whether they do or not, I think you'll find that exchanging such services for money isn't illegal, at least not in the UK it isn't.'

'But soliciting sexual favours in a public place is, Mr McMillan.'

'Then that would be something you'd need to take up with them.'

'Er...excuse me,' Crabtree interrupted, his attention diving between Tanner and Cooper, 'but can either of you enlighten me as to what any of this has to do with the alleged murders you've dragged my client all the way in here to talk about?'

'I was just coming to that,' Tanner responded.

'And I've still yet to see hide nor hair of a single scrap of so-called evidence.'

'That as well,' Tanner added, offering Crabtree a reassuring smile. 'Now, where were we?'

'You were about to let my client go, before offering him your most humble apology for not only having completely wasted his time, but also for having made him suffer the indignity of being arrested in front of half the nation's press.'

Tanner gazed up at the ceiling. 'No, I don't think that was it. Oh yes, I remember now. Mr McMillan, did you ever introduce Claire Metcalf, otherwise known as Amber Vale, to any of your friends?'

'Frequently, but not in the way to which I think you're alluding.'

'And which way would that be?'

'In a way that would make me a pimp, inspector.'

'I see. How about Sir Michael Blackwell? Did you introduce him to any of your dancers.'

McMillan paused for a moment, his eyes studying Tanner's face. 'I thought I'd already told you that I'd never met the man?'

'So you didn't introduce Sir Michael to Miss Metcalf?'

'No!'

'That was a very direct answer.'

'You asked what I believe is called a closed question, being that it only requires a yes or a no answer. If you expect people to speak more freely, I suggest using something a little more open-ended.'

'OK, then let's try again, shall we? Did you send Claire Metcalf to Sir Michael's house with the specific instruction to make sure he was handcuffed to his bed in preparation for either you, or one of your performing monkeys, to pay him a visit?'

'I think you'll find that that was another closed question.'

'And the answer is...?'

'No.'

'To which part?'

'All of it, obviously.'

'I see,' Tanner mused, returning his attention back to his file. 'What about Mr Toby Wallace?'

'Who?'

'He was the other man we discussed, when we were chatting at your club the other day.'

'I'm sorry, you're going to have to refresh my memory.'

'He owned the property you were driving out of, just before you nearly drove straight into us.'

'Ah yes, I remember, the discussion at least. But if you recall, I wasn't in the car at the time.'

'That's right, my mistake. But you know him though, don't you?'

'Sorry, I thought I'd already told you that I didn't.'

'That's correct. I was just wondering if you'd like to change your story, for the record.'

Once again, McMillan paused, this time turning to give his solicitor a questioning glance.

'Is there some reason why you think my client should know the person being referred to?' Crabtree asked, his eyes finding Tanner's.

'It's a straightforward enough question. Either he does, or he doesn't.'

The solicitor narrowed his eyes at Tanner before leaning over to whisper something in his client's ear.

'I *may* know the person you're referring to,' McMillan eventually replied, 'but, unfortunately, I can't be certain. As I'm sure you can appreciate, a successful entrepreneur such as myself does tend to meet a considerable number of people during their day-to-day business activities.'

'OK, then let me ask you something else. Have you ever been inside Mr Wallace's house?'

'That would assume I knew who Mr Wallace was.'

Tanner drew in an impatient breath. 'Let me put it another way. Given what you've told us, that you've only been in Norfolk for a few days, have you stepped inside anyone's house since between the time you arrived and just before you were placed under arrest about three hours ago?'

'I'm sorry, inspector, but again, I simply can't recall.'

'I don't suppose you can remember what you had for breakfast this morning?'

'You must forgive me,' Crabtree interrupted, 'but would you mind me asking how the subject of what my client eats for breakfast could possibly have to do with your investigation?'

'Your client is clearly having problems with his memory. I was merely attempting to establish how bad it was.'

Crabtree closed his leather bound notebook to begin climbing to his feet. 'Right, that's it. We'll be leaving now.'

'Do you recognise this pen?' Tanner asked rather suddenly, sliding a photograph out from the file to position in front of the suspect.

'No, why, should I?' McMillan replied, as Crabtree sank slowly back down into his chair.

'It has the name of your club written down the side.'

'So I can see, but that doesn't mean it belongs to me though, does it.'

'I didn't ask if it was yours, Mr McMillan, I asked if you recognised it.'

'My mistake. Yes, I do recognise it. It's one of several hundred we've had printed over the years.'

'We found it under the table inside Mr Wallace's kitchen.'

With Tanner boring his eyes into the suspect's, the man shrugged his shoulders with ambivalent indifference. 'Sorry, I'm not sure what you want me to say. Well done?'

'I don't suppose you know what it was doing there?'

'Attempting to write its first novel?'

Tanner smiled. 'Any other ideas?'

'The only other reason I can think of is that the kitchen's owner must have dropped it.'

'You'd have thought so, wouldn't you.'

'Er, yes, which is probably why I suggested it.'

'At least, perhaps someone would have, had it not been for the fact that it didn't have his fingerprints on it.'

'Oh dear. Then it must have slipped out of his hands whilst he was giving it a bit of a clean.'

'Do you know whose fingerprints we did find?'

'Your mum's?'

'Er, no, Mr McMillan. We found *your* prints on the pen.'

The solicitor looked up from the photograph to catch Tanner's eye. 'Please don't tell me that this is the extent of your so-called evidence?'

'It places your client at the scene.'

'Er, no inspector. It places the pen at the scene.'

'With your client's fingerprints on, but not those of the person who owned the house.' Tanner knew it was a weak argument, but it was all he had.

'Did you find anyone else's prints on it, other than my client's?'

'I fail to see the relevance.'

'I'm afraid I must disagree, inspector. If it *only* had my client's fingerprints on it, then you *may* have yourself an actual piece of evidence, albeit circumstantial. However, if it had someone else's prints on it as well, then it's equally possible for that other person to have brought it into the victim's house. And when you take into account that my client has an alibi, one that I'm confident will be supported by numerous other people...'

'All of whom just happen to work for him,' Tanner interjected.

'...then I'd have thought it would have been far more likely to have been that other person who left it inside the victim's house, instead of my client, don't you think?'

'I suppose that would depend on if that other person said he was with your client at the time he said he wasn't there.'

'From what you're saying, is it safe for me to assume that you did find someone else's prints on the pen?'

'And if that person is employed by him as well,' Tanner continued, focussing his attention squarely at McMillan.

'Are you going to share the information you have with us, inspector, or are we going to have to continue with this rather childish game of charades?'

Tanner paused for a moment before sliding another piece of A4 paper out from his file, this one featuring a police mugshot of a dangerous looking man with a neck nearly twice as wide as his face. 'We found two further sets of prints on the pen under discussion. The first belong to Mr Dixon, currently employed as a security guard for your client. The second are for this man,' Tanner continued, leaving the first photograph in the middle of the table to slide out another, 'Mr Finch, listed as being your client's driver, both of whom have served time for GBH, amongst other things.'

Having given the images nothing more than a cursory glance, the solicitor once again re-engaged eye contact with Tanner. 'This is all fascinating, inspector, really it is. But it's still just a pen. The most it does is to prove that one of three people may have been inside the victim's house at some point. It's hardly justification for having my client arrested for murder.'

'I assume your client is at least able to confirm that he knows the two men featured in the photographs?'

'Of course I know them,' McMillan replied, 'but that's probably not altogether surprising, given the fact that they accompanied me here, and that they're both currently sitting out in your reception, patiently awaiting my imminent release.'

'Ah, right. I was wondering who they were.'

'Well, now that you know, can I go?'

'Of course, but before you do, there are a couple more things we'd like to discuss.'

McMillan locked his hands together on the table to let out a frustrated sigh.

'The first is something my colleague has been dealing with.' Tanner continued, glancing around at Cooper.

As both McMillan and his solicitor turned to face the young DI, each wearing a similar expression of petulant curiosity, Cooper glanced briefly down to his own more slender file, before bringing his attention back up to the suspect.

'We found something at the scene of Sir Michael's murder, at least what was left of it. I just wanted to ask if you knew anything about it?'

'I suppose that depends on what *it* is?' McMillan replied, his jaw visibly tightening.

'It looks as if someone made an effort to destroy it, albeit rather half-heartedly, but from what we can make out, it would appear to be a blackmail letter.'

Cooper pulled out a photocopy of what was left of the item in question. 'I don't suppose it rings any bells?'

Tanner watched with curious interest as a smile flickered briefly over McMillan's face.

'Well?' Cooper demanded.

'I can honestly say, hand on heart, that I've never seen this before in my entire life.'

'Are you sure about that?' Cooper continued, returning to pull out another photocopied image. 'It's just that we found another one, that one being intact. As you can see, the amount being demanded is exactly the same. Our forensics department also tells us that the paper it's been written on, as well as both the ink and the typeface used, are also identical. In fact, the only difference between the two, other than the fact that one's intact and the other isn't, is the location where it was found.'

'And where was that?'

'Inside the home of a person by the name of Toby Wallace.'

McMillan took a moment to examine the two photocopies. 'Well, I'm no detective, or anything, but from what I can make out, I'd say that it looks like someone was trying to blackmail them.'

'I assume you're going to tell us that it wasn't you?'

'Me?' McMillan queried, a broad grin spreading out over his face. 'Why on earth would I want to do that? More to the point, don't you have to at least know the people you're endeavouring to coerce money out of.'

'And you don't?'

'As I've said before, several times in fact, no, I don't!'

'Well, at least we've managed to clear that one up,' Cooper replied, forcing a grin over at the suspect.

'Anything to help our boys in blue,' McMillan replied, smirking back. 'You said there was something else?'

Taking over from Cooper, Tanner delved back into his file. 'The last thing, for now at least, is what we found in the depths of Mr Wallace's study.'

'Don't tell me it was another pen?'

Lifting out a fairly substantial document, Tanner placed it down in the middle of the table. 'Any idea what this is?'

'A policeman's guide as to how *not* to interview a suspect?'

'It's a copy of an agreement for the sale of the Phantom Exchange, which – if you didn't know – is the night club jointly owned by Mr Wallace and Sir Michael Blackwell, both of whom are now dead. As curious as I think that is, what is far more interesting is the name of the prospective buyer.'

The solicitor dragged the document towards him to begin rifling through its pages.

'You'll find what I believe is your client's signature at the end,' Tanner added, gesturing down at where one of the pages had been marked with a yellow Post-it note. 'The only thing that seems to be missing are the signatures of the two legal owners.'

McMillan set his jaw to re-engage eye contact with Tanner. 'OK, so I was trying to buy their crappy little night club. So what? That's what people in my line of work do: buy and sell businesses.'

'My client is right,' added Crabtree, leafing his way back through the document. 'All this proves is that they knew each other, but only in name. It doesn't prove they'd ever met. This would have been drawn up by a conveyancing company.'

'You're right, of course, but what it does prove is that your client has been lying to us. He did know the two victims, even though he's been adamant that he didn't, since the very first time we spoke.'

'As I seem to remember saying to you before, inspector,' McMillan began, locking his fingers together on top of the table, 'I deal with dozens of people every day. I rarely get to meet any of them, and to be honest, I've never been very good with names.'

'It also provides us with a motive, which I must admit, until finding that document, we had been somewhat lacking.'

The solicitor looked up to stare over at Tanner. 'I'm sorry, but I think that's just about the most ridiculous thing I've ever heard come dribbling out of a policeman's mouth. How can this possibly provide my client with a motive for murdering not just one, but three people?'

'Well, first of all, just between you and me, I don't believe he did kill them.'

The solicitor's expression turned from one of angry frustration to that of bewildered incredulity. 'OK, now I'm confused. If you don't think my client killed them, then what the hell are we doing here?'

'Sorry, my mistake, I meant to say all of them. I

know he murdered Sir Michael, and in the most brutal and theatrical way imaginable. That's why he sent his most seductive dancer over to his house, to make sure he was handcuffed to his bed, in preparation for his arrival. But I believe he only did so in order to make sure his next victim, Mr Toby Wallace, knew he was serious. I don't think he had any intention of killing him as well. Why would he? His death would mean he'd be unable to sign the agreement for the sale of his nightclub. No. I'm sure his death was neither anticipated nor desired. The man simply had a heart attack, probably shortly after realising he was about to be tortured. But don't worry, it will still be classed as manslaughter, given the fact that the collapse of his heart was induced by the threat being made to him. Then there's the dancer, Claire Metcalf, known by your client as Amber Vale. I'm fairly certain he killed her as well. After all, he wouldn't have been too happy leaving her running about the place, telling the police about how he'd instructed her to leave Sir Michael handcuffed to his bed in preparation for his arrival, certainly not after his housekeeper had blurted her name out to the press.'

'This is all fascinating,' the solicitor smirked. 'Really, it is. However, apart from the fact that the entire thing is based on pure conjecture, and that the only piece of so-called evidence is a single pen, of which there are many hundreds just like it, there's nothing here to provide my client with a motive for having done any of this, despite what you said a minute ago. And I'm sorry, but someone offering to buy someone else's nightclub is hardly that.'

'Forgive me, Mr Crabtree, but I'm going to have to disagree.'

'I see. And why is that, may I ask?'

'Because of the amount your client was looking to pay for the property in question.'

Tanner paused for a moment as he watched the solicitor's eyes first narrow, then slowly fall to the document lying half-open in his hands.

'I'm sure we'd all agree that nobody in their right mind would be willing to sell what Companies House show to be a highly profitable business, situated on over a thousand square feet of land, for a single solitary pound coin, unless of course that person had a gun being held to their head, or maybe a pair of pliers to their testicles, by way of persuasion.'

- CHAPTER THIRTY EIGHT -

'SO, WHAT DO you think?' asked Tanner, having suspended the interview until the following morning to lead Cooper back out into the corridor.

'That we're lucky forensics found that document for the sale of the victims' nightclub.'

'I was thinking more about McMillan's overall performance.'

Walking alongside Tanner, Cooper shrugged. 'To be honest, I don't think he's the type to saw open some rich guy's chest with a hacksaw. I mean, did you see his nails?'

'Er...I can't say that I did,' Tanner replied, a little surprised to hear Cooper had.

'Well, anyway, I'd say he had them manicured. Then there's his suit. I don't know, it's just difficult to imagine him up to his elbows in blood, which is what he'd had to have been if he was the one who removed Sir Michael's still beating heart. And if he wasn't directly involved, but only gave the order, then it's going to be even harder to prove, especially if the only evidence we have is a pen with a partial fingerprint. I doubt we've even got enough for an extension.'

Reaching the end of the corridor, Tanner stopped to pull open the door. 'Then I suppose we need to thank our lucky stars that it was Forrester's idea for us to pull him in.'

'Maybe so, but do you think he's going to remember that when we're forced to let him go?'

Tanner cursed quietly to himself. Cooper was right. The second McMillan walked out the door, Forrester would be laying the blame squarely at their feet, or to be more specific, his!

'Then I suppose we'd better hope something else turns up,' Tanner sighed. 'I assume we were able to get a forensics unit over to his strip club?'

'As far as I know.'

Tanner glanced down at his watch, his mind wondering if there would be enough time for him to drop some flowers in to Christine on his way home by way of an apology for having once again been forced to cancel their evening out together. 'OK, then I suggest we call it a day. Hopefully, something will turn up overnight.'

'And if it doesn't?'

'Then we'll have no choice but to let him go, after which we'll be able to look forward to spending a few quiet moments attempting to remind our Commander in Chief that it was his stupid idea to arrest him in the first place.'

- CHAPTER THIRTY NINE -

I N TWO MINDS as to whether he should be there or not, Tanner steered his XJS into Christine's small gravel-lined drive to pull up next to her MX-5. Killing both the engine and the headlights, he peered nervously out over the car's large black leather steering wheel. With the rain still hammering down as the windscreen wipers came juddering to a halt, he could barely make out the house beyond. All he could see was that there was a light on in the hall and another in a room upstairs.

She must be about to go to bed, he thought, glancing down at the clock on his dashboard as a reminder to himself that it had gone eleven.

Regretting not having called ahead first, he was about to re-start the engine to reverse out when he saw the front door swing open to reveal Christine, staring out at him from her doorway, her arms tugging a dressing gown around her slim narrow waist.

In for a penny, he muttered to himself.

Taking hold of the wet stems of the bedraggled flowers he'd hastily picked up from a garage forecourt on the way, he tugged his fluorescent hood over his head and stepped out into the unrelenting rain to hurry over.

'Better late than never, I suppose,' he heard her say, as he arrived under the shelter provided by her low narrow porch.

Tanner removed his hood to offer her a look of humble apology. 'I'm sorry, I should have called.'

'I thought you did.'

'I meant again; to ask if it would be OK for me to drop by on my way home.'

'Well, you're here now.'

Unsure what to say next, he produced the flowers from behind his back. 'I, er, brought you these; by way of an apology.'

He watched Christine cast a rather cool eye over them.

'I was going to put them in water for you,' he thought to add, 'but to be honest, with all the rain, I thought they'd had enough.'

It wasn't the funniest joke in the world, but it was good enough to at least earn him a smile.

A moment of silence followed as her eyes danced briefly with his.

'I saw you on TV again today.'

'You did?'

'You were escorting some dangerous miscreant inside the station.'

'Oh, right, him.'

'Does that mean you've got your man?'

'We'll have to see. I'm sure it's him, but as is often the case, the challenge is going to be proving it. I'm not even sure we've got enough to hold him for twenty-four hours, so don't be too surprised if you see me on TV tomorrow, standing idly by as his solicitor marches him straight back out again. Anyway, how was your day?'

'Wet; a bit like your flowers.'

'Er...they're yours now,' Tanner remarked, holding them out for her.

'Right,' she responded, taking them reluctantly out

from his hand.

'I must admit, they looked a lot better in the shop.'

'You mean the garage forecourt, as in the one just down the road?'

Tanner offered her a boyish smirk. 'Well, yes, but only because the florist wasn't open.'

'Look, John, I really didn't mind that you couldn't make it tonight, and you certainly didn't need to come around bearing gifts, at least not ones that look as if they'd been dragged backwards through a puddle. I know you've got a lot on at the moment. I think I'd just prefer it if you didn't make promises you're unable to keep.'

'Normally I wouldn't, but as I said on the phone, my boss made the unexpected announcement that I had to make an arrest, despite knowing that we had very little in the form of actual evidence.'

Christine took a moment to start re-arranging the flowers. 'I don't suppose you have any idea how long this investigation is going to go on for?'

'I think that's going to depend on if we can find some evidence that's a little less circumstantial between now and eight o'clock tomorrow evening.'

'Is that likely?'

Tanner hesitated. 'Well, it's possible. We've got a team of forensics poring over his nightclub as we speak. Even if they can't find anything that can link him to the murders, there's every chance they'll find something else we'd be able to charge him with, like a large quantity of drugs, for example.'

'And if it turns out not to be him, I assume this will end up going on for months.'

'Hopefully not that long.'

'But more than a few days, though?'

'Probably,' he nodded, lowering his eyes.

Christine's cheeks flushed with colour, as her eyes

danced nervously with Tanner's. 'You know, you could always stay the night, if you wanted to?'

Tanner felt a sudden surge of blood begin flooding through his veins. It was obvious what she was offering, something he could feel every fibre of his being longing desperately for. All he had to do was hold out his hand to be led quietly inside.

He hesitated. 'I – I thought you said we should wait.'

'Maybe we don't have to.'

An image of Jenny, laughing at something he'd either said or done, flickered through his mind.

'Is that a yes?' Christine asked, a questioning frown creasing her forehead.

Reminding himself that Jenny would never have wanted him to be on his own for the rest of his life simply because she couldn't be with him anymore, he returned a smile to take a tentative step forward, only for him to hear the muffled sound of his phone.

'Shit,' he cursed, stopping to unzip his jacket.

'You don't have to answer it.'

'It will be work.'

'All the more reason not to.'

'I know, but forensics may have found something,' Tanner continued, delving a hand inside his suit jacket. 'If they've uncovered the evidence we need, I'm soon going to find myself with considerably more free time.'

Christine stood patiently by whilst Tanner answered the call.

'Tanner speaking.'

Silence followed as he turned to stare out at his Jag, his jaw stiffening as he watched the rain rattling over its elongated bonnet.

'OK, I'll be there as soon as I can.'

Ending the call, he turned back to face Christine.

'That was my boss.'

'No surprises there.'

'I'm really sorry, Christine, but I'm going to have to go.'

'They can't get someone else to cover for you?'

'Not for this,' he replied, his tone flat with regretful despondency. 'The body of another woman's been found. Sounds like she's been murdered.'

- CHAPTER FORTY -

FOLLOWING DIRECTIONS GIVEN, Tanner soon found himself navigating around a series of endless roundabouts on the outskirts of Norwich, eventually swinging his car into a road that looked very much like every other. There he tilted his head to look up to where he could see a series of blue flashing lights at the top of a steep incline, ricocheting off surrounding cars and modestly proportioned semi-detached houses.

After nudging his car onto the curb behind an ambulance, he stepped back out into the unrelenting wind and rain to begin forging his way up the hill where he could see a couple of constables wrestling with a line of Police Do Not Cross tape. Beyond them were three forensics officers, their showerproof white overalls shimmering in the rain as they fought to lift a glistening white tent around the body of a woman he could just about make out, lying slumped in a gutter at their feet. As a particularly savage gust tore into the group, he watched as the tent keeled slowly over to rest on the body they were trying so hard to protect.

'It's no use,' he heard a voice call out. 'It's never going to stay. We're doing more harm than good.'

A familiar voice broke through the foray. 'Fine. Leave it. We'll just have to make do.'

'Dr Johnstone,' Tanner called, putting his

shoulder to the wind as he continued to make his way up the hill.

'Ah, Tanner,' the medical examiner replied, one hand wrapped around the handle of an umbrella, the other clutching at a tablet. 'I was wondering when someone from CID was going to show up.'

'You're lucky I did,' Tanner replied, allowing his mind to drift momentarily back to what he could have been doing instead.

'As you can see, I'm afraid we're not having much luck protecting either the crime scene or the body.'

'No, well; hardly the weather for putting up a tent.'

Keeping a firm hold of the rim of his hood, Tanner stepped forward to stare down at the body, its head submerged under a torrent of water flooding along the gutter where a slim red stiletto could be seen caught in the cast iron grate of an overflowing drain.

'What've we got?' he asked, his eyes resting on a slim stocking-clad leg jutting awkwardly out into the road before lifting them up to an open handbag, its strap caught around a thin delicate wrist.

'Pretty much as you can see. A woman, late teens / early twenties. Death would appear to be from a single blow to the back of the head, very much like the last one. Judging by the shape and size of the injury, I'd say there's a better than average chance that it was the same weapon as well.'

'Time of death?'

'No more than an hour ago.'

'Had she been...?' Tanner began, his eyes moving to a cream-coloured mini-skirt, and the thighs it had ridden to the top of.

'Unless whoever did this took the time to put everything back on afterwards, I'd say no.'

Tanner's eyes trained themselves on her open handbag. 'Any other motivating factors?'

'If you mean the bag, it was like that when we arrived. We found a purse left lying beside it as well. I'd say it had been gone through, but interesting enough, it doesn't look like anything had been taken, certainly not what you'd have expected.'

'Cash?'

'In abundance.'

'But you say someone had been through it?'

'The credit cards looked as if they'd all been jammed back inside, so at a guess, I'd say it had. We found a drivers' licence in there as well. Assuming the handbag, purse and everything inside belonged to the victim, her name is Nicola Bowell.'

Tanner contemplated the idea of digging out his notebook to write it down, but when yet another savage gust of wind tore its way along the street, driving ice cold shards of rain up into his face, he thought better of it. 'Any idea who found her?'

'I believe it was a taxi driver.'

'Do you know if he's still here?' he asked, glancing furtively about.

'The last time I looked he was. Try further up the hill, past the forensics van.'

- CHAPTER FORTY ONE -

WITH THE MEDICAL examiner returning to his work, Tanner continued to forge his way up the hill, the fingers of one hand remaining firmly clasped around the rim of his hood.

Passing a line of emergency vehicles, all double-parked down one side of the road, he eventually saw a couple of police constables huddled beside a non-descript saloon car, its windows clouded over by thick layers of dripping condensation.

'I've been told there's a taxi driver somewhere around here?' he called out, lurching to a halt in front of the two men.

'Yes, sir,' the one nearest replied, standing to attention. 'The taxi driver. He's been waiting inside his car. We told him he couldn't leave until someone from CID turned up.'

'I bet he was pleased to hear that.'

'Not exactly, sir, no.'

'OK, thank you. I'll take it from here. Perhaps you could give your colleagues a hand with getting the area cordoned off? The last time I saw them, they looked as if they could probably do with some help.'

Waiting for them to scurry away, Tanner rapped his knuckles on the car's fogged-up window to see first the sleeve of a coat wiping away at the condensation before the round screwed-up face of a man appeared, gawping out at him through two bleary half-closed eyes.

Gesturing for him to wind his window down, Tanner pulled out his ID, only to see the man roll his eyes to begin mouthing some inaudible complaint.

'About bloody time,' the driver eventually spat, the moment the window began inching its way down. 'Do you have any idea how long I've been waiting here for?'

Tanner thought he'd hazard a guess. 'I'm not sure. Ten minutes?'

'More like a bloody hour!'

'Oh dear. Well, never mind. At least you're nice and dry.'

'I'm supposed to be working. I don't get paid to sit about all day doing bugger all.'

'Surprisingly enough, neither do I.'

'You could've fooled me.'

Tanner drew in a calming breath. 'Maybe you can start by telling me your name?'

'I've already told one of your fellow officers.'

'If you could tell me as well.'

'Alex Barnes,' the driver huffed.

'And how did you find the body, Mr Barnes?'

'I didn't.'

Tanner blinked in surprise to glance quickly about. 'I'm sorry, someone told me you did.'

'I dropped her off back there. It was only when I looked in the mirror to pull away that I saw him.'

'Saw who?'

'The guy who attacked her.'

'You mean, you saw the person who killed her?'

'That's right.'

Tanner tucked his ID away to begin scrabbling around for his notebook. 'Can you describe him?'

'Well, when I say I saw him, I couldn't see his face, exactly. He was wearing a raincoat with a large hood, and what with the weather and everything.'

'But it was definitely a man?'

'I'd say so.'

'Do you know for sure?'

'Well, I suppose I couldn't guarantee it.'

It was Tanner's turn to roll his eyes. 'OK, so...what happened then?'

'I stopped the car and got out.'

'And...?'

'When I saw him trying to take her bag, I shouted at him. That's when he saw me and ran off.'

'Then you called the police?'

Barnes shook his head. 'I went to see if Nicola was alright first. But when I saw the way her head was submerged under the water, and all the blood coming out the back of it...well, it was obvious enough that she wasn't.'

Whilst he'd been talking, Tanner had been staring at him with his mouth hanging open. 'I'm sorry, but am I to understand it that you knew the victim?'

The taxi driver shifted awkwardly in his seat, glancing away as he did.

'Mr Barnes?'

More silence followed before the man finally turned to meet Tanner's penetrating gaze. 'I'd picked her up a couple of times before.'

'I see. And is it normal for you to ask the names of your fare-paying passengers?'

'Well, no, but...'

'So...?' Tanner continued. 'How did you know her name?'

'I'd seen her before, where she works.'

'And where's that?'

'The same place I picked her up. The Riverside. She's one of the dancers there.'

- CHAPTER FORTY TWO -

INFORMING THE TAXI driver that they'd need to arrange a time to collect a sample of his fingerprints and DNA, Tanner waved him off to hear the sound of Vicky's voice calling out his name from somewhere behind him.

Turning his back to the wind to see her traipsing up the hill, her hands clutched at the edges of a beige hooded raincoat, he dug his own into his pockets to wait.

'She's another stripper,' he eventually called out. 'Nicola Bowell. Killed the same way as the other one.'

Vicky came to a breathless halt in front of him. 'I know. I spoke to Johnstone on the way up. He asked me to tell you that they found a stamp on the back of her hand. Looks to be the same as the last one.'

'OK, well that at least confirms what the guy who found her said; that she worked at the Riverside.'

'So – it must be McMillan then?'

'Unfortunately, I think this only goes to prove that it couldn't have been him. She was only killed an hour ago. That's assuming he's still sitting in a holding cell back at the station?'

Vicky nodded. 'His security guards haven't moved either. Could he have used someone else?'

'It's possible, I suppose, but if he had, we'd need to reconsider his motive. I can understand why he'd feel it necessary to kill Claire Metcalf – for knowing about his involvement in Sir Michael's murder – but I can't see any reason for him thinking that this latest victim would have known anything about it.'

'Unless Claire told her, of course, and McMillan somehow found out?'

Tanner considered that for a moment. 'Maybe, but to be honest, it doesn't seem very likely. One employee hearing from another that their boss may have had someone killed is hardly the sort of evidence that would be needed for a murder conviction. He'd have known that. Even if he was worried that she knew, I can't believe he'd risk having her killed in the middle of a built-up residential area such as this with literally dozens of potential witnesses hiding behind an equal number of permanently twitching net curtains. Then there's the question of her handbag, or at least the purse found lying beside it.'

'What was that?'

'Johnstone thinks someone had been through it, as if searching for something, and it wasn't money, not with the amount of cash they found stuffed inside. If it was McMillan, or at least one of his associates, what would they have been looking for?'

Tanner took a moment to cast his eyes down the hill to see Nicola Bowell's body being carefully lifted onto a stretcher.

'If he didn't kill this latest victim,' Vicky began, following his gaze, 'does that mean he didn't murder Claire Metcalf either?'

'I think that's something we're going to have to consider.'

'And what about Sir Michael, and Toby Wallace? I mean, the only reason we thought it was him was because Claire Metcalf admitted to handcuffing Sir Michael to his bed, and that McMillan had told her to.'

'And the fact that he was attempting to buy their nightclub for the paltry sum of a single pound coin, a deal that would have been worth millions had it gone through.'

'So does that mean we're back to looking for three people again? The person responsible for murdering Sir Michael and Wallace, someone else for killing Claire Metcalf and this latest victim, and the person responsible for sending out those blackmail letters?'

Tanner sighed quietly to himself. 'I'd almost managed to forget about those.'

Feeling a sudden wave of exhaustion roll over the top of him, he pulled back the sleeve of his coat to stare down at his watch. 'Anyway, there's nothing more we can do today, what little is left of it. I suggest we head home, get some sleep, and just hope that forensics comes up with something more tangible for us tomorrow.'

- CHAPTER FORTY THREE -

Monday, 30th August

THE FOLLOWING MORNING, as he drove cautiously through the savagely gusting wind and the seemingly never-ending torrential rain, Tanner remained desperately tired. Once again he'd hardly slept. The continuous knocking of his yacht against the patrol boats lashed to either side of his had seen to that. He hadn't even had a chance to put a spacer between the mast and the main sail halyard, as he'd intended, the one slapping erratically against the other making even more noise than the previous night.

With his spirits buoyed somewhat by the sight of the nation's bedraggled press, struggling against the elements to re-set their camera equipment in preparation for yet another day camped outside the station, they fell a moment later when he remembered what they'd be most likely to be filming later that evening; their one and only suspect being led out the front door by his no-doubt gloating solicitor.

Leaving his car in the furthest corner again, he flipped his hood over his head to step out, only to hear his phone ring from the hidden depths of his sailing jacket. Clawing it out to discover that it was Christine calling, he was about to duck back inside the car to answer it when he heard a vaguely familiar voice shouting out his name.

A quick glance over his Jag's low sloping roof was enough to confirm who he'd thought it was; McMillan's solicitor, charging over towards him, his bulging eyes glaring out from underneath a most inadequately sized umbrella.

With no choice but to leave the call unanswered, he tucked the phone back where he'd found it to zip up his jacket and close the door. 'Mr Tree Crab, wasn't it?' he smirked, skirting around the back of his car to find out what was so important that it needed to be addressed in the middle of a carpark during a category three storm. 'How can I help?'

'I'm just curious to know if you're here to release my client?'

With Tanner's attention being momentarily caught by a series of flashing lights erupting from the ever-curious pack of news-starved journalists, Tanner let out a world-weary sigh. 'Don't you think this could have waited until we'd at least made it inside the station?'

'I don't think this can wait a minute longer,' the man continued, coming to an abrupt halt directly in front of Tanner, so blocking his way to the station's entrance. 'Since suspending your interview with my client yesterday evening we've seen neither hide nor hair of you. Nor have we seen anyone else. We certainly haven't had a glimpse of anything more in the form of evidence. That was nearly eleven hours ago. Since then he's been forced to endure what I'm sure has been a most uncomfortable night inside one of your grubby little holding cells. So, unless you have something new to bring to the table, I ask again, are you here to release him?'

'I think that's going to depend on what's come in

overnight from our forensics department, something I'm not going to know until I have the chance to speak to my colleagues. So...if you'll excuse me?' Tanner continued, gesturing for the man to stand to one side.

The solicitor continued glowering at Tanner for a moment longer before finally stepping away. 'You're treading on very thin ice, detective inspector.'

'I'd rather be on thin ice than perpetually stuck out in this bloody storm,' Tanner muttered, nudging past the belligerent solicitor to make a beeline for the station's entrance.

Reaching the glass door, Tanner heaved it open to throw himself inside, only to find McMillan's heavy-set bodyguards glaring at him from what appeared to be the very same chairs he'd seen them slouched in the night before.

Shaking his head, he stepped over to where he could see the duty sergeant, DS Taylor, staring vacantly at a monitor behind the reception desk's thick plastic security screen.

'Have they been there all bloody night?' he whispered, catching the man's eye to gesture over at the men he was referring to.

'Just about. One of them did step out for a while, but only to find them something to eat.'

Tanner fell momentarily silent as he watched Crabtree come crashing through the entrance to begin staring about.

'And our prime suspect?' he continued, in the same low conspiratorial tone. 'He's still here, I take it?'

'I took him a coffee this morning.'

'How's he been?'

'Quiet as a mouse.'

'Well, that's something, I suppose.'

Seeing Crabtree glare around at them to begin

stomping his way over, Tanner glanced quickly down at his watch. 'Is Forrester in?'

'Not yet.'

'And Vicky?'

'About ten minutes ago.'

'OK, good,' Tanner replied, just in time before Crabtree barged past him to step up to the plastic screen.

'I'd like to see my client, Mr McMillan,' the solicitor demanded, deliberately ignoring Tanner to fix the duty sergeant's eyes.

'May I see some identification?'

'I was here yesterday.'

'Even so.'

The solicitor exhaled with frustrated annoyance as he delved into the black leather satchel he'd brought with him. 'Here!' he stated, holding up a laminated identity card attached to a pale blue lanyard. 'Happy now?'

Taylor leaned forward to peer at it through the screen. 'That's fine, thank you. If you could follow me.'

'I assume someone from your CID department will also be looking to speak with him, preferably to offer him a heartfelt apology for having put him through such a humiliating and totally unnecessary experience?'

'Er...' Taylor began, sending Tanner a questioning glance.

Tanner turned to face the solicitor in a bid to garner his attention. 'As I attempted to explain to you outside, Mr Crabtree, I will need a moment to catch up with my colleagues before being able to make a decision as to how best to proceed.'

Crabtree turned to finally acknowledge Tanner's presence. 'You'd better hurry up, then, hadn't you!'

Leaving the duty sergeant to usher the solicitor away, Tanner entered the main office to peel off his still dripping sailing jacket to hook over the back of his chair. Bypassing the kitchen, he headed for Vicky's desk, where he could see her curly mop of dark red hair bobbing furtively up and down behind her monitor.

'OK, so, where are we?' he asked, arriving to find her biting down onto a large fluffy croissant.

'Sorry,' she spluttered, sending him an embarrassed glance as pastry flakes flew out from between her lips. 'I didn't have a chance to have breakfast.'

'I haven't even had a coffee yet,' Tanner bemoaned, saving her blushes by glancing briefly away.

Swallowing hard, she dumped what was left of the croissant onto a napkin to reach instead for her mouse. 'We've had a preliminary report through from Dr Johnstone, for last night's victim.'

'And?'

'As we thought, her name's Nicola Bowell. Local girl; an un-married twenty-three year old. Cause of death was a blow to the back of her head. Death occurred at around eleven o'clock last night.'

'Is that it?'

'Um...' she replied, her eyes scanning over the document displayed on her monitor, '...he thinks she was probably killed with a hammer, possibly the same one used on Claire Metcalf...and that there were no signs of any recent sexual activity.'

'Were anyone's prints or DNA found on her?'

'There's no mention of any, but that's probably not altogether surprising, given the weather conditions at the time.'

'So, he's basically saying there's nothing there to

give us a single clue as to who killed her.'

'Apart from the murder weapon thought to be the same used on both women.'

'Something we don't have in our possession, making it impossible for us to know.'

'That reminds me,' Vicky continued, closing one file to open another. 'I saw something in the forensics report about them finding some tools.'

Tanner pulled up a nearby chair. 'Where abouts?'

'At McMillan's strip club. Here it is. Looks like they found quite a few, locked inside what was otherwise being used as a stationery cupboard.'

'Could any be of potential interest to us?'

'Um...' she responded, her eyes drifting slowly down the list, 'there's a hammer.'

'And look, a hacksaw as well,' Tanner stated, leaning forward to place a finger on the screen at the very end of the list. 'I don't suppose either show signs of having any blood on them?'

'I don't think they've been processed yet. Sounds promising, though, don't you think?'

'Perhaps, but hardly conclusive. There can't be many households in the world that don't have a hammer and a hacksaw lurking inside them somewhere.'

'But stashed inside a locked stationery cupboard?' questioned Vicky, in a more optimistic tone.

'Well, we'll have to see. Can you give them a call for me? Ask them to make those two a priority? We need to know if there are any traces of blood on either; more specifically, Sir Michael's on the hacksaw and at least one of the women's on the hammer.'

Seeing her reach for her phone reminded him of Christine's earlier call. 'Can I leave that with you?' he asked, standing up to dig out his mobile. 'I've just remembered that I need to make a call myself.'

With Vicky nodding, he spun away to stare down at his phone. Seeing she'd left him a message, he was about to listen to it when he saw DCI Forrester burst in through the double doors at the end to begin stomping his way past all the desks, heading for his office, directly opposite to where Tanner was standing.

For a fraction of a second, his mind wrestled with the idea of spinning back to Vicky in order to avoid having to say hello, but it was too late. Forrester had spotted him.

Holding his ground, Tanner pretended to do something on his phone other than return Christine's call. 'Morning, sir,' he smiled, glancing casually up only to see Forrester alter course to begin charging straight for him.

For one disturbing moment, Tanner honestly thought he was going to walk straight into him, but at the last moment he veered away to whisper, 'A word if you will,' rather harshly into Tanner's ear.

'Shit,' Tanner muttered, tucking his phone back inside his suit jacket's pocket to follow what was clearly a rather disgruntled detective chief inspector.

- CHAPTER FORTY FOUR -

'RIGHT,' FORRESTER BEGAN, glancing down at his watch as Tanner eased the door closed behind him. 'You'd better give me an update before Superintendent Whitaker phones me up for what would be the second time in about as many minutes.'

'He's already called you?' Tanner enquired, with a concerned frown; hoping a rare show of empathy may help ease the man's obvious ill temper.

'Before I'd even left my bloody house!' the DCI stated, slumping down into his chair. 'Which is why I'm so late. So, anyway, where were we again?'

As Tanner pulled out a chair for himself, he could feel his boss's eyes endeavouring to bore down into his. 'I was about to give you an update, sir.'

'Oh yes, that's right,' Forrester replied, leaning back in his chair to lock his arms firmly over his chest, 'so you were. To be honest, I was a little disappointed you didn't phone me last night, after the call-out.'

'I assume you're referring to the woman found by the taxi driver?'

'I wouldn't know, Tanner. Nobody seems to tell me much of anything these days.'

'I'm sorry, sir, but as I think I said before, it's only because we've been so busy.'

'That's all very well, but it's not much use when Whitaker phones me up demanding an update, when

I don't even know myself. And why? Because nobody's thought to consider that I may want to know what's been going on!'

With Forrester's vein on his forehead rhythmically pulsating, as if attempting to keep time to the words flying out from his mouth, Tanner sat up in his chair to clear his throat. 'I arrived at the scene to find the body of another woman, lying in the gutter with the back of her head smashed in. As far as we know, she'd been dropped off there by a taxi driver who then saw her being attacked in his rear view mirror as he pulled away.'

'Did he see the person's face?'

'Only enough to think that it was a man, although he wasn't even sure of that. With what the weather was doing at the time, I'm surprised he was able to see anything at all. What he was able to do, somewhat surprisingly, was identify the body, something Johnstone has since confirmed.'

'A Miss Nicola Bowell,' Forrester commented, fishing out his mobile to begin scrolling down its screen. 'I was glancing through his report when Whitaker called. That, and the one from forensics.'

'The taxi driver told us that she works at the Riverside. Another one of their "exotic dancers".'

'I assume you asked him how he knew her?'

'He admitted to being one of the club's patrons, and that he'd picked her up before.'

'You don't think he could have been the one who killed her?'

'If he did, then he'd have to had killed the other stripper as well.'

'And why's that?'

'Because of what Johnstone said in his report; that both the method and the weapon were the same as the ones used to murder Claire Metcalf.'

Forrester tossed his phone onto his desk to stare out the window where a long line of news vans could clearly be seen, cluttering up the road outside. 'I assume that means our prime suspect couldn't have done it either.'

Tanner shook his head. 'Not with him being locked up all night.'

'One of his known associates, perhaps?'

'Well, the two most obvious have been sitting out in reception ever since we brought him in yesterday evening.'

'And they've been there the entire time?'

'We can check our security footage, but it would seem so. Certainly at the time in question. According to DS Taylor they've been there all night.'

'I suppose that means someone else is responsible for what happened to our two female victims?'

'Either that, or it's the same person. Just not the one we have locked inside a holding cell.'

'I sincerely hope not!' Forrester exclaimed, bristling uncomfortably in his seat. 'I've already told Whitaker that we have our man, at least the person responsible for Sir Michael's murder.'

Tanner's mouth fell open as he stared over at his DCI. 'I'm, er, sorry sir, but...I'm really not sure that we have enough evidence to charge him. I don't even think that we have enough to apply for a holding extension.'

'What are you talking about? I thought you said you'd read the forensics report – about what they found at the Riverside?'

'Well, yes, sir, but only briefly. Did I miss something?'

Forrester let out an exasperated sigh. 'They said they found a hacksaw, hidden inside a stationery cupboard.'

'Well – yes – but – '

'One that had traces of blood on it.'

Tanner closed his mouth. 'OK, I must admit, I hadn't read that part. Did they confirm it was Sir Michael's?'

'Not as such, no, but I can't see who else it could belong to.'

Tanner was about to say that he could think of at least a dozen people, anyone in fact who had access to the stationery cupboard, when he thought better of it, electing to remain silent instead.

'When you combine that with the pen found underneath Toby Wallace's kitchen table,' Forrester continued, 'that McMillan had been seen going in and out of his house on numerous occasions, and that he was endeavouring to force the sale of the Phantom Exchange nightclub for the sum of a single pound coin, it's enough.'

'But only if the blood found on the hacksaw matches Sir Michael's, sir.'

'Then it better bloody had, hadn't it!'

'And what if it doesn't?'

Forrester glowered over at him for a moment, the skin around his nose creasing into something akin to a snarl. 'In that scenario, I suppose you'd be left looking for another key piece of evidence.'

With Forrester throwing a problem that was entirely of his own creation straight back at him, Tanner could feel his blood beginning to boil. 'And just how the hell would you propose I do that?'

'I'm sorry, Tanner, for a minute there I thought it was your job.'

'Manufacturing evidence out of thin air is hardly my job, sir, unless you're stating on the record that you're happy enough for me to start going around planting some?'

Tanner watched as Forrester spread the palms of his hands out over the top of his desk. 'Listen, this is only relevant if the blood on the hacksaw doesn't match Sir Michael's. So let's find that out first, shall we?'

Tanner took a moment to get his emotions under control. 'I've already asked forensics to make both the hacksaw and the hammer a priority.'

'They found a hammer as well?'

'Well, yes, but there can't be many households that don't have at least one knocking about the place.'

'But not hidden inside a stationery cupboard.'

'I'm not sure the tools had been hidden, exactly. More just kept inside.'

'But the door was locked.'

'It was, but that could have been more to stop people from helping themselves to free staples than a method of hiding a material piece of evidence from a high-profile murder investigation.'

'Is there any chance you could try to be a little more optimistic, Tanner?'

'I wouldn't have to be if someone hadn't gone and told Superintendent Whitaker that we had our man, when it's far from certain that we have, *sir*.'

'And I wouldn't have felt the need to if the Senior Investigating Officer had made a bit more of an effort to keep me informed as to what's been going on.'

'You made an assumption based on what a forensics report said about some blood being found on a hacksaw, which had nothing to do with what I either had or hadn't updated you about. And now I'm the one stuck with the task of finding enough evidence to charge him.'

'As I said before, Tanner, that's your job!'

'My job is to find out who's guilty, sir, not to try to figure out *how* someone is, just because of what you decided to tell your superior over the phone this morning. If it had been my choice, I wouldn't have even arrested him. Not before we had the evidence first.'

A sudden knock at the door saw the argument come juddering to a breathless halt.

'Yes, what is it?' called out Forrester, almost shouting.

In the silence that followed, the door creaked open to reveal the timid face of young DC Townsend. 'Sorry to – er – bother you,' he began, glancing first at Forrester before focussing his eyes on Tanner, 'there's a man out in reception, asking to speak to you.'

'Does he have a name?' Tanner enquired, grateful for the interruption.

'George Chapman. He said you spoke to him yesterday, him and his daughter.'

Recalling the name, Tanner turned to look at Forrester. 'He's the guy who lives next door to the lighthouse – the one mentioned as being a drop-off point in the letter found at Wallace's house.'

'Didn't you go up there with Cooper, as part of his blackmail investigation?'

'I did, yes, but...'

'Then I suggest you let him deal with it.'

Townsend cleared his throat. 'Er, he did specifically ask for DI Tanner, sir.'

Tanner turned to gaze out of Forrester's window, and the rain rattling off all the cars parked out in front. 'I'd better go, sir. It must be important for him to have come all the way over here in this.'

Forrester let out an impatient sigh. 'Very well. But the moment you're done with him, I want your focus straight back on McMillan. If forensics comes back to say that the blood on that hacksaw belongs to Sir

Michael, I want to see you charging him for the murders of both him and Wallace. If they come back to say it isn't, then you're going to have to ask the local magistrate for a holding extension, whether you think one will be granted or not.'

- CHAPTER FORTY FIVE -

ELIEVED TO BE able to escape from underneath Forrester's simmering glare, with McMillan's goons still parked out in reception, Tanner asked Townsend to show Chapman into one of the interview rooms where they'd be able to talk in private.

Stopping off at the kitchen to grab himself a much needed coffee, Tanner entered the room a few minutes later to find the walk-in slumped in a chair, water dripping down from a soaking-wet raincoat.

'Good morning, Mr Chapman,' Tanner began, placing his coffee onto the table to begin levering himself underneath. 'You asked to see me?'

'I have some rather belated news about the missing girl,' Chapman began, staring down at his hands clenched together on top of the table.

'Sorry...which one was that?' Tanner replied, a sanguine smile tugging inappropriately at the corners of his mouth.

'The one the newspapers said went missing last week. I think her name was Abigail Taylor?'

Tanner took a moment to wade back through the many recent events in a bid to remind himself.

'It was something my daughter told me,' Chapman continued, 'that she thought she'd seen something from her bedroom window, the night the girl was said to have gone missing.'

'And what was that?'

'Her bedroom is at the back of the house, facing out over the cliffs towards the sea.'

'Go on.'

'Well...she said she thought she saw someone fall off the back of a boat, about half a mile off the coast.'

'And she thinks it was this missing girl?' Tanner queried; his voice edged with curious scepticism as his mind considered just how much anyone would be able to see staring out into the middle of an ocean from the top of a distant cliff.

Chapman nodded back in response.

'What makes her so sure? I mean, the view from up there can't be great.'

'She has a telescope in her room. It's a bit of a hobby of hers, watching all the boats sailing past.'

'OK, well, fair enough. I presume she called the coastguard to let them know?'

'I'm afraid not. She didn't even tell me; not until last night.'

Tanner blinked in surprise. 'And why was that do you think?'

Chapman shrugged. 'She said she'd been too scared.'

'Scared of seeing someone fall off the back of a boat?'

'That's the thing. She said she didn't fall, exactly, more that she was thrown.'

'Thrown?'

'She thinks the girl on the boat was dead, and that the men she was on the boat with had murdered her.'

'Jesus Christ!' Tanner exclaimed, frantically clawing out his notebook. 'And she's only thought to mention this now, over a week after the event?'

'I know. I told her how stupid she'd been, and that she should have told me the minute she saw it. But I think she found the whole thing genuinely frightening, which I can understand. I mean, it's not every day you see someone being killed before watching their body thrown over the side of a boat, especially if you're a fifteen year old schoolgirl.'

'Did she actually see her being killed?'

'Not that she said.'

'What *did* she say, exactly?'

'That she saw her lying on the table, in the cockpit at the back, and that she wasn't wearing any clothes. Neither were the men standing around her. Then they tied something around her ankles, threw her body over the side, and motored away.'

'Did she see their faces?'

Chapman shook his head.

'And the boat's name?' Tanner demanded, poised with a pen.

'She said it was too far away.'

'Did she at least see what type it was?'

'All she said was that it was white and had a flybridge.'

'She doesn't know the make?'

'I can ask her; if you like?'

Tanner thought for a moment before tucking his notebook away. 'I think it's probably best if we talk to her directly. Would you be able to bring her into the station?'

Chapman hesitated.

'If it's easier, we can come to you?'

'To be honest, I was hoping if it would be possible to keep her out of this. She's still just a child, and she doesn't know any more than I've already told you.'

'I'm sorry, Mr Chapman, but I'm afraid that won't be possible. With a matter as important as this, we have no choice but to speak to her directly. But as I said, we'd be happy to do so in your own home, and we'd make sure to bring someone from child services with us, to make sure she's as comfortable as possible.'

'Would I be able to sit in?'

'Of course.'

Chapman thought for a moment before eventually capitulating. 'Well, I suppose it will be OK, but I'm not sure when, though. She's at school now.'

'Which school is that?'

'St Martins in Stalham. Then she's got rehearsals for their end of term play, and she'll still have homework to do when she gets back. Can't it wait till the weekend?'

'I'm afraid we'll need to see her as soon as possible, preferably today.'

'Then I'll have to have a think. Would it be alright if I called you a little later to arrange something suitable?'

Tanner rose to his feet, levering out one of his last remaining business cards from his wallet to give to the man. 'OK, but please don't leave it too long.'

'I won't,' Chapman replied, pushing away his chair.

'Then I look forward to hearing back from you soon.'

- CHAPTER FORTY SIX -

LEADING CHAPMAN BACK into the reception area, Tanner thanked him for making the effort to come in before watching him head back out into the storm. With the door swinging closed, he turned to stare about with hesitant indecision. The view of McMillan's so-called security guards crowding around the coffee machine reminded him that their boss was still waiting for him to re-start the interview, but until he had some actual evidence to challenge him with, he couldn't see the point. Then there was what Chapman had just told him. He had to let Forrester know. If he didn't, there was little doubt that he'd be accused of failing to update him once again.

With the plan to get that out of the way first, he made his way back into the main office to head straight for his door.

'Sorry to bother you,' he said, knocking to poke his head inside. 'I just thought I'd better let you know what George Chapman had to say for himself.'

'OK, hold on,' Forrester began, peeling his eyes from off his monitor to make a point of glancing down at his watch, 'but be quick. I've got a conference call coming up.'

'It was about Miss Taylor.'

Forrester sent him an uncertain frown. 'Sorry, who?'

'The girl reported missing last Saturday.'

'Christ, I'd almost forgotten about her.'

'On the night in question, his daughter thought she saw the body of a woman being thrown over the side of a boat from her bedroom window, about half a mile off the coast.'

'But – that was over a week ago!'

'That's exactly what I said. According to her father, she found the whole experience rather traumatic, which is why she waited so long before telling anyone.'

'Even her father?'

Tanner shrugged. 'I admit, it does sound a little odd, but if what she's saying is true, I can understand why she'd be too scared to speak up.'

'And what was that?'

'That she saw the girl lying naked on a table in the boat's cockpit, surrounded by a group of men, also without clothes. Her father didn't mention it, but I think it's likely she saw them having sex with her, possibly murdering her as well. If that was the case, then I can see why a witness could end up being traumatised, especially when you take into account her age, and the fact that she's still at school.'

'Yes, well, I suppose. You said this took place at sea?'

Tanner knew what he was about to ask. 'The father said she has a telescope in her bedroom, and that watching all the boats going past is a hobby of hers.'

'Strange sort of hobby for a teenage girl to have, don't you think? Sounds more like something the father would be interested in.'

It hadn't occurred to Tanner, but Forrester was right. Staring at boats through a telescope did sound far more like what a middle aged man would do rather than a teenage schoolgirl. 'I'll make a note to ask them about that. First we need to speak to the girl, and to be honest, the father doesn't seem keen for us to do so.'

'I take it she didn't come in with him?'

Tanner shook his head. 'She's at school.'

'So, what have you arranged?'

'For him to call me with a convenient time, preferably this evening.'

'OK, keep me posted. How about McMillan? Any news?'

'Sorry, but I've still not had a chance to sit down with him.'

'What about the blood found on the hacksaw?'

'Vicky's supposed to be chasing it up,' Tanner replied, just as her head popped around the door. 'Speak of the devil.'

'Sorry to butt in,' she began, glancing around at the two men, 'but I thought you'd better know that another body's been found.'

'You must be joking!' Forrester stated, his voice strained with incredulity.

'Unfortunately not, although it does sound more likely to be an accident than anything else. The person who found it said they saw the victim trip over a mooring line and fall into the river, over at Ludham.'

A look of relief brightened Forrester's face. 'Thank God for that!'

Vicky gave him a reproachful scowl.

'You know what I mean.'

'Anyway, I was just wondering if you wanted me to pop down and take a look?'

Forrester hesitated. 'Tanner says you've been chasing forensics about that hacksaw.'

'They said they should be able to get back to us by two o'clock - for the hammer as well.'

'Do we have any other leads we need to be chasing?'

Vicky deflected the question over to Tanner.

'All we're waiting on are the tools found in the stationery cupboard.'

'OK, then you may as well both head down to take a quick look, but make sure you're back here by two. Understood?'

'Two o'clock,' Tanner repeated, nodding at Vicky for her to lead the way out.

- CHAPTER FORTY SEVEN -

HALF AN HOUR later, Tanner was driving Vicky cautiously through the village of Ludham, its high street devoid of people as sheets of rain swept over shimmering cars and glistening pitch black tarmac. Turning right onto Horsefen Road they continued along, both peering out through the windscreen as a flurry of leaves flickered down through the rain like falling snow, the branches above being twisted and bent by what appeared to be a still-building breeze.

Avoiding a large broken branch at the side of the road, they emerged out from underneath the canopy of trees to turn right again, into a carpark overlooked by a small red bricked gift shop nestled neatly behind an eclectic mix of tenders and dinghies, all jostling for position along a short narrow dyke.

With Tanner's Jag left parked beside an ambulance they stepped out to follow the directions given by a police constable towards a row of hire boats, each lashed to a purpose built hardstanding marking the edge of the river beyond. As the boats tugged restlessly against their mooring lines, as if fighting to be set free, they hurried over to where they could see Dr Johnston, his shoulders hunched over as he stared down the line of boats.

'We really must stop meeting like this,' Tanner called out, lifting his voice above the noise of the howling wind as they came to a gradual halt behind him.

'I'm not sure what other circumstances we *could* meet,' Johnstone commented, glancing around to take in both DIs through rain splattered glasses, 'unless, of course, it was your body we'd found floating upside down in the river.'

A series of raised voices near the water's edge had them all peering over to see a half-submerged frogman hauling the body of what appeared to be yet another young woman up into the awaiting hands of two police forensics officers.

With her body laid out on the grass, the three of them shuffled forward to find themselves staring down into the open blue eyes of yet another beautiful young woman, her sun-bronzed skin the colour of freshly moulded clay.

Watching Johnstone crouch down to begin his preliminary examination, Tanner stood by with impatient expectation. 'Did she drown?' he eventually asked, unable to wait any longer.

'From what I can see, I'd say that was the most likely cause. The colouring of her lips together with the skin around her mouth is certainly consistent with someone who had. However, as always, I'll have a more accurate idea when I get her back to the lab.'

With a relieved nod, Tanner glanced first at Vicky, then behind them at the seemingly deserted shop they'd passed on the way in. 'Does anyone know where the person is who called it in?'

'I think it was the lady who owns the shop,' commented one of the forensic officers. 'But the body itself was found by a Broads Ranger. That's her patrol boat, moored up in the dyke.'

Staring through the rain to see none other than Christine's boat, Tanner kicked himself. With so much going on, he'd completely forgotten about her call. He hadn't even had a chance to listen to her message, let alone have the decency to call her back.

'I don't suppose you know where the Broads Ranger is?' he asked, staring about.

'No idea. If she had any sense, she'd be inside the shop.'

'OK, thanks,' Tanner replied, wondering if he should make the effort to listen to her voicemail before heading over to find her. At least that way he'd know what she'd said. Deciding that it was probably better if he didn't know, he glanced back over at Vicky. 'Shall we wander over to see if we can find them?'

'After you,' she replied, gesturing for him to lead the way.

- CHAPTER FORTY EIGHT -

HEAVING THE SHOP'S door open against the savagely gusting wind, Tanner ushered Vicky in for them to be met by an eerie silence, the only sound being the rain rattling against the outside of its pretty white-framed windows. The shop itself appeared to be deserted.

'Hello!' he called. 'Is anyone here?'

The muffled clatter of cutlery echoing out from somewhere towards the back was soon followed by the cheerful sound of a woman's voice. 'Sorry about that,' they heard her say, the voice soon followed by the pleasant face of an elderly woman emerging out from one of the aisles. 'I wasn't expecting any customers. Not in this dreadful weather.'

'I'm afraid we're not either,' Tanner responded, taking an apologetic tone. 'Detective Inspectors Tanner and Gilbert, Norfolk Police.'

Digging out his ID, he held it up for the shopkeeper to see, just as another far more familiar face appeared out from the same aisle, one hand wrapped around a steaming mug, the other hooked through the arm of a faded red lifejacket.

'Oh, hi Christine!' Tanner exclaimed, in a surprised but friendly tone. 'Someone said you might be here.'

'Small world,' came her somewhat curt response, the smile that followed perhaps a little forced.

'I'm sorry for not having returned your call,' he continued, now realising it had been a mistake not to have listened to her message, 'it's just been one of those mornings.'

'Don't worry,' she replied. 'I haven't exactly been waiting by the phone.'

'No, of course,' Tanner replied, wondering if he should ask her what she'd said, or move the subject along to make a mental note that he had to listen to it later. Deciding on the latter, he cleared his throat. 'I – er – heard you found the body?'

'Only because Mrs Chapwick here called to tell us that she'd seen someone fall into the river.'

Tanner's attention turned to the shopkeeper. 'You actually saw her go in?'

'Well, yes and no.'

'Doesn't it have to be one or the other?'

'Sorry, that probably wasn't very helpful. I was behind the counter, staring out at the weather, when I saw her running through the rain. I remember shaking my head thinking that she could easily trip over one of the mooring lines and fall in. The next thing I knew, she'd done exactly that.'

'So, you *did* see her go in?'

'Well, as I said, not exactly. Perhaps unsurprisingly, we haven't been particularly busy this morning, so I was making the most of my time by catching up with the accounts. I must have glanced down at the books for a moment; the next thing I knew, she'd fallen in. But I didn't see her trip, or anything. One minute she was there, the next minute she wasn't.' The shopkeeper took a quiet moment to gaze wistfully out of the window. 'Poor girl. I simply can't imagine what she was doing out in such horrific weather.'

'But you must have seen something to have known

she'd fallen in. Otherwise, wouldn't you have assumed that she'd have simply hopped onboard one of the boats?'

The shopkeeper's eyes glazed over in thought. 'I – I think something must have caught my eye,' she eventually replied, 'like a branch falling, close to where I'd seen her. I'm not sure. To be honest, I couldn't see much of anything, not with all the rain.'

'But you saw enough to know that it was a girl?'

'Well, yes. She had a skirt on that was far too short and was only wearing a flimsy-looking raincoat. I think she was wearing high heels as well. Either way, she should never have been running like that, not in the storm, and certainly not so close to all the boats.'

Tanner's mind harked back to one of her earlier comments. 'Do you think it was possible she was hit by a falling branch?'

'Well, as I said, I think I may have seen something.'

'Could it have been someone else – a man, perhaps?'

The woman hesitated, her grey sunken cheeks flickering with colour. 'I'm – I'm not sure,' she began, her thin lips tightening with anxious uncertainty. 'As I said, it was difficult to see much of anything.'

'But there *could* have been someone there with her?'

'I – I'm sorry, I don't know. There could have been, but I wouldn't want to say, not with any certainty.'

Tanner turned his attention back to Christine. 'How long was it before you arrived?'

'Probably about twenty minutes after we were called.'

'I don't suppose you saw anyone when you got here?'

'Nobody,' she replied, shaking her head.

'How about on the way over?'

'You mean, on the water? Hardly a soul. You'd have to be either particularly stupid or incredibly brave to take your boat out in this, not unless you're being paid to, of course.'

'But you did see someone else?'

'Only one that I can remember.'

'A hire boat?'

Christine shook her head. 'If it had been, I'd have stopped them to ask what the hell they were doing, taking it out on a day like this.'

'Did you see what it was?'

'If I was to hazard a guess, I'd say it was a Fairline, possibly a Squadron, but don't quote me on that.'

'How about a name?

'I didn't think to look. It was heading back the other way, towards Potter Heigham.'

'And the helm?'

Christine took a moment before answering. 'A man, I think. Quite tall, with a thin narrow face.'

'Would you be able to recognise him if you saw him again?'

'I doubt it. As you'd expect, he had a hood pulled over his head, and what with the weather and everything.'

- CHAPTER FORTY NINE -

L EAVING VICKY TO make a note of the shopkeeper's phone number, Tanner peeled away to have a quiet moment with Christine.

'I just wanted to say sorry again for not having returned your call,' he began, keeping his voice as low as possible as he guided her down one of the empty aisles.

'It's fine,' she whispered back. 'As you said, you've been busy.'

'Well, yes, but that's hardly an excuse, and I'm not going to give you one now, but you called when I was getting out of my car, just as this solicitor came up to start moaning at me about his client.'

'Uh-huh.'

'After that, I had Forrester dragging me into his office to have a go at me about what amounted to the same thing. Then we had this witness walk in off the street; all that before getting the call to come over here.'

'So, no excuses then?' Christine responded, offering him an acrid smile.

Tanner smirked back in response. 'I was hoping you'd consider them more as reasons than excuses.'

'There's a difference?'

'I'd have to admit, it is subtle.'

Having reached the end of the aisle, Christine stopped where she was to turn and face him. 'To be honest, I assumed your silence was in direct response to my message.'

With Tanner only able to offer her a blank guilty expression, her eyes bored into his. 'You didn't listen to it, did you!'

'Of course,' he lied; regretting doing so before the words had even left his mouth.

Christine hooked her hands around the empty arms of her lifejacket. 'I see. So, what did I say?'

Tanner shook his head. 'Sorry, I meant that I knew you'd left me a message, I just haven't had the chance to listen to it yet.'

'I think all that means is that you've managed to add lying to your growing list of undesirable attributes, together with being generally unreliable, of course.'

Tanner could feel the apologetic guilt he'd been carrying around with him ebbing away to reveal a layer of resentful anger simmering underneath. As far as he was concerned, all he'd done wrong was forget to return her call. But that was hardly surprising, given the day he'd been having. And now with the body of yet another young woman on his hands, with a witness unsure as to whether she'd tripped, or if someone had given her a helping hand, he really didn't need to be standing there listening to Christine bawling him out over it. 'Maybe it would help if you told me what the message said,' he eventually replied.

'You can listen to it yourself, can't you?'

'I'm here now, so you may as well tell me.'

The shop fell into an awkward silence as they both realised they'd stopped whispering a long time before.

'I said,' Christine began, forcing herself to keep her voice down, 'that it's probably best if we wait until we both have a little more time before resuming

227

whatever this is.'

'Doesn't something need to have started first, before it can be resumed? I mean, I haven't even so much as kissed you yet.'

Christine face flecked with colour. 'I think that's exactly my point. You first asked me out over a week ago, and despite having made numerous promises, you've still yet to take me out on an actual date.'

'But that's only because I've had so much going on. I'm not normally this busy.'

'Well, we'll have to see, but from my perspective, since moving off that boat of yours, I've spent more time with you in a work-related capacity than I have in a social one; like now, for example.'

'And I'll make it up to you, just as soon as this investigation is over.'

'Which could take months.'

'Well, yes, but...'

'Which was why I suggested for you to give me a call when you're done.'

'I was going to say that it was possible it could take months, but it's not very likely.'

'Look, John, I just don't think I want to be in a relationship where I'm forever wondering where you are, and if you're ever going to show up when you actually say you are.'

'Then I'll make sure to call more often.'

'It's not just that.'

'Then what is it?'

Christine hesitated, her eyes holding his before falling slowly to the floor. 'I'm – I'm just not sure I want to spend the rest of my life worrying; not so much about when you'll come back, but *if* you'll come back.'

'I'm not about to up and die on you if that's what you mean.'

'And you can say that for a fact, can you?'

It was Tanner's turn to fall silent. Since joining the Norfolk Constabulary they'd lost no less than two of their own, one of whom was his fiancée.

'Anyway,' Christine continued, 'I'm not saying I want to stop seeing you, I just think I'd rather wait; at least until you have a bit more time.'

But the look of immovable resolution in her eyes told him otherwise. It was obvious she'd come to the conclusion that it wasn't working out, and there wasn't a damn thing he could do about it, at least not until the current mess of an investigation had come to some sort of an eventual conclusion.

'OK,' he began, an empty feeling of rejection beginning to churn inside the depths of his stomach. 'Would it be OK if I gave you a call – when all this is done?'

'Oh, I'm sure we'll see each other before then.'

'Is that a no?'

Christine paused for a moment. 'You can, of course, but I can't promise anything.'

They stood there in silence, staring at each other before Tanner blinked to look away. 'OK, understood.'

With Christine's mouth remaining firmly closed, Tanner sucked in a juddering breath. 'Right,' he said, forcing himself to stand up straight. 'I'd better get on.'

Making his way back down the aisle, he turned to stare back at her, opening his mouth as he did to offer her a look of pitiful remorse. But when it came to the moment of actually saying something, the words simply weren't there. He knew that anything he did manage to come out with would make him sound desperate, a male trait he knew to be even less attractive than lying. So he closed it again to head silently away, doing his best to hold his head high as

he began peering down the remaining aisles in search
of the person he'd walked into the shop with.

- CHAPTER FIFTY -

'ARE YOU OK?' asked Vicky, in a concerned motherly tone, the moment they were back outside the shop.

'Why wouldn't I be?' came Tanner's dismissive response.

'Oh, no reason.'

Knowing she must have overheard virtually their entire conversation, Tanner sought to change the subject. 'Do we need to speak to Johnstone again, before we head back?'

They both stopped to look over to where they could see him, crouched over the woman's body.

'I suppose that depends on if he's found anything that would help clarify what the shopkeeper said; that she may not have simply tripped over a mooring line.'

As they continued to stare through the unrelenting rain they saw Johnstone tilt his head towards them, raising a hand as he did.

'That can't be good,' commented Vicky.

Tanner lifted his own in acknowledgment. 'Is it ever?' he replied, before hunching his shoulders to begin leading the way over.

'What've you got?' he called out a minute later, as they came to an eventual halt behind the medical examiner, now staring down at the body.

'We've found her purse,' he began, lifting his head

to cast his eyes along the line of boats. 'It was on the grass, near to where she must have gone in. It still has all her credit cards and ID inside. Assuming it belongs to the victim, her name's Amanda Monaghan.'

Tanner watched Vicky dig out her notebook. 'Anything else?'

Johnstone heaved himself up to face them, water dripping down from the lip of his hood. 'I'm afraid there's an indentation on the back of her head.'

Tanner gave him an agitated look. 'I thought you said she drowned?'

'I still think that was the cause of death, but something hit her before she died, either as she went in, or when she was in the water.'

Tanner thought for a moment. 'The shopkeeper mentioned something about a falling branch.'

They all spent a minute gazing about at the surrounding grass, strewn with dancing leaves and jagged broken twigs.

'I can't see anything that would have been nearly big enough,' Johnstone eventually replied, his focus returning to the body. 'Besides, I'd say the shape of the indentation was more manmade than natural.'

'Please don't tell me it was another hammer?'

'Well, it's certainly similar to the other two. There's something else they have in common as well. There's another stamp on the back of her hand.'

'And that brings us all the way back to McMillan,' Tanner muttered, catching Vicky's eye.

'Who's still back at the station.'

'Which is where we'd better be getting back to, before Forrester calls to find out where we are.'

'What about Iain Sanders?'

Tanner threw her a look of curious confusion. 'Sorry, what about him?'

'According to my notes, he's got a Fairline

Squadron, the same boat Christine saw.'

'The same boat Christine *thought* she saw.'

'And she said there was a man behind the wheel.'

'Isn't there always?'

'And that he was tall, with a narrow face.'

'Which she said she could hardly see. Besides, what possible reason would Sanders have for murdering an exotic dancer who worked at a strip club he'd never been to?'

'He only *said* he'd never been there. For all we know, he was one of their most frequent visitors.'

'Even so, he doesn't have a motive, at least not one we know about.'

'But if both the boat and its driver match the description of the only boat seen sailing away from what is looking likely to be the scene of another murder, isn't it worth having a chat?'

'I suppose,' capitulated Tanner, glancing down at his watch. 'Let's just hope Forrester sees it the same way.'

- CHAPTER FIFTY ONE -

WITH THE ROADS virtually devoid of all traffic, it took them less than twenty minutes to reach the short narrow dyke where they'd first met Iain Sanders.

As they turned into the carpark, for a full moment they thought his boat had gone, only to realise a second later that it was still there, just not where it had been before. When they'd been there last it was up at the far end, near to where the dyke met the River Thurne. Now it was lashed to the hardstanding at the other end, directly opposite the carpark.

Seeing someone move about inside, they forced themselves back out into the torrential rain to begin forging their way through buffeting gusts of turbulent wind, over to the boat's cockpit enclosed by a clear plastic canopy, one of the sections left flapping in the wind.

'Hello!' Tanner yelled, attempting to peer inside. 'Is there anyone on board?'

A moment later the figure of a man could be seen emerging out through the glass patio doors inside, his features clouded by the canopy's thick plastic covering.

'Mr Sanders?' Tanner continued.

'I'm not sure who else I'd be,' came his familiar voice, as they watched him place something heavy down onto one of the cockpit's moulded plastic seats.

'It's DI Tanner and DI Gilbert. Norfolk Police.'

'So I can see,' he continued, pulling back the half open flap to lift a toolbox onto the narrow walkway.

'We have some questions for you – if that's OK?'

'You've certainly picked quite a day for it.'

'Hardly ideal, I know, but time and tide.'

Sanders glared out, first at Tanner, then Vicky, before ducking back inside to disappear once again.

'Have you been anywhere nice?' called Tanner, bringing Vicky's attention to the toolbox he'd left out in the rain.

'Don't worry, I'm not leaving,' came his muffled response.

'I asked if you'd *been* anywhere nice, Mr Sanders,' Tanner continued, 'not if you were making plans to.'

The figure soon appeared through the canopy, more heavy items hanging from the ends of his arms.

'Sorry,' he eventually said, pulling back the cover to lift more toolboxes out. 'I can barely hear anything with all this wind. What did you say again?'

'I asked if you'd been anywhere nice?'

'Only back home, to pick up these tools.'

'But you've just come from somewhere though, haven't you?'

Sanders shook his head whilst holding Tanner's gaze. 'I haven't moved, not since you were last here.'

'But your boat has though, hasn't it?'

'Oh, I see what you mean.'

'OK, so I'll ask you again. Where have you been?'

'Well, I was moored up at the top of the dyke,' Sanders began, gesturing over to where he was referring with just the hint of a smirk. 'Now I'm here, at the other end.'

Tanner failed to be amused. 'Was there any particular reason why you moved?'

'I asked the dyke's owner if I could bring it further

down when news of the storm broke. There's more shelter here. I must admit,' he continued, glancing up towards the threatening sky above, 'I'm pleased I did. I'd no idea it would be this bad.'

'So, you haven't used it today?'

'What, in this weather? Are you mad?'

Tanner took a moment to run his eyes down the yacht's sleek white hull. 'It's a Fairline Squadron, isn't it?'

'That's right, why? Are you in the market for one?'

'It's just that a boat exactly like yours was seen about an hour ago, up near Ludham, which isn't a million miles from where we are now.'

'Then it must have been another Fairline Squadron, one with an owner who's either incredibly brave, or as equally stupid.'

'The person driving the boat also met your description.'

'Good-looking chap, was he?'

It was Tanner's turn to smile. 'I don't suppose you know a young woman by the name of Amanda Monaghan, by any chance?'

'Never heard of her.'

'Her body was found about an hour ago, very near to where the witness said she'd seen your boat.'

'Well, as I said, apart from bringing it down to this end, I haven't moved.'

'How about another young woman by the name of Nicola Bowell?'

'Again, no, sorry.'

'Her body was found by a taxi driver last night at around eleven o'clock. Would you be able to tell us where you were at that time?'

'Probably at home, but I'd have to check.'

'Then there's Claire Metcalf, of course. She was found down an alleyway near to where she lived yesterday morning. I don't suppose you'd know anything about that?'

'Only what I saw on the news.'

'And at that time you were...?'

'Either at home or here. I haven't been anywhere else.'

'How *is* life at home, Mr Sanders?'

The sudden change of subject had the man stopping to glare out at Tanner. 'What the hell's that got to do with anything?'

'It's just that you mentioned before that you were happily married.'

'And I still am, thank you very much.'

'Have you ever been to a place called the Riverside Gentlemen's Club?'

'What? No. Why?'

'But you've heard of it, though?'

'Well, yes, but only because Mike and Toby used to go there.'

'But not you?'

'As I think I mentioned before, inspector, nightclubs really aren't my thing.'

'But it's not really a nightclub, though, is it?'

'I wouldn't know. As I said, I've never been.'

'But your friends used to?'

'I just told you, didn't I?'

'Do you think that's where they'd meet the girls they'd bring back to your boat?'

Sanders eyes fixed onto Tanner's, his mouth remaining firmly closed.

'We spoke to one of your neighbours,' Tanner continued, 'when we were last here. She said she'd seen numerous young women being "entertained" on board, whilst you were on it, I may add.'

'That's as may be, but I wasn't the one doing the "entertaining", at least not in the way which I suspect you're referring. Neither was it my wish to have them on board. That was all down to Michael and Toby.'

'But you did meet their attentive young female friends, though?'

'Of course, but as I said, I didn't do anything with them.'

'I'm not suggesting you did.'

'Then why do you keep asking about them?'

'Because, Mr Sanders, it would appear that of the three women who've turned up dead over the last two days, they all worked at the same club, that being the Riverside, the same place your now deceased friends would go to pick them up, before bringing them back for you to do God knows what to them.'

'I told you, I never so much as laid a finger on them!'

'Of course, you said; you're happily married,' Tanner smirked, just as the sound of his phone could be heard, ringing from inside the depths of his coat.
'If you'll excuse me for just a minute,' he said, turning around to dig it out.

'Forrester?' questioned Vicky, catching his eye.

Stepping away from the boat, Tanner stared down at the rain-splattered screen to shake his head. 'It's nobody from the office. It could be forensics. I'd better take it. Whilst I do, maybe you could ask Mr Sanders if he has either a hammer or a hacksaw hidden somewhere within his burgeoning toolbox collection.'

Seeing Vicky nod with a conspiratorial smile, Tanner lifted the phone up to his ear whilst heading off to seek the shelter provided by a local corner shop.

'Hello, Tanner speaking?'

'Detective Inspector John Tanner?'

'Yes, speaking,' he repeated, struggling to hear what the caller was saying.

'Sorry to bother you. It's George Chapman.'

It took him a full second to place the name. 'Mr Chapman. How can I help?'

'You asked me to call, to arrange a time for you to come round to speak to my daughter.'

'Indeed I did.'

'I'm afraid the only time we can do today is later this evening, at around nine o'clock.'

Tanner rolled his eyes.

'Unless you can wait until the weekend?'

'You can't do any earlier. Say around six?'

'I'm sorry, but as I said, she has rehearsals for her end of term play after school. Then she has to revise for her GCSEs. The only time we have is after we've had supper.'

'Then I suppose that will have to do. Have you spoken to her since this morning.'

'Er, no, why?'

'I was just wondering if she may have remembered anything else that could help us.'

'Only what I told you, that she thought she saw three men throwing the missing girl over the side of a large white motorboat.'

As Chapman's words drifted out of Tanner's phone, he turned slowly around to stare back at the boat moored up no more than ten metres away. Kicking himself for being so incredibly stupid, he ended the call to come jogging back.

'Sorry about that,' he eventually said, coming to a gradual halt beside the boat. 'Now, where were we?'

'For some unknown reason, your colleague has been asking if I owned either a hacksaw or a hammer,' Sanders replied, securing the latch of one of his toolboxes.

'How many people did you say you bought this boat with again?' Tanner queried, replacing his phone for his notebook.

Sanders opened and closed his mouth, his focus shifting between the two police officers. 'I told you before, didn't I?'

'If you could remind me?'

'I bought it with Mike and Toby, but I've never said anything different.'

Tanner turned his head slowly to face Vicky. 'What date was it when Abigail Taylor went missing? Last week sometime, wasn't it?'

Vicky flicked quickly back through her open notebook. 'She was reported missing on Saturday night, the 21st of August.'

'Mr Sanders,' Tanner continued, returning his attention back to the man standing inside the boat's sheltered cockpit. 'I don't suppose you'd mind telling me where you were on that particular evening.'

'I've no idea.'

'Didn't you say the three of you used to go fishing together on Saturday nights?' Tanner continued, leaning his head to the side in a bid to stare through the half-open canopy.

'I – well – yes, then we probably were.'

'I don't suppose you can remember where you went?'

'Where we always go, at least we used to.'

'And where was that?'

'Heading south, normally to anchor just off Lowestoft.'

'So...nowhere near Happisburgh Lighthouse, then?'

'We used to go up that way, but not for a long time. We generally had more luck heading south.'

A moment of silence followed as Tanner continued doing his best to stare inside the man's boat. 'Aren't you curious to know why I'm asking, Mr Sanders?' he eventually queried, raising his eyes to watch as the man shifted his weight from one foot to the other.

'I assume it has something to do with that missing girl – the one you were talking about.'

'That's right. You may or may not be interested to know that we have a witness who says they saw a boat – once again very similar to yours – just off from Happisburgh Lighthouse on the night in question.'

'That couldn't have been us. We were down the other way.'

'This witness saw something which I think would be best described as a little...unsettling, shall we say.'

'OK, well...'

'Three men, none of whom were wearing any clothes, standing around an equally naked young woman, whose body the witness then saw being thrown overboard.'

'As I said, detective, that couldn't have been us, as we were down near Lowestoft.'

'Yes, I see. I don't suppose there'd be anyone there who'd be able to vouch for you?'

'Well...no, but...'

'I didn't think so.'

Sanders closed his mouth to stare silently at Tanner.

'Anyway, sorry to have taken up so much of your time, Mr Sanders. Next time, if you could let us know before moving your boat again, even if it is only from one end of the dyke to the other, I'd be very grateful.'

- CHAPTER FIFTY TWO -

TANNER WAITED UNTIL they were back in the car before opening his mouth. 'That was all rather interesting,' he mused, tugging on his seatbelt.

Vicky did her best to shake the rain from her coat before stepping inside. 'Who was that on the phone?'

'The guy I met when I went up to Happisburgh Lighthouse with Cooper. I'm not sure I told you, but he came into the station this morning. His daughter was the witness I was talking about, the one who said she saw the body of a young woman being thrown over the side of a boat. That was him calling to arrange a time for us to go over there to interview her.'

'She didn't come in with him?'

Tanner shook his head. 'She was at school.'

'And why is that so interesting?'

'I'm afraid I've been incredibly stupid. I should have made the connection a long time before now, probably when he came into the station. It's the old "three men in a boat" scenario, just with the addition of a young woman by the name of Abigail Taylor.'

'You think they're responsible for her disappearance?

'Well, we have three men in a boat, one of whom has already admitted to having been out at sea at the time in question.'

'But – why would they have killed her?'

'Maybe they didn't, at least not on purpose. If they'd being doing drugs, it's possible she simply overdosed. That would have left them in a position where they'd be unable to tell us, not without leaving them wide open to a criminal enquiry. If that's true, then I think there's a strong possibility that we have the wrong man in custody.'

'I assume you're thinking that Sanders killed his two friends because they were the only other witnesses to what they'd done.'

'If it was Sanders' fault the girl died, I was actually thinking that he may have killed them because they were the only witnesses to what *he'd* done. Maybe he was the one who gave her the drugs, or maybe he accidently choked her to death during intercourse.'

'OK, so if he murdered Abigail Taylor, Sir Michael Blackwell and Toby Wallace, are we still saying that he killed the other three girls as well?'

'The evidence does seem to be pointing that way.'

'And the blackmail letters? Could they have been written by him, to try and throw us off the scent?'

'It's possible, I suppose, but for now I suggest we focus on the murders. What did he say about the contents of his various toolboxes?'

'He admitted to owning both a hammer *and* a hacksaw. He was even happy enough to show them to me.'

'OK, I suppose that doesn't mean much. If he had half a brain he'd have dumped the ones he used in the river.'

'What if forensics comes back to say that the blood on the hacksaw found at the Riverside club belongs to Sir Michael?'

'Then we'll have to have another think, which reminds me. The results should have come in by now.'

Glancing at the dashboard to look at the time, Tanner saw a figure walking slowly through the rain towards them, its face and form left blurred by the water cascading down the Jag's sloping windscreen.

Vicky looked up to follow his gaze. 'Another lunatic out for a pleasant afternoon stroll.'

'Probably taking the dog out for a walk,' Tanner commented, flicking on the windscreen wipers to briefly glimpse the face of a strikingly attractive young woman.

Vicky lifted her head to peer down at the grass the girl was traipsing over, a pair of black over-sized wellies hanging from the ends of her feet like two clanging church bells. 'I can't see one.'

They took a moment to watch her step around the Jag, seemingly on her way towards the dyke.

'Where the hell is she going?' Tanner questioned, as a particularly savage gust of wind nearly sent her flying to the ground.

'She must live on board one of the boats.'

'But even so. To be out in this?'

'You know what they say. When a dog has to go, a dog has to go.'

'But as you said, there isn't one.'

'Then it must have blown away, and she's out looking for it. Either that or she popped out for some milk.'

'*She'll* be blown away if she's not careful,' Tanner replied, just as they saw Sanders' head re-appear through his cockpit's canopy to dump a large holdall onto the decking beside his boat, staring out at the woman as he did. 'You know, I think she may be going to see our brand new friend.'

The moment he said it, another violent gust of wind tore into the woman, sending her stumbling away from the dyke to begin skirting around the edge of the carpark.

'My money's still on the flying dog,' Vicky mused, watching as she disappeared somewhere behind them.

Tanner let out an exhausted sigh. 'Anyway, I suppose we'd better be heading back to the station. If the wind gets any stronger than this, Forrester really will have to send out a search party for us.'

- CHAPTER FIFTY THREE -

T HE MOMENT THEY entered the main office, even before Tanner had reached his desk, they saw Forrester come bursting out of his to begin marching his way over towards them.

'Looks like someone's been missing us,' whispered Vicky, leaning her head into Tanner's.

'You'd better let me deal with this,' he began, his eyes drifting over towards the kitchen and the coffee machine he could see perched on its counter. 'I suggest you get back to that desk of yours. See if you can find out what happened to that forensics report. You know the question we need an answer to. Does the blood found on that hacksaw belong to Sir Michael?'

'Will do.'

'When you've done that, could you do me a favour?'

'That probably depends on what it is.'

'Can you make me a coffee?' he asked, sending Vicky a look of imploring desperation before gazing ahead to meet Forrester's rapidly approaching glare. 'It looks like I'm going to need one.'

Seeing Vicky nod before slinking quietly away, he pulled himself straight as Forrester came storming up to him.

'Where the *hell* have you been?' the DCI demanded, his voice kept menacingly low.

'Sorry, sir, we had another lead which I felt necessary to follow up.'

'Despite my having told you not two hours ago to keep me more informed as to your whereabouts?'

'I know, but a couple of things happened which I didn't think could wait.'

'Neither of which you've bothered to tell me about.'

'Which is why I'm telling you now, *sir*,' Tanner replied, feeling his blood pressure beginning to rise.

'Then you'd better get on with it, hadn't you!'

Tanner drew in a calming breath. 'Someone saw a boat motoring away from the scene of the girl's murder.'

'Sorry, which girl's murder was that? There have been so many, I'm beginning to lose track.'

'The one Vicky and I went to look at this morning, over at Ludham.'

Forrester fell into a sullen silence, his eyes boring steadily down into Tanner's. 'I thought...' he began, his voice rumbling like a brooding volcano, '...the witness said that the person had tripped over a mooring line before falling into the water?'

'That *was* her initial impression, but after questioning, it turned out that she wasn't quite as sure as she'd first thought.'

'So you've come to the conclusion that she was murdered, have you?'

'Johnstone came to the initial conclusion that she drowned.'

'Right, good.'

'However,' Tanner continued, 'he also found an indentation on the back of her head.'

'For fuck's sake,' Forrester muttered quietly to himself, turning his head to glare wildly about.

'The witness *did* say she thought she may have been hit by a falling branch, which could have been the cause of the head injury, as well as for her going into the river.'

'I assume you didn't find one?'

'I'm afraid not, at least nothing large enough to have caused such an injury.'

'That's just great.'

'Johnstone's eventual opinion was that whatever caused the injury was more man-made than natural. He also thought it was similar to those found on the previous two women.'

'Even better,' Forrester replied, his tone soaked in acrid sarcasm. 'And where did you go after that? On a camping trip up to the Lake District?'

'I think that's where we might have some more positive news,' Tanner continued, doing his dogged best to ignore Forrester's on-going barrage of flippant acrimonious remarks. 'I mentioned before about another witness saying they saw a boat motoring away from the scene. She – I mean – the witness said the boat was a Fairline Squadron, just like the one Iain Sanders owns.'

Tanner could almost see the cogs of Forrester's mind turning slowly around inside his head.

'And this witness – she's reliable, is she; in that she can tell one boat from another?'

'She's a – er – Broads Ranger, sir.'

Forrester's eyes narrowed to the point where Tanner could barely see them. 'I do hope you're not about to tell me it was that woman you've been seeing so much of recently?'

'If you're referring to Christine, she just happened to be the Broads Ranger who was called to the scene.'

Seeing Forrester shake his head, rolling his eyes as he did, Tanner thought it was probably best for him to move the conversation along. 'Anyway, that's where Vicky and I went afterwards, to see if we could find him.'

'And did you?'

Tanner nodded. 'He was on board his boat.'

'And...?'

'Well, he didn't exactly admit to murdering the girl, but his boat had been moved off its mooring since we were last there, and he was packing up to go somewhere, amongst his possessions being a large collection of tools which included both a hammer and a hacksaw.'

Forrester waited expectantly for a moment before eventually opening his mouth. 'Is that it?'

'Not quite. Whilst we were talking, I had a call from the guy who lives next to Happisburgh Lighthouse, the one whose daughter said she saw a woman being thrown over the side of a boat. He was calling to arrange a time for us to speak to her, but it made me realise something that I'm afraid I should have worked out a long time before. She'd told him that there were three men on board the boat the girl was thrown out of.'

The malevolent frown Forrester had been wearing since the start of the conversation began to ebb slowly away. 'I assume you're thinking that the three men she saw might have been Sir Michael, Toby Wallace and this Iain Sanders chap?'

Tanner nodded in response.

'OK, I'd have to admit, that is interesting, at least more so than I was expecting.'

Vicky's appearance beside Tanner with the coffee he'd requested held out in her hands had him smiling gratefully around. 'Did you manage to get hold of forensics?' he asked her, taking the proffered mug.

'I spoke to someone who said the tests were completed this morning.'

'So, why haven't we received the results?'

'He's not sure.'

'Don't tell me they've lost them?'

'He seemed to think it was more likely they'd been miss-filed than actually lost.'

'You must be joking, surely,' Tanner muttered, with mounting frustration. 'Did you tell them just how important that one piece of evidence is to our entire investigation?'

'I can't say that I did, although I'm not sure what difference it would have made if I had.'

Forrester made a point of glaring down at his watch. 'You do realise, Tanner, that we only have three hours before McMillan's solicitor is legally entitled to march his client straight out the front door, meaning that any evidence we've collected so far will be as good as useless.'

'Forgive me, sir, but it's hardly my fault our forensics department seems to lack the ability to do basic filing.'

'Did you apply for an extension, like I told you to?'

'I've been waiting on forensics. The blood on that hacksaw is the only piece of non-circumstantial evidence we have.'

'Then I suggest you get over there to help them find it!'

Tanner stopped to stare over at him. 'You're not being serious?'

'Does it look like I'm joking?'

'But – I don't even know where they're based.'

'Yes, I can see how that's going to be a problem,' Forrester replied, folding his arms to place a pensive finger against the lose skin hanging from his chin. 'Vicky, do you have any idea how Tanner here would be able to find somewhere he's never been to before?'

'Er...' Vicky began, a playful smirk beginning to tug gently at the corners of her mouth, '...it was a while ago now, but didn't someone invent something called a map?'

'My God, you're right!'

'And with the recent invention of the internet,' she continued, seemingly enjoying herself, 'these days I think you can access them via a computer. And when you find something called a postcode, you can use another clever bit of kit known as satellite navigation. Apparently, it will take you straight there.'

'Well, there we are!' beamed Forrester, his attention returning to his senior DI. 'Problem solve-ed!'

'Most amusing,' commented Tanner, without looking as if he had been. 'Even if I was to go all the way over there, wherever they're based, I can hardly imagine they'd allow me to start ploughing my way through all their files.'

'Frankly, I don't give a shit. I want those results found, and before eight o'clock. Under absolutely no circumstances am I having McMillan waltzing out of here one minute, only for the evidence proving he's guilty of carving up Lord Blackwell's son turning up the next, do you understand?'

'And what if the forensics report comes back to say that the blood found on the hacksaw *doesn't* belong to Sir Michael, whilst the real culprit is happily motoring his way down to the Caribbean?'

'Then I suggest you arrange for a search warrant before he does.'

'I'm sorry, I thought you wanted me over at forensics, emptying out their wastepaper baskets?'

'Fortunately for us, you're not the only person who works here.'

'*Could've fooled me*,' Tanner muttered, loud enough for both his colleague and boss to hear.

'Always good to know my work here is being

appreciated,' Vicky said, forcing a jaded grin over at him.

'Present company excepted, of course.'

'I'm sure Vicky is more than capable of organising a forensics team to head over to Sanders' boat.'

'What about Cooper?'

'What about him?'

'Why can't *he* go on a fishing trip for the missing evidence?'

'Because you're the SIO.'

'Yes, of course. I nearly forgot. By the way, I'm not sure I ever did thank you for that.'

'Which means it's your responsibility to find it,' Forrester continued.

'I'd have thought, being that I am the SIO and everything, it would have been my choice who went.'

'Just get yourself over there, Tanner, that's an order!'

Tanner waited for Forrester to spin around to start heading back to his office before offering the back of his bald head an exaggerated salute. 'Yes *sir*,' he added, with undiluted sarcastic irreverence.

Turning to find Vicky glaring at him with her arms folded, he offered her a concerned frown. 'Are you alright?'

'If you want me to continue fetching coffee for you at a drop of a hat,' she began, 'as if I'm some sort of snot-nosed work placement student, may I suggest that you refrain from insinuating that I do bugger all around here.'

'Ah, right. Sorry about that. It was said in the heat of the moment.'

'I don't care if it was said inside a pre-heated microwave.'

'Er...I'm not sure you can pre-heat a microwave.'

'You know what I mean.'

'I do, yes, and sorry again.'

Vicky glared at him for a moment longer before her features gradually softened. 'So – I suppose you want me to arrange for a forensics team to head over to Sanders' boat.'

'If you could, but first, I don't suppose you could help me work out where our forensics department is based?'

'Have you seriously never heard of Google?'

'I must admit, I have, but to be honest, I've never been very good with search engines.'

'How is it possible for someone not to be very good with search engines?'

Tanner shrugged. 'I'm not sure. I just never seem to know what to type in.'

Realising he was joking, Vicky couldn't help but smile. 'Then I suppose it's fortunate for you that I've been there before. They're over at Thorpe End. I'll dig out their address, but I suggest you give them a call before you head over, just so they know to expect you.'

'Makes sense.'

Seeing her about to head off, he glanced down at the still full coffee mug held at the end of his arm. 'Er...before I do, I don't suppose there's any chance you could make me another coffee? This one seems to have gone cold.'

'I do hope you're joking?'

He looked up at her with an amused smirk. 'Don't worry. I'll just have to get some snot-nosed work placement student to heat this one up in a pre-heatable microwave, although they may have to invent one that has the ability to pre-heat first, of course.'

- CHAPTER FIFTY FOUR -

JUST OVER FIFTEEN minutes later, Tanner arrived at the Norfolk Constabulary's forensics department in Thorpe End, a small village lying on the border between Norwich City Centre and the Norfolk Broads.

Leaving his XJS in the waterlogged carpark outside, he hurried in through a narrow inconspicuous door marked only by a small sign above. As he peeled off his hood to wipe the rain dripping from off the end of his nose, he stepped up to the reception desk to find that there was nobody behind it.

'Hello!' he called, staring about whilst digging out his formal ID. 'Is anyone here?'

A moment later, a rotund man with a bald head and thick tortoiseshell rimmed glasses came hurrying through a door to the side. 'Hello, yes, sorry. What can I do for you?' he enquired, navigating himself behind the desk.

'DI Tanner. I called earlier.'

'That's right, but as I said on the phone, I'm not sure how we can help.'

'And as *I* said on the phone, the results you've somehow managed to lose are vital to a multiple murder investigation.'

'We're fully aware of that, thank you, I just don't see how your presence here will enable us to find them any quicker.'

'Can't I help go through your files?'

'What – for every case we're working on?'

'Obviously not. Just the ones relating to our investigation.'

'I'm sorry, but I can't allow you to go through *any* of the files on our system, whether they're related to your investigation or not. Apart from it being highly inappropriate, you simply don't have the authorisation. Even if you did, had they been in the files you're referring to, we'd have found them a long time before now.'

'But – there must be something I can do?'

'I'm afraid you're just going to have to be patient,' the man continued, pushing his glasses up the bridge of his nose. 'But don't worry, they'll turn up soon enough. They've just been misfiled, that's all.'

'You don't seem to understand. We have a man sitting in a holding cell who we believe murdered at least two people, maybe more. If we don't find those results in – what...' Tanner glanced up at a large white clock marking the time against the wall, '...two and a half hours he's going to walk free, at which point it won't matter even if you did find them. Even if we had the opportunity to arrest him again, they'd be completely useless to us.'

'I'm fully aware of the law, thank you, inspector, but I'm afraid there's nothing more we can do. All I can say is that we're working as hard and as fast as possible to find them for you, and your presence here is only holding that process up. Now, if you'll excuse me, I need to re-join my colleagues in attempting to find them.'

Tanner let out an exasperated sigh as the man spun around to disappear back through the door he'd entered through.

Unsure what to do next, he reached inside his sodden jacket in search of his phone.

'Vicky, it's me. I'm at the forensics lab.'

'Any luck?'

'Nothing. They wouldn't even let me look. They said I don't have the authorisation, despite the fact that I'm the bloody SIO.'

'OK, so, what now?'

'I guess we're just going to have to keep our fingers crossed that they find it in time. Any luck with that search warrant for Sanders' boat?'

'Not yet, but in fairness, I've only just submitted the application.'

'I suppose time isn't such an issue with that one, as long as he doesn't do a runner out into the North Sea, of course.'

'In this weather, I doubt it. Speaking of which, we're not headline news anymore.'

'Really? How come?'

'The MET Office has just upgraded the storm to a category four. They're saying the worst is yet to come, advising everyone to stay home and to travel only if absolutely necessary.'

'Did they say anything about driving around in a thirty plus-year-old Jaguar XJS whilst trying to solve multiple murder investigations?'

'Not that I heard.'

'Shame. I could have had the day off.'

'It is beginning to look pretty serious, though. Loads of trees have come down, one person died when a wall fell on top of him, and most of the shops in Norwich have already closed. Half the schools didn't even bother to open today.'

Tanner stopped to stare absently out at the trees thrashing wildly about in the gale force wind outside.

'Are you still there?' Vicky questioned, her voice

nothing but a distant echo.

'Half the schools or all of them?' Tanner eventually asked, his attention returning to the room.

'Er...I've no idea.'

'Do you remember that girl we saw, walking past the car near Sanders' boat?'

'The one looking for her flying dog? Yes – why?'

'I've got a nagging feeling that I've seen her before, inside the cottage next to the lighthouse. I could be wrong, but I think she was the owner's daughter.'

'I'm sorry, but what would his daughter have been doing wandering about during in the middle of what is now being classed as a category four storm?'

'I'm not sure, but when her father called me earlier he said she was at school. That's why we couldn't go round to interview her.'

'Maybe her school was one of the ones that decided to stay open.'

'And maybe it wasn't. Do me a favour, will you?' he asked, digging out his notebook to begin rifling through its pages.

'What, another one?'

'Give her school a call for me? It's St Martins in Stalham. Find out if they were open today, and if they were, was Alice Chapman there.'

'OK, no problem.'

'Whilst you're doing that,' Tanner continued, his gaze returning to the storm raging outside, 'I'm going to see if I can get hold of her father.'

- CHAPTER FIFTY FIVE -

FINDING CHAPMAN'S NUMBER, Tanner dialled it to begin pacing up and down, listening to it ring endlessly before finally being sent through to voicemail. With the slim hope that he'd simply not been able to make it to the phone in time, he tried again, only for the same thing to happen a minute later.

Cursing quietly to himself, he left a brief message, asking him to call, before phoning Vicky back.

'Any luck with the school?' he asked, the moment she picked up.

'There was no answer.'

'Shit.'

'How about you?'

'Same thing.'

'I'm just taking a look at the school's website,' he heard Vicky continue. 'There's no mention anywhere about them having been closed for the day. If they had, I'd have thought they'd have posted up something about it.'

Tanner thought for a moment. 'Sod it,' he eventually said. 'I'm going to have to go over there to find out.'

'Is it really that important?' came Vicky's enquiring voice.

'If Chapman has been saying that the reason his daughter can't speak to us is because she's at school, when the school in question has been closed all day, then there has to be a reason, and I'm beginning to get an idea as to what that might be.'

'I assume you're thinking that they're the ones behind the blackmail letters?'

'If they'd seen three men dumping the body of a young woman over the side of a boat, then they'd have been in a very strong position to.'

'Then why would the father have walked into the middle of Wroxham Police Station to tell everyone what they'd seen? If you're attempting to blackmail someone, surely the idea is that you know something nobody else does, making the idea of telling the entire Norfolk Constabulary about as sensible as murdering the people you're endeavouring to coerce the money out of.'

'If you remember, it was over a week after the girl disappeared before Chapman stepped forward to tell us, by which time they only had one blackmail victim left, Iain Sanders, his other two friends having turned up dead. And maybe he was refusing to pay up, saying they had no proof. With nobody from CID knocking on his door asking awkward questions about what happened that night, Sanders could have easily thought his secret was safe enough. Chapman telling us at least part of what they'd seen may have been their way of increasing the pressure on him to cough up the money. After all, if they were the only witnesses, it would be easy enough for them to say they'd be willing to stand up in court, their hands resting on a bible, to swear it wasn't him they'd seen, on the condition that they received the sum being demanded, of course.'

'But that doesn't tie in with what the letters said,' Vicky continued, her tone still edged in doubt, 'at least not the one we found at Toby Wallace's house.

"Leave fifty thousand in cash at the base of Happisburgh Lighthouse by midnight tonight, or else I'll be doing unto you as you so kindly thought you'd done unto me." That sounds more like the blackmailer was the aggrieved victim, a living one at that, not a father and daughter duo who'd watched them murder someone through the end of a telescope.'

Tanner's gaze drifted out of the window, his mind deep in thought. 'You know,' he eventually said, 'it could be that that was their intention.'

'Sorry, I'm not with you.'

'To make them think that the girl whose body they thought they'd disposed of in the middle of the North Sea had somehow survived, and that Chapman has been using his daughter, Alice, in an effort to convince them. That's why the letter found at Wallace's house had "by hand" written so clearly on its envelope. That could also be why we saw her making her way towards Sanders' boat in the middle of a category four storm, only to veer away when he caught sight of her. The problem is, I think they may have done too good a job at trying to convince him.'

'How d'you mean?'

'If Sanders now believes the woman they threw over the side of their boat is still alive, then it's possible that he doesn't only think she's been trying to blackmail them. He may think she must have murdered Sir Michael and Wallace as well, possibly after they refused to pay-up, or simply to exact vengeance. If that was the case, then it would be logical for him to conclude that he was next on her rather short list.'

'You think Sanders has been killing those women because he thought one of them was the girl they'd thrown over the side of their boat?'

'I think it's possible, especially in light of the way Sir Michael had his heart cut out of his chest whilst he was still alive. If he thought for one moment that she was planning on doing that to him, I can understand why he'd be just a tad keen to make sure he didn't end up suffering a similar fate.'

'OK, I suppose I can understand why he may have killed the first woman – Claire Metcalf,' Vicky continued, 'being that Sir Michael's housekeeper told the national press that she'd allowed her to walk in through the front door, not long before he was murdered, but why the other two?'

'He must have reached the conclusion that he'd killed the wrong person. That must have been why he came into the police station yesterday, trying to find out if Wallace had been murdered, and at what time. Don't forget, they all worked at the Riverside.'

'The missing girl didn't,' stated Vicky.

'Not that we know of, but that doesn't mean she didn't. She could have used a stage name, in much the same way Claire Metcalf did. Now that I think about it, that could explain why Sanders doesn't know who she is – because the name she gave them wasn't her real one, and also why he's been going through their bags, looking for ID. Either way, we need to find out if Chapman's daughter has been at school today. If she hasn't, and Sanders is under the impression that she's the girl they thought they'd left at the bottom of the North Sea who has already murdered two out of the three people who'd left her for dead, then there's every chance she's in real danger.'

There was a momentary pause from the other end of the line. 'What do you want me to tell Forrester?' Vicky eventually asked.

'Why? Has he been asking after me again.'

'Not yet, but he's currently staring at me through

his partition window, no doubt wondering who I'm on the phone to.'

'OK. If he does, you'd better tell him I'm still at forensics, helping to find that missing evidence. If you say that I'm off on what he'll no doubt consider to be another pointless wild goose chase, he'll probably have a cardiac arrest, which he'd subsequently blame me for. Worse still if I rock up to find the school's been open all day, Chapman's daughter has been there since half-past eight this morning and she's currently up on the stage, rehearsing for their end of term play, just as her father said she was.'

- CHAPTER FIFTY SIX -

LONG BEFORE TANNER found himself driving past a sign warning him that there was a school ahead, it had become increasingly obvious that the storm had reached a new level of ferocity. The roads on the way were now strewn with broken branches, some of which were so large he was forced to steer carefully around, and he'd seen more than one ancient solitary tree ripped from its roots to lie twisted and bent on surrounding fallow ground, like fallen soldiers, left for dead by their brothers-in-arms.

Following the signs for the entrance, he turned left off the road to find himself slamming on the brakes as a pair of green wrought iron gates loomed up in front of him, blocking the way ahead.

'Well, it's closed now,' he muttered to himself as he stared about, looking for some sort of an intercom device.

Spying one on the curb to his right, too far for him to reach, he contemplated the idea of stepping out to press the plastic button before deciding against it. Instead, he edged his car back out into the thankfully deserted road behind, spinning the steering wheel to bring it forward again.

Opening his window just enough to squeeze his hand through, he pressed the buzzer and waited.

With no response, he pressed it again.

Still nothing.

Unsure if the thing even worked, he was about to swing the car around to see if he could find some other way in when a metallic voice came blaring out from the machine.

'School's closed!'

'I can see that, thank you,' he replied, rolling his eyes. 'Detective Inspector Tanner, Norfolk Police.'

With no immediate response, Tanner found himself glaring at the machine. 'Are you still there?'

'I said, the school's closed!'

Tanner shook his head in quiet frustration. 'I heard you the first time. I was just wondering if it would be possible for you to tell me *when* it did?'

'I'm just the caretaker. I'm not responsible for when the school opens and closes.'

'*Unbelievable,*' Tanner muttered, a little louder than he'd meant to.

'What was that?'

'I'm trying to establish if the school has been open all day, as usual, or if it's been closed, because of the storm?'

'I don't know about this morning, but there was no one around when I started.'

'And when was that?'

'Ten o'clock.'

'What, this morning?'

'No, last Tuesday,' the caretaker replied.

Tanner took in a breath. 'If it was closed at ten, then it must have been closed all day.'

'I suppose, but as I said, I wouldn't know. I'm never here that early.'

'OK, thanks for your help. Really appreciated,' Tanner replied, just as sarcastically as he knew how.

Winding his window up, he pulled out his phone to try calling Chapman again. 'Where the hell are you?' he said to himself, listening to the phone ring.

Eventually being put through to voicemail, he hung up to call Vicky instead.

'Hi, it's Tanner. Any news?'

'The search warrant for Sander's boat still hasn't come through. You?'

'I've just been speaking to some idiot school caretaker. He says he doesn't know if the school's been closed today as he didn't start till ten.'

'What, at night?'

'No, in the morning. As I think it's unlikely they'd have opened for only a couple of hours before changing their minds, I think we can assume it didn't open this morning. Even if it did, Chapman called me at around eleven to tell me that his daughter was in school when she couldn't have been, so he was definitely lying. It must be them who've been writing those blackmail letters.'

'Have you been able to get through to him?'

'Still no answer. How's Forrester doing?'

'Hasn't he called you?'

'Not that I know,' Tanner replied, pulling his phone away from his ear to stare momentarily at the screen. 'Was he supposed to?'

'He came over about two minutes ago, asking if I knew where you were.'

'And...what did you say?'

'What you told me to – that you're still at forensics, helping to find that missing report. That's when he said he was going to call you.'

'OK, he's probably trying to get through now. I'd better give him a call – see if I can beat him to it. Let me know when that warrant comes through.'

- CHAPTER FIFTY SEVEN -

T HE MOMENT HE ended the call, his phone rang in his hand. He didn't need to look at the screen to know who it was.

'Tanner, it's Forrester.'

'I was just this second about to call you, sir.'

'Does that mean you have some good news for me?'

'Not regarding the missing forensics report, I'm afraid; at least, not yet.'

'You do know that we only have two hours before McMillan walks out the door?'

Tanner glanced down at the Jag's analogue clock, mounted onto its somewhat dated heavily varnished dashboard. 'I'm aware of that, thank you, but unfortunately I'm not sure what else I can do.'

'So...why were you about to call me?'

'Something else has come up that I think needs to take priority.'

'Over charging a suspect for multiple murder?'

'In order to stop someone else from being, sir.'

Tanner's statement was initially met by silence.

'OK, you have my attention.'

'George Chapman has been lying to us about the whereabouts of his daughter, Alice.'

'You mean, the girl who said she saw a body being thrown over the side of a boat?'

'That's the one.'

'What the hell has that got to do with anything?'

'I think they're the ones who've been writing those blackmail letters.'

'Wasn't it the father who came into the station, telling us what his daughter had seen?'

'Well, yes, it was, but...'

'Isn't that rather an odd sort of thing for him to have done, if they were endeavouring to convince Sir Michael and his friends that they knew about some heinous crime they'd committed, one that nobody else was supposed to?'

'I can only assume they must have had some other motive for doing so. Perhaps it was because nobody was coughing up the cash they were demanding, so they decided to apply some additional pressure by providing us with some clues as to what they'd been up to.'

'Either way,' Forrester continued, 'what I'd really like to know is why you think a case of attempted blackmail should take priority over a multiple murder investigation?'

'Because of the blackmail method they've been using, and what I believe Sanders has been up to since.'

'I'm sorry, Tanner, but you're going to have to explain yourself.'

'I think they've been endeavouring to make Sir Michael, Wallace and Sanders believe that the girl they threw over the side of their boat survived, and that she's the one who's been attempting to blackmail them.'

'What on Earth would make you think that?'

'It's the wording used on the letter found at Wallace's house. "Leave fifty thousand at the base of Happisburgh Lighthouse by midnight tonight, or else I'll be doing unto you as you so kindly thought you'd done unto me." It's in the first person. And in an attempt to further convince them, I think the father has been using his daughter effectively as bait – sending her out to parade herself in front of them. Vicky and I saw a girl today, just after we'd finished speaking to Sanders. She walked straight past his boat. I swear it was Alice.'

'This is all well and good, Tanner, but I still don't see why you're making such a fuss. It's still just blackmail, and by all accounts, a failed one at that.'

'Not if Sanders ends up being the one who's been killing all those women, and his motivation for having done so.'

'Which is?'

'Because he's become so convinced by the Chapmans' blackmail attempt – that the woman they threw over the side of the boat did somehow survive – he's come to the conclusion that it must have been her who murdered Sir Michael and Wallace, and that he's next. If that's true, and he now thinks Chapman's daughter is the girl he'd previously thought was lying at the bottom of the North Sea, then I think she's in real danger.'

Tanner heard a distant knock on a door from the other end of the line, followed by the muffled voice of a woman.

'Hold on a sec, Tanner, Vicky's at the door.'

Trying to overhear what was being said, Tanner waited patiently for his DCI to come back over the line.

'Sorry about that. The search warrant for Iain Sanders' boat has just come through. I've told her to see if she can dig up any forensics officers to head straight over there. I assume that's OK with you?'

'Yes, of course.'

'As for Chapman's daughter. If you're right, then

we need to find her. When was the last time you spoke to her father?'

'Not since he called me earlier to try and arrange a time for us to speak to her. He said she was still at school.'

'How do we know that she isn't?'

'It was on the news - that the schools have closed.'

'What, all of them? Are you sure?'

'I'm currently parked directly outside their school's gates, having just been speaking to the caretaker about it.'

There was a momentary pause from the other end of the line. 'I thought you were at forensics, helping to find that missing report?'

'Well, I – er – was, sir, but they said I was being more of a hindrance than actually helping, so I thought I'd come down here instead.'

Tanner could almost hear Forrester shaking his head in disbelief.

'So, what do you intend to do now?' the DCI eventually asked.

Tanner cleared his throat. 'I thought I'd head over to Chapman's house. Hopefully, that's where his daughter is.'

'Wouldn't it be easier just to phone him up to ask?'

'He's not picking up. He must think we're onto him about his attempted blackmail endeavour, without having a single idea as to the danger his actions have placed his daughter in.'

'OK, then I suppose you'd better get over there. Meanwhile, I'll get the word out that she needs to be found. Do we have her picture?'

'Not that I'm aware of.'

'Then I'll ask Sally to start trawling through the social media sites. Hopefully she'll be able to find something.'

- CHAPTER FIFTY EIGHT -

A RRIVING AT THE entrance to the lane that led up to Happisburgh Lighthouse, Tanner took a moment to watch its giant sweeping beam push back against an amassing army of billowing black clouds.

Turning in, he proceeded up the single-track road, one eye on the glistening tarmac ahead, the other on the line of telegraph poles to his left, the wires stretched between each rattling like the final death-throes of a dying snake.

Once in the carpark he tried opening his door, only to find the wind was blowing so hard against its side, it took all his strength to force it open. For the first time since the storm had started a prickle of fear pinched at the corners of his mind. Two years at sea had given him a taste of just how terrifying the wind could be, leaving him with a sense of humble respect for such an overwhelmingly powerful force.

As a particularly savage gust tore its way underneath the car, momentarily lifting up its vast steel structure before leaving it rocking back on its suspension, he stepped out into a maelstrom of turbulent wind and razor sharp rain to begin staggering over to the gap in the hedge, beyond which Chapman's cottage lay. Pushed along by the sheer force of the wind, he fell against the cottage door, ringing the bell before hammering on it with his fist.

Hearing nothing but the howling gale and the distant sound of giant waves crashing against the nearby cliffs, he was about to hammer again when the door suddenly swung inwards.

'Mr Chapman,' he said, pulling himself up. 'DI Tanner.'

'What are you doing here?' Chapman demanded, glaring out.

'I'm looking for your daughter. Is she here?'

'I thought we agreed that you wouldn't come until nine?'

'Is she here?' Tanner repeated, his voice cracking with immediacy.

Chapman first opened, then closed his mouth, his eyes darting between Tanner's as if searching his mind for what to say in response.

'Why did you lie when you phoned me this morning?' Tanner continued, unable to wait for whatever it was that he was going to come out with.

'About what?'

'You told me your daughter was at school.'

'Yes, and...?'

'I've just come from there. It was closed.'

'I know. They all are.'

'Then how could she have been there?'

'It was open this morning. I only heard about it closing after I'd spoken to you.'

Tanner narrowed his eyes. 'OK, so, where is she?'

'In bed. Sick I'm afraid. She came back soaking wet. She must have caught a cold. I was about to call to postpone our meeting to another day.'

'Can I see her?'

'I'm sorry, inspector, but as I said, she's in bed, hopefully asleep. I don't care who you are, there's no way I'm going to allow you inside her bedroom.'

Tanner watched him take a firm hold of the edge

of the door before returning his attention to his face. 'What time did she get home?'

'Sometime after I called you.'

'You know, that's funny.'

'What's funny?'

'At around half-past-three this afternoon I saw a girl bearing a striking resemblance to your daughter, walking down by Acle Dyke.'

Chapman's eyes recommenced their erratic dance.

'The question is,' Tanner continued, 'what was she doing all the way over there, if she was supposed to have been making her way back from school at the time?'

'Isn't the answer to that rather obvious?'

'Not to me it isn't.'

'You must have mistaken her for someone else. As I said, she came home and went straight to bed.'

'Unfortunately, Mr Chapman, I don't believe you.'

'Frankly, I don't care if you do or not.'

'That's fine, but I'm still going to need to speak to her.'

'I'm not waking her up to bring her to the door, just to prove to you that I'm telling the truth.'

Tanner shook his head with mounting frustration. 'Mr Chapman, I don't think you have the slightest idea just how much danger your daughter is in.'

'I'm sorry?'

'I assume you've heard of a man by the name of Iain Sanders?'

'Why should I have?'

'How about Sir Michael Blackwell?'

Chapman stopped for a moment; his eyes fixed on Tanner's. 'Only what I've heard about on the news.'

'And Mr Toby Wallace?'

'Same thing.'

'I suppose that means you didn't know that they all

owned a boat together; a fifty foot Fairline Squadron by the name of Medusa?'

'What's any of this got to do with either myself or my daughter?'

'Because, Mr Chapman, their boat bears a striking resemblance to the one you said your daughter saw through her telescope.'

'Then why are you here pestering me about it? Shouldn't you be out there, arresting them?'

'Well, I would have done, of course, had it not been for the fact that two of them are dead.'

'I still don't understand. Are you suggesting we killed them?'

'I'm thinking more along the lines that you've been trying to blackmail them.'

'Right, yes, of course. And that's why I drove all the way to your police station to tell you what she'd seen. I thought the whole idea of blackmail was that nobody knew what the culprits had done, only the person doing the blackmailing.'

'Unless you felt that the people you were trying to coerce large sums of money out of weren't taking you seriously enough, possibly because they were certain that nobody had a clue what they'd done, apart from you and your daughter. So you thought you'd pop down to help steer us in the right direction. Even then, they probably thought you wouldn't have been able to prove it, as the body they'd dumped over the side of the boat would have been lying somewhere at the bottom of the North Sea, being feasted upon by about a billion hungry fish. But I think you must have realised that, which was why you decided to write the blackmail letters as if they'd been written by the victim herself, making the three men you'd seen think that she'd somehow survived her horrific ordeal.'

'This is ridiculous!'

'When that didn't work,' Tanner continued, 'I think you began sending your daughter out, pretending to be her, in a last ditch attempt to help persuade them. But what you could never have known was just how effective your strategy had been, leading one of them to believe that not only had the girl survived, but when Sir Michael and Mr Wallace turned up dead, he thought she must have decided that money on its own wasn't going to be enough.'

'I'm sorry, but even if we had decided to blackmail them, which we haven't, obviously, I still don't see what any of this has to do with us?'

'Because I believe that the last remaining boat's owner has become so convinced that the girl he thought they'd left for dead is killing them off, one by one, he's decided to take matters into his own hands.'

'I still haven't got the slightest idea what you're going on about.'

'No less than three women have been found dead in the past forty-eight hours, Mr Chapman. If that *was* your daughter beside Acle Dyke this morning, and if Sanders saw her face...'

Chapman's skin drained of all colour.

'Where's your daughter, Mr Chapman?'

'I – I...' the man spluttered, his eyes becoming as wide as discs. 'I don't know.'

'She's not in bed?'

Chapman shook his head.

'Did you send her out, pretending to be the girl she saw thrown over the side of that boat?'

'Alice didn't see what happened. It was me. I was the one with the telescope.'

'I suppose you saw the boat's name, tracking the owners down before sending them those letters?'

'You've no idea how difficult it's been,' Chapman began, his mouth quivering uncontrollably as tears began circling the edges of his eyes. 'My wife's illness left us without a penny, nobody will give me a job, and I'm about two weeks away from losing the house. I've barely got enough money to put food on the table, and there are these stinking rich bastards, out in their fat pretentious yacht, doing the most unimaginably disgusting things to this poor girl who couldn't have been much older than Alice, before discarding her body over the side of their boat as if she was of no more value than a sack of rotten potatoes.'

'Does your daughter know – about your blackmail attempt.'

'Nothing.'

'You sent her out to deliver the letters, without telling her what they said?'

'She'd have never understood. I just told her where to take them.'

'*Was* that her we saw, near Sanders' boat today?'

'She was supposed to ask if he'd received the letter. He wasn't paying up. None of them had.'

Tanner caught the man's eyes. 'You do realise that your actions have led to the murder of three innocent women?'

'That's got nothing to do with me!'

'You're right, it doesn't. It's your daughter who may find herself paying the price.'

Chapman's expression transformed from fearful dread to one of pleading desperation. 'You've got to find her for me. You've got to find her!'

Tanner drew in a short shallow breath. 'Does she have a phone?'

Chapman nodded, tears now falling freely down the sides of his sunken grey face.

'I assume you've tried calling her?'

'Of course. It just keeps going through to voicemail.'

'Where was she supposed to go, after seeing Mr Sanders?'

'Straight back here. There's a bus that stops at the end of the lane. Number 42. It only comes once an hour.'

'When's the next one?'

'I saw it go past, just before you arrived.'

Hearing the faint sound of his phone ringing, Tanner delved a hand inside his coat to find it. 'Hold on,' he said, digging it out to see that it was Vicky. 'I need to take this.'

Answering the call, he turned away, pressing the end against his ear. 'How's it going?'

'Not great, I'm afraid.'

Tanner held his breath. 'Why? What's up?'

'We've just pulled up at Acle Dyke. Sanders' boat isn't here.'

'Is it not up at the other end?'

'I've already looked. I'm sorry, John. It's gone. He must have taken off.'

Tanner cursed quietly under his breath. 'Any sign of the girl, Alice?'

'Nothing!'

'OK, call Forrester. Tell him to get an all-ports warning out for both the girl and our estranged suspect. And make sure to let the coastguard know as well.'

'You think he'll be heading out to sea – in this?'

'Just because we wouldn't, I don't think we should assume that he won't.'

'Anything else?'

'Ask him to send some police patrol boats to where you are now. I think it's more likely he'd have been planning on finding a quiet sheltered mooring nearby, at least until the storm passes.'

'What about you?'

'I'm heading over to you now. Don't move until I get there.'

Ending the call, Tanner straightaway began making another.

'What's going on?' he heard Chapman demand behind him.

Tanner lifted his phone back to his ear to glance around. 'The guy you were trying to blackmail – his boat's gone.'

'What about my daughter?'

'No sign, I'm afraid,' Tanner replied, turning away again to begin another conversation.

'Christine, it's John. I don't suppose you're anywhere near Acle Dyke, by any chance?'

- CHAPTER FIFTY NINE -

ARRIVING AT THE carpark opposite Acle Dyke, with Chapman following in the car behind, Tanner skidded to halt besides Vicky's to clamber out. After staring momentarily about, the fingers of one hand clamped firmly onto the rim of his hood, he spotted her taking shelter under the narrow entrance to the local shop. The moment he saw Chapman open his door, he called over to him, pointing to where Vicky was before turning to begin forging his way towards her through savage gusts of turbulent wind.

'Any news?' he shouted, tucking himself under the shop's narrow alcove.

'I told forensics to go,' Vicky replied. 'I couldn't see any point in them sticking around.'

'I meant about Sanders?'

'Nothing good. One of the locals said he saw a tall middle-aged man dragging a young girl on board his over-sized boat before motoring away in a cloud of diesel fumes.'

'Jesus Christ! Didn't he think to call the police?'

'He said he assumed it was the man's daughter.'

Tanner shook his head in disbelief. 'So Sanders definitely has her.'

'I'd say so,' came Vicky's despondent reply.

'Any idea which way he went?'

'He didn't see.'

'Great,' Tanner replied, just as Chapman came running up.

'Has there been any news? Have you found my daughter?'

'This is George Chapman,' responded Tanner, by way of introduction. 'He's the one who's been attempting to blackmail Iain Sanders and his two now deceased friends.'

'Have you found her?' the man repeated, his eyes lurching between the two police officers.

'I'm afraid it looks like your one surviving blackmail victim has her on board his boat.'

Chapman froze, the skin of his face tightening with angst-ladened fear. 'Where's he taking her?'

'That's what we have to find out,' Tanner replied, his attention returning to Vicky. 'Did you get Forrester to send boat support?'

'Uh-huh,' she replied, peering through the rain towards the end of the dyke. 'I also mentioned about the all-ports warning and the coastguard, although he didn't sound particularly convinced that either would be necessary.'

'But he did call them, though?'

'He said he would. He also said he was going to send Cooper down.'

Tanner gave her an indifferent shrug. 'The more the merrier, I suppose.'

'Townsend as well. They should be here any minute,' she continued, glancing down at her watch.

Tanner nodded over towards the entrance to the carpark as a pair of headlights swept into view. 'Looks like that's them now,' he commented, seeing the sleek muscular shape of Cooper's Audi A5 emerge out through the deluge of rain.

An intermittent sliver of blue flashing light glinting off the tops of the surrounding trees had

Vicky looking past the Audi to the road behind.

'I don't think that's a squad car,' commented Tanner, his own attention being drawn to the river. 'I'd say it's more likely to be a patrol boat.'

- CHAPTER SIXTY -

WAITING FOR COOPER and Townsend to join them, the burgeoning group fought their way through the elements to reach the River Thurne at the end of the short narrow dyke. There to meet them were no less than two police patrol boats, each battling against wind and wave in a bid to secure themselves to the river's slippery grass bank.

'What's the plan?' yelled the nearest driver, shutting off his engine to help his colleague make fast the mooring lines.

'Our suspect is a man called Iain Sanders.' Tanner shouted back. 'We believe he has a hostage. A girl by the name of Alice Chapman. She's only fifteen, so it's imperative that we find them.'

'Do we know what sort of boat he's in?'

'A fifty-foot Fairline Squadron called Medusa, so he shouldn't be too difficult to spot, unless of course he's already made it out to sea.'

'Is that likely?' the police officer asked, taking hold of the railing as his boat lifted and fell in the river's rolling water.

Tanner shrugged. 'I've no idea. He could have, but I think it's more likely that he'll try to haul up inland somewhere, at least until the storm's passed.'

The driver lifted his head to stare first upriver, then down. 'Then I think our best bet will be to make our way to the end of the Bure at Great Yarmouth. There's no other way out to the sea from here, so if he does try, it should be possible for us to head him off. Meanwhile, my colleagues in the other boat can help search the waterways inland, although it would be useful to have a few more boats.'

'There should be a Broads Ranger joining us,' Tanner replied, glancing up to see one of their patrol boats speeding into view. 'That should be her now. Would you be able to take some of my people?'

'We keep spare waterproofs and life jackets down in the cabin.'

Tanner nodded before turning to face the group huddled behind him. 'Cooper and Townsend, you go in this boat. Make your way down to Great Yarmouth; just in case he's stupid enough to try and make a run for the sea. On the way, radio ahead to the yacht station. Tell them to keep their eyes open for a fifty-foot Fairline Squadron. If they see it they have to tell us immediately, but under no circumstances are they to try and stop it, not if there's a hostage on board.

'Vicky, you take the boat behind. Follow the River Bure up to Horning. Take a look down Fleet Dyke on the way. If he's not lurking along there somewhere, try Malthouse Broad.'

Vicky nodded her confirmation. 'How about you?'

'Mr Chapman and I will catch a lift with Christine. We'll see if he's headed up the Thurne before swinging back to take a look along the Ant. Three rivers, three boats. With a Fairline the size of his, one of us should be able to find him.'

- CHAPTER SIXTY ONE -

D RAGGING CHAPMAN WITH him, Tanner made his way upriver to where he could clearly see Christine, frantically trying to steer the boat into the bank against the vicious twisting wind.

'Thanks for coming!' he hollered, catching the line thrown to him to begin heaving back. 'Christine, this is George Chapman. It's his daughter who we believe has been taken. Is it alright if we come aboard?'

Christine gave him the briefest of nods, her attention focussed on endeavouring to keep the boat parallel with the bank. 'You'll find lifejackets below. There should be some waterproofs down there as well.'

Keeping hold of the rope with one hand, Tanner used the other to help Chapman on board before stepping on himself.

Spinning the wheel between her hands, she caught Tanner's eye. 'OK, so, what's the plan?'

Tanner waited for the boat to safely clear the bank before lifting his voice to answer. 'I've got a patrol boat heading down towards Great Yarmouth; just in case he's stupid enough to head out to sea. The other is making its way towards Horning,' he continued, waving at Vicky as she surged past them in the second police boat. 'I've told her to take a look at South Walsham and Malthouse Broad on the way.'

'How about us?'

'I thought we'd start with a quick trip up the Thurne.'

'But he won't be able to pass under the bridge at Potter Heigham, not if he's in a fifty-foot Fairline Squadron.'

'Which is why I thought he might try hiding somewhere this side of it, thinking it would be the last place we'd look.'

'OK, well, Womack Water is up that way,' added Christine, easing forward on the throttle. 'The willow trees at the end would give him enough cover. It's sheltered from the wind as well.'

- CHAPTER SIXTY TWO -

Wripe ITH TANNER HELPING Chapman on with a lifejacket before clawing into one himself, Christine began blasting them up the River Bure, back the way she'd come. With barrels of white water flying past both sides of the hull, it wasn't long before they were making the gradual turn into the River Thurne.

As the giant white windmill standing at the edge of Thurne Dyke disappeared to their right, Christine yelled over to Tanner. 'Shall I keep heading up to Potter Heigham, or make a left for Womack Water?'

Tanner glanced over from where he was crouched on the side of the boat, his abandoned fluorescent hood left flapping in the wind. 'Let's try Womack first,' he bellowed. 'What you said makes sense. If he did come up this way, that's where he'd be.'

Nodding in agreement, Christine steered the boat around a gradual bend before slowing to make a hard left, forcing Tanner to grab hold of one of the handrails to stop him being hurled down onto the cockpit's floor.

With the channel instantly narrowing with lines of boats cluttering up one side, Tanner stood up to begin staring about.

'Anything?' asked Christine, as they motored slowly past the dyke at the bottom of which stood the infamous Falcon's Yard.

Tanner cast his eyes down to the boatshed he could see at the end. As memories of him falling in to become entangled by the lifeless limbs of long-dead bodies began creeping their way to the forefront of his mind, he shook his head clear, forcing himself to stare ahead. 'Nothing yet,' he eventually replied, as trees began appearing on either side, the tops of their branches being lashed by the vicious unrelenting wind.

A moment later, something caught his eye. It was a sliver of white about twenty metres away, hovering between the water and the cascading branches of a giant weeping willow. 'I think I can see something,' he eventually replied, holding up his hand as a signal for Christine to slow the boat to a crawl.

As they glided effortlessly through the water, a vortex of gusting wind came twisting through the gaps in the trees above, forcing apart the willow's low-hanging branches to reveal the outline of what he knew to be Sander's Fairline Squadron.

'It's him!' he stated, glaring ahead.

'Can you see my daughter?' came Chapman's voice, Tanner's words bringing him stumbling out from the patrol boat's cabin.

'Not yet,' Tanner eventually replied, as the three of them did their best to both watch and listen for even the vaguest signs of life. But with the Fairline almost completely hidden by the veil of vertically hanging branches, and the unrelenting noise of both rain and wind, it was impossible to tell if there either was or wasn't.

'Can't we just climb on board to find out?' Chapman questioned, a stark pleading tone to the edge of his voice.

Tanner shook his head. 'I'm sorry, I don't have a search warrant.'

'We don't have to go inside – just take a look through the windows.'

The moment he said it, a shadow flickered behind the canopy at the back, immediately followed by the shrill but muted sound of a young girl's scream.

'ALICE?' Chapman shrieked, his voice slicing through the air like an angle-grinder held against toughened steel.

A sudden lull in the wind left his voice echoing out through the haunting silence that followed. As the three of them stood there, eyes open, mouths closed, the sound of a muffled scuffling noise came from somewhere inside the boat, followed a second later by the shrill sound of a single word, one that resonated deep inside the darkest corners of Tanner's fractured soul.

'DADDY!'

- CHAPTER SIXTY THREE -

AN EERIE MOMENT of unnatural silence fell over the sheltered waterway before the wind and rain came crashing back down, this time with such intense ferocity, even Tanner found himself casting a wary eye up at the billowing clouds above.

With the return of the wind came an avalanche of words, tripping and stumbling out of Chapman's contorted mouth. 'She's in there! My daughter – she's in there! ALICE!' he screamed. 'DON'T WORRY, DARLING. WE'RE COMING FOR YOU!'

As his words were wrenched away by the gusting wind, a rumbling noise could be heard echoing out from the surrounding trees. At first Tanner thought it was the sound of distant thunder, rolling in from the sea. It was only when the Fairline began inching forward did he realise his mistake.

'He's going to make a run for it,' he said, glancing around at Christine to plunge a hand inside his coat, his cold wet fingers reaching for his phone.

'Then stop him!' Chapman demanded, just as the Fairline's huge bulbous white bow came flying out of the water like a harpooned whale, piercing the willow tree's branches to begin charging away.

With their patrol boat left pitching and rolling in its mammoth-sized wake, Christine had to fight for control, spinning the wheel first left, then right, leaving Tanner grasping hold of whatever he could to stop himself from being thrown over the side. It took a full agonising minute for her to flatten the boat, by which time all that was left of Sanders' opulent motor yacht were two foaming white lines, disappearing away into the troubled water ahead.

'You can't let them get away!' came Chapman's whining voice, picking himself up from where he'd fallen.

'Don't worry, we won't!' Christine stated, placing her hand back on the throttle to lever it forward.

As the patrol boat's hull lifted up to begin surging away, Tanner was finally able to dig out his phone.

'Vicky, it's Tanner. We found him.'

'Where abouts?'

'He was hiding at the end of Womack Water.'

'Not anymore?'

'Sadly no,' Tanner replied, his eyes resting briefly on Chapman's. 'Someone alerted him to our presence. He's definitely got the girl, though.'

'Any idea which way he's heading?'

'Hold on,' Tanner continued, bracing himself as Christine careered the boat around a bend in the narrow stretch of water. With the entrance to the River Thurne coming into view, he lifted his head to stare over the wheelhouse roof. There was still no sign of the Fairline; but drifting over the water ahead were the parallel lines left by its twin propellers. 'He's turned right,' he said, the phone back against his mouth. 'He must be headed for Great Yarmouth.'

There was a momentary delay before Vicky's voice came back over the line. 'OK, we're turning around now.'

'How far did you get?'

'We'd just reached the end of Fleet Dyke.'

'Then we should see you at Thurne Mouth.'

'Shall I call Cooper, to let him know?'

'If you could. And make sure to tell him not to do anything stupid. That boat of Sanders' makes ours look like nothing more than floating matchsticks.'

- CHAPTER SIXTY FOUR -

APPROACHING THE EXPANSIVE entrance to the River Bure, Tanner lifted his head to peer over to his right. Over the tops of the reeds being thrashed by the wind he could see fragmented shards of blue flashing light, ricocheting off the near horizontal rain.

'Careful as you come round,' he called down to Christine. 'The other patrol boat is going to be right on top of us.'

Nodding back a response, she expertly began easing the boat around the bend, straightening up a few seconds later to find the police patrol boat Vicky was on tagging along behind.

With Tanner raising a hand over to its driver, the two boats continued careening their way down the meandering River Bure, the boat behind holding a steady course on the curving edge of their starboard-side bow wave as they banked first left then right in perfect unison.

'Whoever's driving that boat behind certainly seems to know what they're doing,' Christine called out, her jaw set firm as her emerald eyes focussed on the river ahead.

'As do you,' complimented Tanner, with the utmost sincerity. He was fully aware of the skill needed to drive a boat at full speed down such a narrow stretch of river with limited visibility and a savage buffeting gale.

Seeing the corners of her mouth lift ever-so slightly, he glanced back at the boat behind them to pull out his phone.

'Did you manage to get hold of Cooper?' he asked, staring over at Vicky as he watched her answer his call.

'They're heading back this way,' she nodded, 'hopefully to head him off.'

'You did tell him not to do anything stupid.'

'Well, yes, but as he made clear, he's not the one driving the boat. Anyway, are we sure he'll be going that way? I can see loads of places he could have turned off.'

'Not once we're past Acle Dyke. It's a clear run, all the way down. Besides, he's leaving a remarkably generous trail of breadcrumbs for us to follow.'

'I'm sorry, for a minute there I thought you said breadcrumbs?'

'They may as well be. The wake from that monster yacht of his is huge. If you look ahead, you'll probably be able to see it.'

He watched as she lifted her head briefly before ducking it back behind the windscreen.

'I'll have to take your word for it,' came her voice from the other end of the line. 'We can hardly see a thing from back here.'

Seeing Christine catch his eye to deliberately gesture ahead, Tanner quickly ended the call.

'What's up?' he asked, his phone returning to the depths of his coat.

'I don't think he's able to go as fast as us,' Christine replied, re-fixing her eyes on the water ahead. 'Not around these tight narrow bends. Look!' she continued, lifting a hand off the throttle to gesture ahead. 'His wake is more pronounced. I could be wrong, but I'm fairly sure we're catching him up.'

- CHAPTER SIXTY FIVE -

PLOUGHING THROUGH THE water to round the next bend, Christine's prediction soon proved to be true. As the lattice blades of the Stacy Arms Windpump flickered their way past, appearing through the rain ahead was the sleek white silhouette of Sander's majestic Fairline Squadron, banking hard to starboard to begin careening around the next rapidly approaching bend.

'Looks like you were right,' Tanner observed, as they watched it disappear once again.

'Did you see my daughter?' Chapman queried, stepping forward to stand directly behind them.

Tanner shook his head. 'Sorry, they were just too far away.'

He paused for a moment before glancing around at Christine. 'I don't suppose there's any chance we could go a little faster?'

'I sincerely hope you're joking?' she replied, her greying blonde hair whipping violently about her face as she sent him an unamused look of stern reproach.

'OK, but from what I can make out,' Tanner began, offering her a coltish smirk before staring past Chapman to the police patrol boat behind, 'my colleague seems to be gaining.'

A quick glance over her shoulder had Christine

glaring back. 'They're doing no such thing! If anything, I'd say they're struggling to keep up.'

Tanner shrugged back in response. 'What can I say? From where I'm standing, it looks like they're catching up.'

Christine rolled her eyes to offer him a curt unamused smile. Setting her jaw to stare ahead, she eased the throttle forward until its leading edge stopped up against its black plastic casing.

'That's as fast as it will go,' she eventually replied, the knuckles of her hands visibly whitening.

'That'll do,' Tanner replied, finding his own grip of the wheelhouse roof's edge had already tightened.

As they tore around the next bend for the Fairline to come into view again, the gap had closed to the point where they could just about make out Sanders, ducked behind the smoked glass windshield surrounding its voluminous sweeping flybridge. Glimpsing him turn his head to stare momentarily back, Christine placed both hands on the steering wheel. 'OK, so he knows we're here. Not sure what he's going to do now.'

'Well, he's not slowing down.' Tanner replied. 'If anything, I'd say he's doing the opposite.'

Christine nodded. 'I think you're right, but he better be careful. A boat that size going flat-out down here isn't going to end well. One mistake and he'll flip it; that's assuming nobody's coming up the other way.'

'Shit; Cooper!' Tanner exclaimed, burying a hand down inside his coat, his cold clammy fingers in urgent search of his phone.

Dragging it out, he dialled his colleague's number to press it against his ear, just as Sanders' Fairline disappeared around the following bend, a giant wave soaring high off the leading edge of its portside bow.

'He's not picking up,' he eventually said, re-taking hold of the wheelhouse roof as Christine began steering them into what was rapidly becoming an unexpectedly tight corner.

'Jesus Christ!' she shrieked, slamming the wheel first one way, then the other, as the pointed nose of Cooper's police boat burst out through the Fairline's bow wave to blast past the starboard side of their hull, missing them by just a fraction of an inch.

As Tanner was thrown first one way, then the other, he managed to turn his head to stare back at them as they swept their way past.

'Are they alright?' Christine asked, still fighting to maintain control.

'Just about,' he replied, wincing as it missed Vicky's boat by a similar margin to end up careering safely into a bed of reeds.

'How about the boat behind?'

Seeing Chapman trying to pick himself up from the cockpit's floor, he gave him a hand whilst looking back again, this time to see Vicky staring directly ahead, her normally reddish face now the colour of bleached chalk. The driver, however, didn't seem to have even raised an eyebrow. 'I'd say they're a little shaken-up,' he smirked, 'at least Vicky would appear to be.'

As he watched the driver slow the boat to begin spinning it around, Tanner returned to staring ahead. 'Looks like they're stopping to make sure the others are OK. Where did Sanders get to?'

'He's gained,' came Christine's begrudging reply. 'Judging by how much, I doubt he even bothered to make an effort to steer clear of your colleagues.'

'Which was probably why Cooper's boat ended up in the Broad's equivalent of a hedge.'

Chapman stepped up to wipe the rain from his

face. 'What happens now? How do we stop him?'

Tanner looked at Christine for an answer, but from her pallid expressionless face, it was obvious she didn't have one.

'We've already informed the coastguard,' Tanner eventually replied, unable to meet Chapman's gaze.

'Seriously? Is that it?'

Tanner remained silent, leaving Christine to offer him a glimmer of hope.

'Well, all this rain means the river's running high, so there's a chance he won't make it under the bridge at Yarmouth.'

'If he can't, what would happen then?'

'He'd have no choice but to moor up and make his way by foot.'

'And if he has a car waiting for him?'

Taking heed of his words, Tanner once again reached for his phone. 'I'll give the office a call. We should be able to get a couple of squad cars standing by, just in case.'

- CHAPTER SIXTY SIX -

FLANKED BY WALLS of tumbling water, after twenty minutes of sombre silence during which time none of them had caught so much as a glimpse of Sanders' boat, Christine began banking them around a long meandering bend.

'It's a straight run down to Yarmouth after this,' she announced, her words snatched instantly away by the howling wind. 'With any luck, we should be able to see them as we come round.'

Sure enough, as the boat levelled off they could see the sleek white silhouette of Sanders' Fairline Squadron ploughing through the water ahead.

'We're catching up,' Tanner observed, peering through the windscreen, the patrol boat's short clunky wipers struggling to keep up with the seemingly never ending deluge of rain.

Christine lifted a hand to gesture ahead. 'You can see the arch of Vauxhall Bridge.'

'You're right about the water being too high,' said Tanner, leaning forward to stare out at its complex lattice work of iron red girders growing wider and higher with every passing second. 'He's never going to make it underneath.'

'Then someone better tell the driver. From what I can make out, he's not slowing down.'

The moment she'd said it the back of the Fairline thrust itself suddenly into the air, the surrounding water exploding into a billion shards of brilliant white.

'Jesus Christ!' Tanner exclaimed, as Christine threw back the throttle, spinning the wheel hard to port.

With the starboard side of the patrol boat digging into the water, it first lifted, then fell, throwing its passengers violently to the side.

Somehow managing to stay on his feet, with the engine spluttering to a halt, Tanner stared out with his mouth hanging open to see that they'd ended up less than a metre away from the back of the stricken Fairline. 'What the...!' he exclaimed, blinking cold dirty river water away from his eyes. 'The idiot just drove straight into it!'

'ALICE!' came the deafening roar of Chapman's voice.

Glancing up, Tanner caught sight of Sanders, scrambling over the crumpled remains of the Fairline's once elegant flybridge, one hand clawing his way up onto the bridge's grimy iron girders, the other clamped around the fragile skinny arm of Chapman's teenage daughter.

The moment she saw them, her eyes punched themselves open. 'DADDY!' she screamed, the solitary word giving birth to a lifetime of emotion as it sliced its way through the gale force wind. 'HELP ME, PLEASE!'

Tanner glanced around at her father, just in time to see him step up onto the still rocking patrol boat's side, the man's eyes frantically assessing the rapidly-growing distance between themselves and the back of the Fairline. He was about to jump when Tanner grabbed hold of his lifejacket to heave him back.

'Get the fuck off me!' the man growled, his head turning to snarl down at the detective inspector.

'You'll never make it,' Tanner replied, staring down.

'Then I'll swim!'

'The tide is too strong. You'll be swept away. Look!'

Tanner was right. During the few seconds they'd been talking, the distance between the Fairline and them had already more than doubled.

'Then *you* do something! We can't just stand here watching my daughter be carted away by some deranged fucking lunatic!'

Tanner's mind whirled as he stared frantically about. Catching Christine's eye he called out, 'Can you start the engine?'

'I'm trying,' she replied, her body hunched over the throttle, frantically twisting and re-twisting the key. 'Nothing's happening. It must have flooded.'

The distant sound of sirens had him lurching up onto the side. 'OK, try dropping the anchor. I'm going to see if I can talk to him. I think there's a squad car approaching; maybe two. If I can hold him up long enough for them to get here, we may just have a chance of stopping him.'

- CHAPTER SIXTY SEVEN -

L EAVING CHRISTINE TO launch herself down the side of the boat, heading for where the anchor was stowed, Tanner stood high on its side. 'Mr Sanders!' he bellowed; a hand cupped around his mouth. 'Detective Inspector Tanner, Norfolk Police.'

'I know who you are,' came the man's aggravated response as he continued clambering his way over the wreckage.

'Then you know why we're here?'

Instead of replying, Sanders raised a foot up onto the solid steel girder spanning the bridge's length, heaving Chapman's daughter kicking and screaming with him as he went.

Hearing the clatter of the patrol boat's anchor chain rattling out over its bow, Tanner once again lifted his voice. 'There's no way we're going to be able to let you get away, Mr Sanders, not after you've murdered no less than four innocent women.'

'I only count three,' the man barked back in response, stopping to catch his breath. 'I'd be willing to admit that I did take their lives in error,' he continued, his eyes finding Tanner's, 'but don't worry, inspector, it won't be long before I correct that mistake, which should end up with us both being right.'

'Then let's discuss a deal,' Tanner offered,

watching Sanders continue to inch his way along the base of the bridge, dragging Alice Chapman after him. 'The girl in exchange for a reduced sentence. But you're going to have to let her go first.'

Sanders stopped again. 'And why the hell should I do that? She's the one who started all this. It's her you should be after, not me!'

'But, Mr Sanders, she's done nothing wrong!'

'Oh, right! You mean apart from murdering my two best friends?'

'You're mistaking her for someone she isn't,' Tanner continued. 'She's not the same girl whose body you discarded over the side of your boat.'

Sanders took a moment to stare down at the swollen river, hurtling its way beneath his feet before returning his gaze to Tanner, the first signs of uncertainty rippling over his brow.

'Whoever killed your friends,' Tanner continued, 'it wasn't the girl you were with that night. It certainly wasn't the one you're dragging behind you now. Her name's Alice Chapman. She's just a schoolgirl, not one of your friends' part-time prostitutes. It was her father who saw what the three of you did, watching through a telescope. He's the one who's been trying to blackmail you.'

Tanner could now see clear signs of doubt stabbing at the corners of Sanders' eyes as the sound of sirens grew ever closer, disjointed lines of blue flashing light beginning to dance in the downpouring rain.

'If that's true,' Sanders began, 'then who killed Michael and Toby?'

'I'll admit, we don't know the answer to that – not yet – but it wasn't Alice. I mean – look at her, man! She's barely fifteen years old!'

Tanner watched as Sanders took a moment to stare into the sobbing petrified face of the girl held in his vice-like grip, before his eyes swung slowly back to meet Tanner's. 'But – the girl on the boat. I saw her swimming away. It must have been her.'

'The girl you threw over the side of your boat is dead, Mr Sanders. Even if she was still alive when you did, she'd never have survived long enough to make it back to the shore.'

Sanders hesitated for a fraction of a second, restless indecision playing out over his eyes. 'Fine!' he eventually spat. 'Have her! She was slowing me down anyway.'

With that, he let go of the girl's wrist, shoving her away as he did.

Tanner looked on in horror as he watched Alice's feet immediately slip on the girder's greasy wet surface, her body plummeting over the edge. For one frantic moment he thought she wasn't going to stop, continuing down into the turbulent water below, when he saw one of her flailing hands latch itself around the beam she'd been standing on moments before, leaving her gangly legs dangling helplessly underneath the low hanging bridge.

'ALICE!' the father screamed, launching himself onto the patrol boat's side.

'Daddy, help me! I – I can't hold on!'

Chapman shot a desperate look at first Tanner, then Christine, scrambling her way back to the wheelhouse. 'Can't you get this damn thing started?'

'We're doing the best we can,' Tanner stated, as the patrol boat snagged hard against its newly set anchor.

Taking a moment to glance frantically about, Tanner threw a glance over at Sanders, side-stepping his way along the girder to where the bridge met the land. He then looked at the girl, rain dripping from her soaking wet body as she stared desperately up at her pale delicate hand, as if willing for it to maintain its eroding grip. From there his eyes fell to the water separating them from the stricken Fairline. It may have been only a few metres away, but it may as well have been a million miles. There was no way they'd be able to get to her, not from where they were, snagging against their anchor as the overflowing river swept relentlessly past.

The distant whine of an engine had his head jolting around. Blasting down the river towards them was a powerboat, its pointed white hull stark against the unforgiving landscape beyond.

'That must be Vicky,' he muttered to himself.

Turning his head back, he could see Alice's elongated fingers beginning to slip. Making a rapid assessment of the distance between the approaching patrol boat and the base of the bridge, he shook his head. 'They're never going to get here in time.'

The sudden appearance of a police constable's head, gawping down at them from over the top of the bridge had Tanner gazing up. 'Can you reach the girl?' he shouted, dragging the man's attention down to where Alice was hanging, only the whitened tips of her fingers now hooked around the girder's edge.

Seeing him nod to immediately throw himself over the top of the iron red structure, Tanner dared to let out a juddering breath. *If she can just hold on a little longer.*

It was then that she fell, her pale skinny body slipping gracefully through the air to instantly vanish into the swirling blackness of the water below.

Stunned into silence, with his heart pounding deep inside his chest and the father's voice endlessly screaming out her name, Tanner trained his eyes on the water's foaming surface, doing his best to follow the surging current from the point where he'd seen her fall.

Precious seconds passed as nothing but gallons upon gallons of river water swept its way past with cruel unforgiving dispassion. As the section of water he'd been doing his best to follow flooded past the hull above where he stood, with still not a single sign of the girl, Tanner was about to turn to face the father to offer him a look of sorrowful remorse, one he'd borne so many times before, when something caught the corner of his eye. It was the girl, a metre away, her head facing down as her body rotated slowly around.

Without daring to think, he launched himself off the boat, plunging headfirst into the unseasonably cold swirling river.

As his borrowed lifejacket inflated around his ears, his head burst out through the surface, his mouth gasping at the air. Wiping water from his eyes to see the girl's body, just up ahead, he kicked hard with his feet, his hands jutting forward to drag themselves back. One more stroke and he'd reached the girl, flipping her body over so that her nose and mouth were facing the sky. With one arm locked around the base of her chin, he swivelled her around to try and drag her back through the current to the boat from which he'd leapt. But it was no use. The force of the water was just too strong. The harder he tried, the further away he seemed to become.

As savage burning pain began tearing at the muscles in his legs and arms, he was about to give up to leave themselves at the mercy of the tidal flow, when looming into view came the hull of the boat he'd seen before.

'John!' came the sound of a woman, her voice he instantly knew.

Blinking water out of his eyes, he gazed up to see Vicky's face, her arm stretching out towards him.

'Take my hand!' she called again; her jaw clamped

together as her body strained to reach still further.

He didn't need to be told twice.

Sucking in a breath, he lifted himself up, his hand reaching for hers.

For one paralysing moment he thought he was too late, when he felt his wrist suddenly snatched from the air. As water began surging past, he used the last of his strength to hoist the girl up into waiting hands before climbing up himself.

Collapsing onto the wheelhouse floor, he turned to see the patrol boat's driver breathing air down into the young girl's lungs before pumping his hands down onto her chest. He continued to watch in silence as the man cycled between the two, eventually stopping to breathlessly press two fingers against her neck, searching for signs of a pulse. But the way her eyes were staring up, and the purple hue surrounding her nose and mouth, it was obvious to everyone on board that she'd taken her last breath a long time before.

- CHAPTER SIXTY EIGHT -

W ITH HIS FLAGGING wet limbs trembling uncontrollably from the cold, Vicky accompanied Tanner to the shore to help guide him into the awaiting hands of two paramedics.

'D-did we c-catch Sanders?' he stuttered, beginning to follow them over to where their ambulance was parked.

'Looks like it,' Vicky replied, steering his attention over to where a young police constable could be seen placing a hand on top of his head to lever him down into the back of a squad car.

Silence followed as Tanner was helped up into the ambulance. As one of the paramedics gave him the once over whilst the other threw a blanket over his shoulders, Vicky sought to catch his eye. 'What are we going to do about Chapman?'

Tanner's mind was instantly transported back to the sight of the man's daughter, her lips the colour of lavender, her eyes dead and vacant. Inhaling deeply, he let out a capitulating sigh. 'I suggest we let him go.'

'But – what about his blackmail letters?'

'I think his greatest crime was to have successfully convinced Sanders that the girl they threw over the side of their boat that night had somehow survived,' Tanner began. 'If he hadn't done, Sanders wouldn't have had a single reason to have laid so much as a finger on those women he killed; more to the point, his daughter would still be alive. That's something he's going to have to carry with him for the rest of his life. Anyway,' he continued, glancing up at the nearest paramedic. 'Will I live?'

'You have a mild case of hypothermia. Ideally, we need to get you out of those wet clothes.'

'I'll get changed after work,' Tanner replied, glancing down at his watch to push himself up to his feet. 'I doubt if a few more hours is going to make much difference.'

'And where do you think you're going?' Vicky demanded, watching him barge his way past the paramedics.

'Back to the station. Where did you think?'

'We can handle Sanders.'

'No doubt you can, but there's the question of McMillan. According to my watch, we've got less than twenty minutes before he's legally entitled to walk, and I need to know if that missing evidence found the light of day before allowing him to do so.'

'Then I can phone them to find out,' she replied, searching for her mobile.

'I'm sure you could, but I'm also fairly convinced that Forrester is expecting me to be there in person, whether the evidence has turned up or not.'

- CHAPTER SIXTY NINE -

HITCHING A RIDE in a squad car, Tanner and Vicky made their way in convoy back to Wroxham Police Station, Sanders safely handcuffed in the back of the vehicle directly in front of them. On their arrival, amidst a storm of flash photography courtesy of the bedraggled press pack, Tanner stepped back out into the still torrential rain to escort Sanders safely inside.

After formally checking him in with the duty sergeant, he turned to make his way through the double doors into the main office when he came face to face with DC Townsend, a folder clasped in his hands.

'Afternoon, sir,' the young man began, bringing himself to attention. 'I think this is for you.'

Taking the folder being held out for him, Tanner quickly scanned his eyes over the report found inside. With Townsend waiting patiently to be dismissed, the flicker of a smile tugged at the corners of his mouth, just as the voice of McMillan's solicitor had him turning slowly around.

'If you came to see us off, inspector, there really was no need. I'm sure you must have far more pressing matters to attend to.'

'Mr Crabtree!' Tanner exclaimed, fixing his eyes first on the solicitor, then over at his client standing next to him offering him a broad malevolent grin.

'And Mr McMillan! I didn't know you were still here.'

'Not for long,' the solicitor proclaimed, a guiding hand being placed behind his client's back as he continued ushering him towards the station's exit.

'Before you go,' Tanner called out, spying McMillan's two weary bodyguards rise slowly to their feet. 'I thought you might be interested to hear that our forensics department was finally able to unearth some evidence.'

The solicitor stopped where he was to stare over at him. 'That's fascinating, inspector, really it is. But as you can see, your time with my client has officially expired.'

'Aren't you curious to know what it was?' Tanner questioned, his eyes glancing furtively down at the file left open in his hands.

'I'm fairly sure that neither my client, nor myself for that matter, could care less.'

Tanner flicked over a page. 'The hacksaw found locked inside the Riverside Gentlemen's Club stationery cupboard: their report says that the blood found on its blade did indeed belong to Sir Michael Blackwell. It also says that your client's fingerprints were found on its handle as well.'

'Then I suppose it's a shame that you weren't able to produce the evidence a little sooner.'

'Perhaps,' Tanner replied, looking up with a wistful smile. 'But then again, technically speaking, you haven't left the building yet.'

The solicitor opened his mouth as if in preparation to present Tanner with some indisputable legal caveat.

Watching him close it again a second later, Tanner glanced behind him to catch Townsend's eye, gesturing for him to block the exit.

'Mr Terrance McMillan,' he continued, turning

back, 'I hereby charge you with the murders of Sir Michael Blackwell and Mr Toby Wallace.'

Seeing the way McMillan was gawping at him with a look of abject horror, Tanner almost felt sorry for him. 'Not the best news, I know,' he added, taking an apologetic tone. 'However, looking on the bright side, at least you'll be able to continue your stay with us, free of charge, I may add. You also won't need to go scrabbling about in search of a solicitor, as there appears to be one standing right next to you. I'd have to admit that he's probably not the best one in the world, else he'd have waited until you'd left the building before saying his goodbyes, but I don't think it will make much difference. Apart from having caught you in the act, so to speak, I'd say the evidence we have is about as conclusive as it's going to get.'

- EPILOGUE -

Thursday, 2ⁿᵈ September

TANNER STOOD ON the boggy edge of Breydon Water, the Wellington boots he was wearing planted firmly on the surrounding marsh. Taking a peaceful moment to stare out to where he could see Great Yarmouth, shimmering in the heat of a steadily rising sun, his head continued up to a pristine blue sky marred only by a handful of solitary clouds, each one drifting effortlessly out towards the North Sea beyond.

Drinking in the crystal clean air purified by the recent storm, his attention returned to why he'd been called out there; the remains of a body discovered earlier that day by an elderly couple out for their daily walk.

'What've we got?' he called down to Dr Johnstone, knee deep in mud, his shoulders hunched over what remained of a rotting corpse.

'A white female. At a guess I'd say she was somewhere between the age of fifteen and thirty.'

'Any idea how long she's been there for?' Tanner continued, his attention momentarily distracted by what looked to be a police patrol boat, chugging its way over the sparkling water towards them.

Johnstone batted a fly away with the back of his hand. 'Stuck out here, I've got no idea, but I reckon she's been dead for at least two weeks – maybe three.'

'I don't suppose there's anything in the form of identification?'

The medical examiner cast his eyes back over the body. 'Well, she doesn't seem to have her handbag with her, if that's what you mean.'

'I was thinking more along the lines of distinguishing marks,' Tanner replied, rolling his eyes.

'Oh, OK. There would appear to be a tattoo; if that helps.'

'Can you describe it?'

Johnstone tilted his head, his eyes still fixed on the body. 'It would probably be better if you took a look for yourself.'

Tanner stared at the fly-infested mud that the body was half-protruding out of before casting his eyes down at the suit trousers he was wearing, the ones he'd only recently picked up from the dry-cleaners. 'How about emailing me a photograph?'

Johnstone turned his head to narrow his eyes up at him.

'Alright, hold on,' Tanner moaned, taking a few cautious steps down the marshy bank before beginning to squelch his way over the thick black mud.

Reaching the body, he carefully eased himself down onto his haunches.

'I'd say it looks like a butterfly,' Johnstone continued, gesturing down at what was left of the girl's arm.

'Er, it *is* a butterfly,' stated Tanner, 'something I'd have thought would have been remarkably easy to describe.'

'It could be a moth,' Johnstone commented, suppressing a smirk.

The call of a familiar woman's voice drifting lazily towards them through the light summer's air had them both glancing up.

'I heard another body had been found?'

Tanner pushed himself up to wave over at the welcoming sight of Christine, peering out from the side of what had turned out to be a Broads Ranger's patrol boat.

'I thought you were the police,' he called back in response.

'Why? Have you done something wrong?'

Tanner smiled. The last time they'd been anywhere near each other was three days before, when Iain Sanders had ploughed his boat straight into Vauxhall Bridge. Seeing her there now made him realise how much he'd missed her.

'I don't suppose you'd know if it would be possible for someone to have been washed up here from the sea?'

He waited a moment for her to turn off the engine.

'I'm not sure that's very likely,' she eventually replied, her patrol boat beginning to drift slowly away in the water's strong ebbing tide.

'What about during the storm?' Tanner continued, forced to tug his feet out of the mud to begin traipsing his way after her.

'That would make it more likely,' Christine continued, pulling a stray lock of hair out of her eyes. 'Is it the missing girl? The one seen being dumped over the side of that boat?'

'Probably. At least the tattoo would appear to be the same.'

The conversation stalled as Tanner did his best to keep up with the increasing speed of the patrol boat.

'Listen, Christine, how about that meal I've been promising you?'

'Sorry, what was that?' she cried, cupping a hand around one of her ears.

'That meal I've been promising you?' he repeated, lifting his voice. 'How about it?'

'When were you thinking?'

'What about tonight?'

He could almost see her weighing up his proposal.

'Are you sure you don't have anything else on?'

'I promise. Look, I'll even turn my phone off,' he continued, wrenching it out to hold in the air.

Forced to give up trying to keep up with the boat that was been carried ever further away, he stood with his boots sinking slowly into the water-logged mud, waiting in anxious silence.

'Can you pick me up at eight?' came her eventual reply.

A broad grin spread out over Tanner's face. 'No problem. Any idea where you want to go?' he added, almost as an afterthought.

'As long as we actually make it there this time, I'm not all that sure I care.'

*DI John Tanner
will return in
Long Gore Hall*

- A LETTER FROM DAVID -

Dear Reader,

I just wanted to say a huge thank you for deciding to read *Storm Force*. If you enjoyed it, I'd be really grateful if you could leave a review on Amazon, or mention it to your friends and family. Word-of-mouth recommendations are just so important to an author's success, and doing so will help new readers discover my work.

It would be great to hear from you as well, either on Facebook, Twitter, Goodreads or via my website. There are plenty more books to come, so I sincerely hope you'll be able to join me for what I promise will be an exciting adventure!

All the very best,

David

- ABOUT THE AUTHOR -

David Blake is an international bestselling author who lives in North London. At time of going to print he has written nineteen books, along with a collection of short stories. When not writing, David likes to spend his time mucking about in boats, often in the Norfolk Broads, where his crime fiction books are based.

Made in the USA
Monee, IL
14 August 2021